Don't

From reviews of previous novels in the series:

Mary Tant carries the narrative forward almost entirely in dialogue and the style suited this country-house murder mystery perfectly. There were plenty of red herrings among the clues as to who had carried out a brutal attack... and plenty of motives too. Of course, it's up to the family to sort it all out...

Strong distinct characters, a delightful setting and further books to follow make this a winner... *Stow Times*

✱✱✱✱✱ rating – One to watch. This is very reminiscent of Agatha Christie with its West-of-England country house setting. A good plot, very good dialogue and the first of a series. I can envisage it adapting well to the small screen...

Philip Richards, *Amazon.co.uk*

...an intriguing tale about familial relationships and friendships with an idyllic pastoral setting and skilfully drawn characters.

Miriam Reeves

Mary Tant in [a] Christie-style classic murder mystery gathers a small group of polite characters in a rundown Tudor mansion and ruined Cistercian priory in the West Country. It has been owned by the Rossington family for generations ... in the Christie tradition, murder ensues, followed by a tense denouement *Oxford Times*

THE ROSSINGTON SERIES

The Rossington Inheritance

Death at the Priory

Friends ... and a Foe

Players and Betrayers

The Watcher on the Cliff

Don't Come Back

The Gathering Storm

The Witness

The Theme is Death

A Deadly Plot

MARY TANT'S WEBSITE

http://www.marytant.com

MARY TANT

Don't Tell Tales

Threshold Press

First published 2025 by Threshold Press Ltd,
www.threshold-press.co.uk

British Library Cataloguing in Publication Data
A catalogue record for this book is available from the British Library
ISBN 978-1-903152-38-6

Printed in Great Britain by Short Run Press, Exeter EX2 7LW

PROLOGUE

What did she want, this woman? She was here because of the restoration of the garden, Elowen Garden. That was well known. But the garden did not stand alone, isolated. It was the story of the people who had lived and worked there, and in its vicinity. People who had loved and hated there, who had died there.

The woman's long black hair fell in heavy waves around her face. And that face looked so innocuous, with its creamy complexion and rose-tinted cheeks. Her dark blue eyes sparkled with interest as she listened, bending forward slightly, intent on following the story that was being told to her, absorbing all the details and wanting more.

Oh yes, she was here for stories. She was curious. And persuasive. She could be a problem. There were plenty of stories to be told, but more than one of them should never be repeated. The storyteller knew that. And the storyteller's heart beat faster, harder, knowing which particular story must never, ever, be told. Not unless it was useful.

Anna Evesleigh must be watched. Her reputation was well known. Local people were mainly proud that an actress, one some of them had seen at the theatre, and even more had seen on television, should be part of their community. But her reputation covered more than that. She was a catalyst, she caused things to happen, she uncovered events long past, events that still affected people now. That could not be allowed to happen here.

The storyteller paused before bringing this particular story to a happy end. But the storyteller knew that not all stories have a happy ending.

ONE

Anna put her mug down reluctantly. 'That was fascinating,' she said, brushing back her dark hair from her face. 'You know so many local stories.'

'Most of them too scandalous to be repeated in public.' The voice made her turn round, a smile of welcome on her face as she saw the short stocky figure standing in the doorway of the mobile home.

'Hello, Gareth,' she said, as the collie beside her got to his feet, tail wagging furiously, and went eagerly towards the newcomer. 'I expect you've heard it before.'

He nodded as he stroked the dog's head, before pulling up a chair to join them around the low driftwood table, crowding the small sitting area. One of his hands gently pulled the dog's ears as the collie laid his head in Gareth's lap. His other hand rested on the arm of the chair. Both hands were clean, the dark hairs that covered their backs still damp from recent washing, but there were clots of clay in his hair and pale wet streaks on his thick fisherman's jumper.

'I've heard all Edward's stories before,' he agreed as he looked across at her, his voice deep and lilting, even though most of his native Welsh accent had faded from his words. 'That's how I know he'll be sued for slander if he's not careful. It isn't right, telling stories that might still affect living people.'

Edward leaned forward, carefully picking out the clots of clay from his partner's smooth grey-tinged hair, watched curiously by the collie. 'I'm always careful who I tell them to,' he said soothingly. 'I've got lots that would be alright for the Women's Institute.'

'But you weren't telling Anna one of those,' Gareth replied. 'Were you?'

'No, of course not. Anna's getting the best ones.' Edward's tone was light, amused.

But Anna intervened, knowing Gareth's serious and rather sober character did not always appreciate the other man's levity. 'I've heard far worse already,' she said, glancing back at Gareth. 'This seems to be an area of born storytellers. I was at the last Storytelling at the village hall, and so many people wanted to tell tales that some of them didn't get a turn.'

'It's still a tradition in some rural areas,' Gareth said, allowing himself to be diverted. 'Stories were told down the generations, and still are, a living history of the families that go back for centuries.'

'Yes, exactly.' Anna's dark blue eyes lit up. 'I'd like to get Lucy, or maybe Hugh, to record some of them. I'll even do some recording myself if I can. Carefully selected stories,' she added hastily, seeing Gareth frown. 'I'd like to keep an archive of them in the garden.'

'And,' Edward said, with a malicious shrewdness in his pale eyes, 'they'll make fantastic plays.'

Anna gurgled with laughter. She nodded. 'Of course. Community plays are now a big part of my repertoire.'

'So I've heard,' Edward said. 'You're getting quite a reputation as a writer and producer. I'll have to take Gareth to see your Rossington play this year.'

Gareth groaned with real feeling. 'You go. It's not my scene.'

'But you'd like to see the manor house where Lucy and Hugh live,' Edward tempted. 'It's a real Elizabethan place.'

'They don't,' Anna said quickly. 'Lucy and Hugh. Live there, that is. It was Lucy's childhood home, but it belongs to her brother Will now. Lucy and Hugh live in an old farmhouse, roughly between the manor and here.'

'It doesn't seem to me,' Edward said sweetly, the malice evident in his voice now, 'that Hugh does much living there. Dear Lucy isn't often there either. Even her dog,' he nodded towards the collie, 'seems to live with you these days.'

Anna recognised the curiosity that lay behind the comment and chose her words with care. 'Lucy is just finishing a big project in South America for the Seed Bank, but after that she'll be working for them part-time on smaller jobs, which will mean less time away from home. Then she'll be spending more time at Elowen, in the garden. She's done a lot of work on the apprentice scheme, and on the young offenders' resettlement scheme. Now she's got to bring it all together ready for the autumn when she hopes to have them both running full time.'

'But I suppose Hugh will still be in the States,' Edward persisted. 'He does seem to like it so much.'

'He's been very tied up there since his publishing company was bought by the American publishers, but he'll be back for the official opening of the garden,' Anna said. Really, she thought, I can't explain Hugh's actions; I'm not sure he knows himself what he wants to do. And will he be back for the opening?

She blocked the thought, glancing at her watch, and exclaimed in surprise, 'Heavens, it'll be dark soon. I'd better get going, I'm supposed to be meeting Mike at Soldiers' Meadow.' She stood up with easy grace and reached for her cape as the collie came to join her. Her shapely figure was already well-concealed by the heavy scarlet jumper she wore over her black woollen trousers, but she expertly wrapped the vividly patterned cape around her body, cocooning herself against the early spring chill outside. She leaned down to kiss Edward on the cheek, but when she turned to Gareth he fended her off with an upraised arm.

'I'm probably still covered in clay,' he said, getting to his feet. 'Anyway, I'll walk up to the meadow with you. I'd like to see how

Mike is getting on.'

He glanced down at his partner, who sprawled comfortably across the sofa beside the stove that made the small sitting area cosily warm. 'I don't suppose you want to come too.' It was a statement, not a question.

'Definitely not.' Edward shuddered, closing his eyes in horror. 'It's wet out there, and cold. You have a good time,' he finished encouragingly. 'I'll be here when you get back.'

Gareth grunted, and followed Anna to the door.

It was only three o'clock, but it was already gloomy under an overcast sky, and the mid-March afternoon was heading towards the dimness of dusk. The fading light did nothing to disguise the derelict farmyard where the mobile home stood.

The farmhouse that had been on one side of the yard had only been a single storey building, a post-war concrete-block rebuilding of the original house. Most of this later construction had crumbled, leaving uneven walls at about head height. The yard still retained its original barns, stables, and dairy, old, Anna knew, but how old she would need Mike to tell her. Or Hugh, if he ever came back. Plants sprouted from the granite walls, doors hung crookedly from their hinges, slates had fallen, shattering into sharp-edged shards as they hit the ground, leaving gaping holes in the roofs.

She hated to think what the interiors would be like. Damp at the very least, probably hosting a community of rats. Possibly even foxes came here to shelter from the weather. Neither Edward nor Gareth were likely to mind their presence. And Ben, the collie, was happily sniffing around, enjoying the scents.

Anna followed a track trodden through the greenery that flourished in the yard, picking her way with care over the cobbled surface that was barely visible under a thick covering of weeds and grass. They had benefited from the wet winter, making the track dangerously slippery underfoot so she was relieved to reach the gateway, where a couple of wooden bars dangled precariously, the only remnants of the gate that had once hung there.

She had passed another track through the emerging cow parsley and hogweed in the yard, leading to what Anna knew to be the old dairy that Gareth had skilfully restored to use as his pottery. This was a narrower track, no doubt because Gareth did not encourage visitors when he was working, not even Edward. The esoteric shapes Gareth created there were sold through various galleries, and he had no contact with the buyers, which suited him well. He could rarely be persuaded away from this isolated spot, except to wander the cliffs, gaining inspiration, Anna supposed, for his creations.

Gareth had not spoken by the time they emerged from the yard. They paused to look at the grassy slope ahead, where a path led past a network of small fields to the cliff path and up to the meadow where Mike was checking the site of the community dig he had recently received funding for. Ben had been ranging ahead, and he stopped too, looking back at them, resigned to human dithering on walks. A light misty haze was already drifting across the ground, likely to settle damply over the buildings during the night.

As they set off along the path, Gareth broke the silence. 'He can't help himself, he just wants to know about everyone,' he said roughly. 'He's intensely curious, and some people just like to gossip, so he encourages them very skilfully. He's had a lot of practice.'

Anna had been thinking of Mike and brought her mind back to Gareth's words with an effort. Of course, he was talking about Edward, she realised.

'He does know a lot about the area,' Anna said. 'And he isn't even local. Neither are you, but you both seem to have fitted in very well.'

'Edward is a Londoner at heart, but he came here for his holidays every year as a child. He knows the area and the people as well as any local, and loves it well enough to have the urge to live here. Says it inspires his muse. So here we are,' Gareth said, only a faint hint of irony in his tone. 'Me, I'm definitely a Tenby lad. My father's family were fishermen from way back. Not much future in that, of course, but I still feel at home by the sea. I even get out in a boat here now and again, to do some line fishing.'

He paused, turning to look back at the farmyard below. The buildings were now a darker grey than the descending dusk. Only a faint glimmer of white showed where the mobile home stood behind a sheltering stack of rotting straw bales, and a shaft of light shone from the window by the little sitting area, where Edward was no doubt dozing on his sofa.

'One day,' Gareth said quietly, almost to himself, hand resting absentmindedly on the collie's head as Ben came back to stand between them, 'I'd like to restore this place and build another house here. Although sometimes I wonder if it would just be better to move.'

'You shouldn't move, build your house instead,' Anna said. 'This is a superb setting. Sheltered from the sea, but close enough to walk there in a few minutes.'

Gareth's teeth gleamed in a sudden smile. 'A bit more than a few minutes. Come on, or Mike will be storming down here looking for you.' As they resumed their walk, shortly joining the cliff path which twisted more steeply upwards, Ben bounding ahead, Gareth went on, 'I'm surprised he can do any work yet. Isn't the ground too wet?'

Anna gurgled with laughter. 'Of course it is. He can't really do much yet. But you know Mike, he can't wait to get started. He got Tony Zennor to take off the turf over the excavation area and he's up there whenever he can, opening the trial trenches. He says the water runs off well, so the ground drains quickly.

'Lucy had a quick look at the meadow last autumn to check the plant life, when we knew Mike's new company might get the funding for a trial dig. She's sure that there's nothing rare there, the ground has been ploughed too often in the past.'

Gareth nodded. 'Yes, Edward loves telling the story of how a body was turned up once, about a hundred years ago, when a farmer was "tilling the soil".' He corrected himself, 'At least, a skeleton, or some of its bones. One of those poor damned soldiers.'

'He told me about it,' Anna said, her breath coming a little harder as they approached the top of the slope. 'But it's mainly been bits of metal and a few pistols that get uncovered, hasn't it?'

Gareth shrugged. 'That's what I've heard. Probably a few coins too. Though I'm never sure about the truth of these old stories. They change fractionally with every telling. And I've never actually seen a pistol that looks of the right period.' He glanced across at her ruefully. 'And I'm not even sure what the right period is. Some say the ship that was wrecked was from the Napoleonic wars. But I've heard other people swear it was older, a Spanish ship from the Armada fleet, naturally carrying a huge cargo of gold bars. Although why a warship would be loaded down with them I have yet to work out.'

'Mmm,' Anna agreed as they reached the top of the field. The clouds had cleared, so it was much brighter here than it had been when they set off.

They walked on a short distance and by mutual unspoken agreement they stopped by an outcrop of rock beyond the path. On the far side of the outcrop the rock had split centuries ago, and a flat wedge of granite kept the split sides apart, forming a natural seat completely sheltered from the path. They stood beside this, looking across the spreading expanse of the sea, as if they were at the foot of the golden path the setting sun cast to the far horizon.

'But,' Anna remarked, as Ben came to sit alertly in front of them, 'the remains of the *Queen Charlotte* were found five years ago just off the coast here, so there is at least some truth in the story of the shipwreck. And Mike says there's proof that she was carrying soldiers for the war in Spain, part of the fight against Napoleon, long before coastguards and lighthouses prevented ships from sailing onto the rocks. Maybe that's why people get confused with the Armada, the Spanish connection. But,' she went on reflectively, 'I've never understood why the bodies weren't buried in churchyards, whatever century they're from. Hawker did that on the north coast. I mean, he buried shipwrecked sailors from the shores below his church at Morwenstow. I went to see the place once.' She paused, thinking back, 'It's very atmospheric. I could almost see him perched in that hut of his above those terrible ridges of rocks, watching, waiting, for something he dreaded, something that happened time after time, a ship driven in by the storms, thrown against the rocks, stranded, trapped, sinking. I could almost hear the shouts and screams from on board, it seemed so vivid.' She shivered slightly as she turned to look up at Soldiers' Meadow, just below the rocky promontory. 'It seems a bit grim to leave bodies out here, away from everyone else.'

'I don't know,' Gareth said prosaically. 'It's a beautiful spot. Look at the panoramic view of the shore,' he gestured towards the horizon, 'and you can see how wide a view there is of the sea. This outcrop is in an ideal spot, no wonder the rock seat is so popular. I expect earlier watchers stood here too, after all there's a fort on the promontory.' He gestured again, to the north. 'Iron Age, I think, but Mike will know. It must have been a perfect spot for local people to look for approaching ships. They'd have seen invaders and had time to summon help. They'd have recognised traders, so they knew when it was safe to come down to the beach to barter. Although I've no doubt the wreckers came here too, when the weather was bad, hoping for a wreck, perhaps waving a lantern to entice a ship onto the rocks. It's not like Morwenstow's coast, but ships can't safely come in too close here either.' Gareth shrugged. 'But overall it's not such a bad place to rest for eternity. I wouldn't mind, myself.'

Anna knew what he meant. The sea was calm, its waves moving gently, tipped with light, and the sky above it was streaked pink and yellow. Gulls flew across it in convoy towards a distant roosting site, black silhouettes against the brightness.

Gareth said abruptly, 'I want to look at those studios you're creating at Elowen.'

Anna was surprised. 'Are you thinking of working there? I thought you liked where you are.'

'I do.' He clarified his agreement. 'Like where I am. But Edward gets bored with the isolation. He'd like to meet more people, so I thought this might be a good way to arrange it. I'll keep my own working studio at the farmyard, but I can make standard pieces at Elowen on certain days, and use it as a selling point, which Edward can manage.'

'What about his own work?' Anna asked cautiously. 'He won't be able to write there, will he?'

Gareth gave a bark of laughter. 'His poetry? He writes that in the middle of the night. He never needs much sleep.'

Anna lifted one shoulder in an elegant shrug, tactfully not asking how well the poetry was received by the reading public. 'Then come over and look around. One studio has already gone, Aaron Tregonan is taking the largest to showcase his dolls' houses, but you'll have a good choice of the others if you come soon. I'm seeing somebody else about them tomorrow. You probably know her, Martha Zennor from the farm over there. Carne Farm.' She gestured to her left, down the slope. Closer to the sea than the pottery, a huddle of buildings crouched in the shelter of a small copse of stunted and bent trees, carved into contorted shapes by the winds from the sea.

'Yes, I know Martha. An amazing woman. She has about ten children running wild around that place.' He heard Anna's indrawn breath of surprise. 'Oh, not all her own. She's got a very large number of cousins all living round and about, so a selection of their offspring is always mingling with her own. I doubt she knows how many are there at any one time.' Gareth smiled with appreciation as he went on, 'But there's always a pot of stew on the range, and cakes and biscuits in the oven. I reckon she does most of the work on the farm too, since Tony had the accident.'

'I heard about that,' Anna said. 'It was in the tractor, wasn't it?'

'Yes. Up here, in this field, not the meadow next to it that Mike's working in. The tractor turned over, pinning him under-neath. Happens to lots of farmers. He's mobile again, but it'll be a while before he's out and about under his own steam. Meanwhile, Martha and the older kids cover his work.'

Anna was frowning. 'It doesn't sound as though she'll need a studio yet then.'

Gareth gave his barking laugh again. 'You don't know her. Nothing will stand in Martha's way if she wants to do something. And her work is superb. Edward gave me one of her jumpers for Christmas, all terracottas and golds. I don't know how he could afford it, her prices are sky-high, but knowing him, he probably persuaded her into a special deal. He thought the colours would remind me of my work.'

'She uses her own alpaca wool, doesn't she?'

'Yes. I don't think she shears the animals herself, although I have heard she's planning to train up her eldest son and one of his mates to do it. But she does everything else. She spins the wool and makes her own plant dyes. But it's the designs that are special. Wait until you see some of the things she's made. She weaves too, she has a large loom set up in one of the barns.' He waved his hand towards the cluster of buildings. 'That farm looks a tip, not like ours, a ruin, but a heavily occupied tip. But it's completely organised, she has a place for everything, it's just that there are a lot of people around the place, and a lot of clutter. When are you going there?'

'First thing in the morning,' Anna said, 'then, if she's still interested, she can come over to Elowen and look round the studios later in the day.' Anna still stood looking out to sea, and asked idly, 'Do you know the farmer on the other side of the headland? I guess his land borders this, so I wonder if he's helping the Zennors out. Farmers generally support each other, don't they?'

'In a dream world.' The words were loud, belligerent. 'Bloody farmers! Who'd have anything to do with them? Not that Trago really counts as a farmer.'

Anna's smile flashed out as she turned around, her hands held out to the man with the tousled red hair who stood close behind her, the collie wriggling with excitement in front of him. 'Hello,

Mike. How long have you been there? I didn't hear you coming.'

'You were too busy talking,' he said, taking her hands in his and pulling her closer to wrap his arms round her.

She turned in his hold, looking back out across the sea. 'It's a beautiful sunset.'

Mike grunted, looking at Gareth. 'And do you know the farmer up there?' he demanded.

Gareth's expression was shuttered. 'We've met,' he said shortly.

Mike freed one hand to rub the collie's head as Ben pushed against his knees. 'I've met him too. Far too often. He was in the meadow just now, ranting about the dig.'

'Oh dear,' Anna said placidly. 'Is he still upset about it? I've never understood why.'

'He claims the land is his,' Mike said through gritted teeth. 'Tony Zennor has legal ownership and he gave me permission to have the dig, and we'll access it through his driveway, so Trago doesn't have a leg to stand on. But that doesn't stop him sounding off. I can't see him helping out a neighbour, not his style.' Mike drew a deep, steadying breath. 'On the other hand, Tony's good to work with. He's really interested in the old stories about the shipwreck and burials, and wants to see if there's any truth in them. And a couple of his kids are taking part. So is Trago's daughter, she's even thinking about studying archaeology, poor fool, and I'm trying not to put her off.'

'Not a good career choice then?' Gareth asked.

Mike glared at him. 'What do you think these days?'

'Bit like making pots,' Gareth said.

'Not if you're making them,' Mike retorted.

'I'll take that for a compliment,' Gareth said. 'Peace, Mike. I don't mind your dig, and I don't like Andrew Trago either. He wants to buy our place.'

'Why?' Anna asked in surprise. 'Doesn't he have a lot of land already?'

'He does,' Gareth said shortly. 'He says he needs it for the horses. His wife, the current one, has ambitions as a breeder. Of equines, that is. She's not as keen on kids as Martha.'

Mike was frowning. 'I wouldn't have thought you'd have enough land to interest him.'

'We don't,' Gareth replied. 'But we link his land with Soldiers' Meadow. Rumour has it that he wants to build a holiday park across it and the fields above, which he does own, with access down beside the headland to the beach. But he's not sounding off widely about that kind of plan.'

'What!' Mike exploded. 'So that's why he's so het up about the dig. He's afraid we'll find something that will upset his crafty plans. Doesn't the fool realise he'd need to have an excavation anyway if he wants to develop the land?'

'Even these days?' Gareth asked quietly.

The grinding of Mike's teeth was audible, and Anna pulled out of his encircling arm before he could say anything. 'Don't let the man get to you. You've got permission to do the dig. Get on with it. And now,' she said, turning towards the track that led down towards Carne Farm, 'let's get home. I expect you're hungry.'

'Of course I am,' Mike said indignantly, as Ben looked up at him, eager to get moving. 'It's you that's been standing here talking.'

'We were just arranging for Gareth to see the studios,' Anna explained. She mentally considered her diary. 'Will sometime tomorrow suit you too, Gareth? Say two-thirty, if you don't mind perhaps overlapping with Martha who's coming at three o'clock if she wants to see the studios.'

'It'll be fine for me,' Gareth said. 'But don't mention anything to Edward yet. Not until I'm sure.'

Mike was grinning. 'That'll be interesting for you,' he said. Glancing at Anna, he asked, 'Won't Will be coming over as soon as he gets back?'

'If he can,' she agreed, 'but Will won't be a problem.'

'Will?' Gareth queried.

'Lucy Rossington's little brother,' Mike said genially. 'He'll just be back from India. No doubt he'll be full of interesting stories. He'll love another audience.'

Gareth's bark of laughter sounded. 'I'm a good listener. I've had a lot of practice.'

'Practice at tuning out might be more useful,' Mike said. He turned as he spoke, pulling Anna with him.

She raised a hand in farewell, before stepping closer to Mike to walk down the track as Ben set off ahead of them. 'That was a bit mean,' she said. 'Will is a nice bloke.'

'Very nice,' Mike agreed, watching the collie pause to sniff a clump of gorse with intense concentration. 'Especially when you can get him off the subject of his latest enthusiasm. What do you think it will be now? Indian life? Elephants? Tigers? Maharajahs? God knows what other possibilities there are. I guess it'll still be India that gets him going. He was keen enough to defer his university place last year to get back there for a while longer.'

'Curry? Tea? Mogul palaces?' Anna suggested lightly. 'We haven't seen him since last autumn, Mike. He's probably changed a lot, but his chief interest is still likely to be something to do with conservation. I don't think that's going to change, especially as he's got that good place he wanted to read Wildlife Biology and Conservation. I've always liked his enthusiasm for things he believes in, and I hope he hasn't lost it.'

'Hmmmph. Four years' study will be testing it alright. Even though he seems to have found a course that allows him to do field work anywhere he fancies in the world. He's fallen on his feet with that.'

They walked along in silence, Ben keeping close now, as they gradually descended the track past Carne Farm. The track was some distance from the house, which was partially screened by its barns. The whole property was a dark mass tucked into the sheltering trees, but lights shone from all the windows of the house. Voices were raised above the loud beat of music, although it was impossible to tell if they were singing along or shouting to be heard above the noise. A door opened, sending a beam of brightness across the garden, lighting bikes strewn across the garden path, and a heap of pallets beside it. 'Have you shut up the hens yet, Sue?' a woman's voice demanded, as a dog barked loudly from the neighbouring yard. 'Supper's ready,' the woman added, her voice carrying clearly through the night air.

There was an answering shout, but the words were not audible to Anna or Mike. The door shut again, leaving the garden in darkness, but not silence as the sound of a television suddenly competed with the booming music.

'I'm visiting there tomorrow morning, to discuss the studios with Martha Zennor,' Anna said, as she and Mike approached his battered Passat estate, tucked tightly against the hedge at the end of the track. 'From all Gareth said, it should be an interesting experience. He said her work's amazing.'

'You seem to have got a lot of interest in the studios,' Mike commented absentmindedly.

'Yes,' Anna agreed. 'I hope that's a good sign. We do have ten to fill. Nine, as Aaron definitely wants to take the biggest one. And Gareth is interested in having one as well, although you must remember not to mention it to Edward yet. So that may leave us with eight to fill. Seven, if Martha has one, too.'

'Ahh,' Mike muttered.

Anna glanced sideways at him as they reached the car and he opened the back for Ben to jump in. She could not quite make out Mike's expression, but she could tell that he was not really listening. She thought back to what he had said when he had joined her and Gareth.

'Did you have trouble at the meadow?' she asked.

His head jerked back as he pulled the driver's door open. 'Trouble?' he snarled. 'Yes.' He flung himself into the seat, banging his hand against the gear stick and swearing loudly. 'I told you I had bloody Andrew Trago up there again, going on about the land being his. He's only been back in the area for a year or so, and he behaves as if he owns it all.'

Mike snorted, although Anna detected a half laugh in the sound. 'I only got rid of him because he nearly fell into one of the trial trenches I've dug. He didn't look where he was going. He just slipped on the edge, but he messed up his nice clean cords and his tweed coat.' Mike's laugh was nearly disguised by the slamming of his door. 'You'd never take him for a real countryman, one who grew up around here. His ten years away have made him a townee, determined to turn his decent sixteenth century farmhouse into a modern monstrosity.'

Anna steadied herself against the rocking of the car as she edged into her own seat, shutting the door with deliberate care. 'But is he really local?' she queried, wondering if she had misheard Mike.

'Yes really, for generations back, from one of the old farming families,' Mike agreed. 'But he's grown well away from his roots. He's talking about going to court to stop the dig,' Mike continued more calmly, starting the engine as he turned the subject back to the meadow. 'I don't really understand what this is all about. Even if he thinks we may find something important there, he must know he can't stop the dig.' His voice brightened. 'Maybe he does know we'll find something.'

'It sounds as though he's got a control complex,' Anna commented practically. 'If he really thinks the land is his, maybe he doesn't like things happening to it without his permission.'

Her brows drew together as Mike drove through the narrow lanes, the car's headlights illuminating the hedgerows. These still looked stark and bare, the newly emerging spring shoots not visible in the gathering darkness of night. 'Why does he think he owns the land? Surely there's proof of the ownership?'

Mike's hands gripped the steering wheel tightly. 'Don't ask me,' he growled. 'How should I know how the idiot's mind works?' He contradicted himself immediately. 'Ownership is registered with Tony Zennor, I checked myself when Trago started kicking off. It's been in Tony's family for generations, but Andrew Trago says there was a gentleman's agreement between their great-grandfathers, passing the land over to the Tragos in return for services rendered.'

Anna's imagination was fired by Mike's words. 'Maybe Trago Senior saved Zennor Senior's life somehow. At sea, or maybe,' she tried to calculate dates in her head, 'at war. Or perhaps Zennor Senior bargained for a treasure map. Or ...'

His tight grip of the steering wheel relaxing, Mike glanced at her with some amusement as he interrupted her. 'It's likely to be something more sordid – gambling, wenching, smuggling, something like that. If it was a heroic story, other people would know about it, and it would probably be public knowledge.'

'Maybe it is,' Anna countered enthusiastically. 'Edward may well know about it. I'll ask him when I see him. I guess it wouldn't do to ask Martha, although I think she's the better storyteller. But if Andrew Trago has proof that he does own the meadow, why doesn't he just produce it?'

'Because he doesn't. And just watch what you say to Martha or Edward,' Mike said. He slowed the car as a fox paused in the lane, turning to stare at them, before it continued a leisurely trot along the base of one of the hedgerows until it reached its route up over the bank and out of sight. 'Edward will repeat anything he finds interesting, and I don't want too much made of Trago's behaviour.'

'Okay. Shall we go to the pub in Genarren for something to eat? I don't fancy cooking, and I'm sure you don't.'

'Too right,' Mike said. 'I'll need fortifying if I've got to listen to Will's India stories tomorrow.'

'Don't be mean, Mike,' Anna reproached. 'It'll be interesting, and we don't know how long he'll be here this time. His last visits were only flying ones. He's sent some stunning pictures to Lucy, but hasn't written much, I think.'

'Is she coming over tomorrow too?' Mike asked, turning down the lane that led to Genarren, the local village. 'I can never keep track of where she is. At least I know if Hugh isn't here, he's likely to be in London or New York.'

'She's in South America, you should remember that's become her specialist field. Peru again, I think, encouraging the development of local seed banks. You know, for small farmers to collect and keep crop seeds as a protection against some kind of natural disaster. She likes doing that best, really, but she spends time searching for seeds of rare plants too, sending them to safe banks around the world. Again, that's insurance against some disaster, and there do seem to be a lot more of those, somehow.' Anna frowned slightly. 'I think she's having more meetings with government officials to schedule in these days too, which she's not so keen on.'

'I can't see how she'll ever be able to put in the work at Elowen,' Mike said, ignoring this resumé of Lucy's work, as he drove up the main street in Genarren.

'You know she's reducing the amount of time she's working for the Seed Bank,' Anna said patiently. 'And Lucy is a brilliant organiser. She always does the things she says she will.' She wondered, though, just for a second, if Mike might be right.

'She hasn't organised such a brilliant marriage,' Mike said brutally.

'It isn't just her marriage,' Anna said mildly. 'Hugh's as responsible for its state as she is.'

'I suppose you've told him so,' Mike said, pulling the Passat to a halt outside The Lanyon Arms.

'Not yet,' Anna said ruefully, as he turned towards her, resting one arm along the steering wheel. 'I thought things were improving last year, but they've barely seen each other this year.' She lifted one shoulder in her usual shrug. 'Some people prefer it that way. But neither of them seems particularly happy.'

'No,' Mike agreed. 'But successful. Maybe that's enough.'

Anna bit her lip. 'I wouldn't have thought so once. But perhaps we all change.' Her brilliant smile flashed out as he glanced at her. 'After all, who'd have ever thought we'd end up together.'

'True.' He turned to the door, 'Well, let's get in here and eat a good steak and kidney pie while we're still talking to each other. It's bound to beat the sushi Hugh's likely to be eating, wherever he is.'

Hugh Carey was not eating sushi. He was swallowing his last bite of the main course of a very fashionable meal in a very beautiful London house, at a table surrounded by the great and interesting of the literary world. His head was turned slightly towards the woman seated on his right, an air of attentiveness about his posture as he listened with one ear to her general publishing chatter. But his attention had wandered.

What was Lucy doing? The thought flashed through his mind, surprising him. He did not often think of his wife. And that realisation startled him considerably. Where was she now? He tried to calculate her diary, but without looking at his own he could not be sure if she was still in Peru or had arrived back in England. It was Peru, wasn't it, he asked himself guiltily. He couldn't remember which country Lucy had gone to this time.

His thoughts fractured as he gathered his wits to answer a question from the woman next to him. He parried the query lightly and greeted the arrival of an artistically decorated cheesecake with secret relief. He returned to his own thoughts. Elowen, that's right, that's where Lucy would be now, or perhaps only on her way there.

Damn, Hugh thought abruptly. There was a party there soon, the garden's opening party, and he had said he'd try to get to it. When the hell was it? He knew he hadn't really meant to go. It would be too difficult to fit into a schedule that had got more demanding rather than less.

It wasn't how he'd expected it to be when he sold his niche publishing company last year and accepted the proffered directorship in the new owner's organisation. But these were interesting times, he reminded himself wryly. And he could never resist a challenge. And yet, the idea flashed across his mind, life generally had become boring. So maybe, just maybe, he'd moved beyond these kinds of challenges. They were getting repetitive. Perhaps he should be looking at something new.

He realised with a start that the woman on his left had turned and said something to him. 'I'm so sorry,' he said apologetically, 'I was wool-gathering.'

'That's such a quaint expression,' she said humorously, with a strong transatlantic accent. 'But,' she looked puzzled, 'what does it mean?'

'Thinking about something else,' he admitted.

'I guess it's hard not to sometimes,' she said. 'You are a man of many parts, aren't you?'

He raised an enquiring eyebrow.

'Hugh Carey, right? Your photographs,' she said. 'I got the book of your photographs a couple of years back. They were quite something. Especially the landscapes.'

Hugh was astonished. Nobody had ever mentioned his book to him before. He looked more closely at the woman. Middle thirties, he guessed, although it was hard to tell. A compact figure, shoulder-length silver-blonde hair in casual waves, an expression of genuine interest on her rounded face. He tried to remember who she was, squinting unsuccessfully to see the name on her place setting.

'Laney Scholz,' she said helpfully.

Hugh's eyes widened. Laney Scholz was a hugely well-known wildlife photographer. He could not believe it was this woman next to him.

She grinned suddenly, as if she had read his thought. 'It's been some time since I went scrambling over cliffs in this country,' she said, glancing down at her black dress. 'But I still get out in my trekking gear with my cameras whenever I can.'

'I know you do,' he said. 'I've seen your recent pictures of Patagonia. Amazing.'

'It's an amazing place. Have you been there?'

'No, I seem to mostly be here or in New York these days,' Hugh said. 'But my wife is in South America a great deal, working for one of the major English seed banks.'

'You should go,' Laney said simply. 'With your own cameras. Meet your wife out there sometime.' She studied him thoughtfully. 'Are you bringing out another book of your work?'

He shook his head, a rueful smile twisting his lips. 'I haven't really done any more in that line. There's never any time.'

'Shame,' she said abruptly. 'You've got a good eye. There were some fine shots in that book. And you got the sense of the landscape well, it gave me a real urge to visit your South West.'

'Well, why don't you?' he said on a sudden impulse. 'Lucy, my wife, and I are involved with a garden restoration down there and there's a big launch party, this weekend, I think. Come and visit us, and I'll show you around.'

Laney considered him. 'D'you know, I think I might just do that. I've always had a fancy to visit that part of England, and I think I've heard of this garden restoration. Elowen, right?' She saw his nod of agreement, and went on, 'You must tell me how to get there. It sounds a real exciting place to be.' She leaned forward to pick a handful of grapes from the fruit bowl in the centre of the table.

Hugh sat back, a feeling of unease creeping through him as he watched her. Just what had he done? He had not been back to see Elowen and the work done there for some time, and now he'd be turning up with a complete stranger, when he hadn't really meant to go at all.

Ah well, Hugh dismissed the qualm, it would work out. He leaned forward to help himself from the fruit bowl that Laney held out to him.

Lucy Rossington stood in the airport watching the luggage carousel chugging around. Part of her mind was scanning the bags and cases for her own. But the main part was reviewing the trip she had just finished in Peru.

It had gone well, very well. She knew that. Local farmers and villagers understood very clearly the need for saving seed, they'd always saved a proportion of their crop seeds in a safe place against poor harvests. Both nature and humans could cause those, the peasant farmers understood that only too well. Now a growing number were accepting the importance of saving the rainforest flora too, understanding the dangers of losing their biodiversity, and she found that very satisfying. She enjoyed working with the local people, absorbing their knowledge, and passing on some of her own.

Lucy frowned as she thought of the high-level scientific and political meetings she had endured as well. Those she did not enjoy at all, but they were necessary. And she was sure they had been successful too. She felt a pang of regret that her next trip, to Ecuador in the summer, would be her last before she spent more time at Elowen.

'Hi, Lucy,' a man's voice broke into her thoughts. She turned, startled, at the familiar tones.

A young man grabbed her in a vigorous hug and then held her away from him. 'Didn't you get my text? Gran said you'd be arriving about the same time as us, so I told you we'd meet you and we can all go home together.'

Lucy stared at her brother, gathering her wits. She had not seen him for six months, and had not been expecting him now. It startled her to see how much he had changed. His slender build was similar to hers, but his shoulders were broader now and he had developed more muscle. His crisp dark hair was longer than it had been, almost touching his shoulders, and his blue eyes were very startling in his thin tanned face.

The brother and sister had their slight stature in common, but not their colouring. Lucy's thin pointed face was only lightly browned by southern suns, and her chestnut hair was cropped very short. But there was an indefinable air of kinship about them, clearly marking them as related.

Will stepped back and reached out for the woman who stood just behind him. Niri Chaudry was watching the reunion with some amusement and stepped forward to touch his outstretched hand.

'I don't think that text got through,' she said. 'I hope you remembered to send it.' She moved away from Will to embrace Lucy fondly. 'It's good to see you.'

'Niri.' The embrace was returned. 'It's such a surprise to see you both here, my thoughts were still in Peru.' Lucy was relieved that Niri still looked the same as she remembered her. She was slightly shorter than Lucy, with a creamy brown complexion and the jet-black hair that reflected her Indian origins. She still wore her long hair twisted into a casual knot, and had on a familiar outfit of jeans with a loose linen shirt, and a thick suede jacket. She looked as calm and imperturbable as always, and Lucy felt a strong pang of affection at the sight of her.

As the women stepped apart Lucy added, 'You're both looking very well. India clearly agrees with you.'

'It does,' Will said emphatically. 'And it sounds as though you've covered most of South America while we've been away.' He was looking around at the other passengers, searching their faces. 'How's Hugh?' he asked.

'He's not here,' Lucy said, noticing his search.

'I know that.' Will grinned at her. 'I'm looking for Gran. She's coming in from Italy shortly, so we can all go home together.'

Lucy was surprised how pleased she was at the thought. She had not seen Isobel Rossington either for several months now and frequently missed talking to her.

It had been Isobel who had brought up the young Rossington siblings after their mother's early death. Their father had been an explorer, rarely at home in the West Country and generally too busy writing to spend time with his children when he was at their family manor. Lucy had wondered recently if she, and perhaps Will, had inherited their father's travel gene, or if they had just learned from his behaviour.

Isobel had been the one who had provided the stability the children had needed at home and had been the anchor of their family life. It had been Lucy who was most taken aback by Isobel's departure from this life a while ago when Will reached his majority. She had moved to live for part of the year in a small mews house in a nearby town.

By then, Lucy had been instrumental in saving the family manor for her younger brother after their father's death. It had been at the cost of her own planned career, put on hold, she had thought, but then she had met Hugh Carey, older, certainly more cosmopolitan than her. He too was changing his life, moving from a career as a successful barrister to explore publishing and photography opportunities. After their marriage, Lucy had followed a different career path as a seed conservator, something she perhaps would not have thought about earlier.

Isobel's departure from the manor, and then, shortly after, from England to mainly live and work in Florence had been a shock to Lucy. Isobel's embroidery business there was booming, with an increasing international following, and she rarely managed visits back to England. Those she did make had not usually coincided with Lucy's stints at home, so Lucy was pleased that this time they would see each other.

'Oh,' Will said casually, his eyes on the flight board, 'I've got some help for you at Elowen.'

His sister looked at him suspiciously. 'What sort of help?' she demanded, remembering how enthusiastic he was about the working Shires he had acquired at their family home.

He laughed. 'Nothing controversial,' he said. 'I expect Hugh would be interested in doing it, but I knew he wouldn't have time.' He broke off to check the time on his iPhone. 'Gran should have landed by now. I don't suppose you have your car here, do you?'

'Of course not,' Lucy said. 'I go down by train and get a taxi out to Withern unless Anna or Mike can meet me.'

'Okay,' Will said agreeably. 'I was just hoping we wouldn't have to lug the baggage much more, like over to Paddington and onto the train.'

Lucy looked at the two trolleys that Niri was standing beside. Both were loaded high with canvas bags, rucksacks, holdalls.

'You're only back for a couple of weeks. I thought you

believed in travelling light,' she commented wryly.

'I do. We do,' he amended, glancing at Niri. 'But people kept giving us stuff,' he waved one hand towards the piles of luggage, 'when we were leaving, even though they know we'll be back soon. We couldn't leave it behind. Rude,' he explained thoughtfully.

She stared at him. This was definitely a different Will. 'Of course,' she managed. Her thoughts reverted to what he had said earlier. 'What about this help you've got for Elowen, Will? You should run it past Anna before arranging it. She's the one doing most of the work there, and they manage the overview of what's happening and who's doing what. There are quite a few people involved in it now.'

'Oh, this will be alright,' Will said breezily. 'Ferdi is just a Dutch chap I know from India. He wants to come down to visit our area, and I thought he could be useful. He's a mad keen bird-watcher like Hugh, so I've set him up to do a bird count in and around the garden later in the year. It'll be interesting, at least,' Will amended conscientiously, 'Ferdi reckons it will.'

'Well, Hugh certainly won't have time to do it,' Lucy agreed. 'But be sure to run the idea past Anna before you arrange anything definitely.'

'Okay,' Will said. 'But Ferdi is coming to stay at the manor in May and he'll be at a loose end without us as we'll be back in India soon after he arrives. That should be time enough to sort out a house in Plymouth for the autumn. I wouldn't bother to view any, but Niri thought we might as well as we had to come back until May. I've got some work to do at the zoo and her Mum's got a big birthday. Forty, I think. Anyway,' Will reverted abruptly to the matter he was more interested in, 'Ferdi will be keen to get started, get to know his way around the area. He's very enthusiastic.'

Will had not changed all that much, Lucy thought. As soon as he thought of an idea, he had to put it into practice. 'I can't see that it'll be a problem,' she said. 'But don't just take him round to Elowen when he gets here, discuss it with Anna and the committee first.'

'Yeah, yeah, I got the message. Look,' his voice changed, suddenly eager, 'there's Gran.'

Isobel Rossington had almost reached them. She bore a strong physical resemblance to her granddaughter. Her build was slight too and her thin pointed face was similar to Lucy's, although her skin was sallow from several years of early married life with her husband on their tea plantation in Kerala. She had always been well dressed in an English countrywoman fashion while she had brought up her grandchildren in England, in the quintessentially English setting of an ancient manor house in the West Country. Even when she had lived in India nobody could have taken her for anything but an Englishwoman abroad.

But now those who liked to guess nationalities would have marked her down as Italian, possibly French. Her iron-grey hair was still worn in a short bob, but this had lost its earlier severity and was now slightly longer and artfully styled to swing against her face. She was dressed today in a well-fitting blue dress, a darker-blue coat open over it, and, carrying one of her own beautifully embroidered bags, she had an indefinable continental aura about her. And an air of confidence, born of the success of her recently developed business. This had grown out of her long-term interest in embroidery, and her growing knowledge of early work across the continent. Her first ventures into embroideries based on this skill and knowledge had been turned into bags for her own use, and gifts for her friends. Now the unique creations were sought after by the wealthy and famous, and Isobel had branched into more areas, most lately shawls, employing an increasing number of home-based embroiderers to bring her designs to exquisite life.

'Hello, Gran,' Will said, stepping forward and seizing her in his usual enthusiastic hug. 'It's good to see you again. We can't wait to come over to Italy for another stay.'

Another stay, Lucy thought. She had not known Will, and

presumably Niri, had been before.

Will was still talking as Isobel freed herself gently from his grasp and turned to her granddaughter. 'Lucy, my dear, I'm so glad we have all arrived together. It's so long since I've seen you.'

They exchanged more genteel embraces, as Lucy asked, 'No baggage, Gran?'

'Of course I have,' she said as they moved apart. 'Fabio is taking care of it for me.' She indicated the man standing silently apart, with a trolley containing two cases, and a carpet bag in another of Isobel's designs. 'Will,' she glanced at her grandson, 'you remember Fabio.' She turned to Niri. 'My dear, it's very good to see you too. It hardly seems any time since you were discussing designs with me. You'll remember Fabio too.'

'Of course I do,' Niri said. She had moved over to the older man and was lightly kissing him on both cheeks. She was joined by Will, who shook his hand enthusiastically.

Isobel smiled at him over their heads. 'Fabio, you must come and meet my granddaughter, Will's sister. We're fortunate she's here, she has a very busy life.'

Fabio came over to them, hand extended to grasp the one Lucy offered. His dark hair was streaked with grey, and Lucy thought he was at least her grandmother's age, possibly older.

'Lucy, how do you do? I have heard so much about you and your work from Isobel. It is a pleasure to meet you at last.'

Lucy hoped she did not look as dumbfounded as she felt. The others knew this man, he knew about her, but she had not the faintest idea who he was.

He was still talking to her, and she concentrated on what he was saying. 'It is so kind of Isobel to ask me to the party. I have been following all the progress on Elowen that Isobel tells me about, so I look forward greatly to seeing the garden at last.'

'Let's get home,' Will said to his grandmother, before Lucy had a chance to find out exactly who Fabio was. He seized one of the trolleys, and began to push it towards the exit, adding, 'I can't wait to see the manor again.'

Niri and Fabio brought the other two trolleys into line behind him, and Lucy, who had only a small holdall, fell into step with Isobel. 'Fabio seems very nice,' she tried tentatively.

'He is,' Isobel replied. 'He's a textile consultant for many of the major Italian museums. I got to know him through my research, and he's been very supportive of my work. He also has a great knowledge of garden history, hence his interest in Elowen.'

'Hi,' Will called, 'let's get a taxi to the station. With all these bags it'll be easier.'

'Yes, that's a good idea,' Isobel agreed, and Lucy lost any immediate opportunity to ask questions.

Much manoeuvring later, they were all seated on the train to the West Country. There was plenty of talking, India, Italy, animals, designs, and questions about Lucy's work. But, somehow, she did not feel part of the group and was not quite sure why.

'Why don't you all come and spend the night at the manor?' Will suggested suddenly, glancing at Niri, who sat beside him. 'Niri's coming back with me, and her parents are coming over tomorrow, but we could have tonight to catch up with everything. We could ask Anna and Mike, too. Wow,' he went on, his eyes widening with amusement, 'I still can't believe those two have got together.'

'I always thought it was likely,' Isobel said. 'There was such a distinct spark between them.'

'I'll say,' Will said. 'An explosive one.'

Isobel glanced at Fabio, and said, 'It's a nice thought, Will, but Fabio and I will go straight to my house. I'm keen to get settled in before all the garden events start. And I must admit, I miss my dear little Juno when I come back to the manor. I sometimes think about getting another spaniel, but it wouldn't really be fair, I do so much travelling now.'

'Okay,' Will agreed. 'What about you, Lucy? Is Hugh back? We could ask him over too, or we could arrange a general catch-up for another time.'

The thought of going to the manor was appealing, but Lucy said, 'Thanks, Will, I'd like to get back to Withern.' She had suddenly realised why she felt left out. Will and Niri had clearly gone beyond friendship, they had become a couple while they were in India, a very well-matched couple. And Isobel and Fabio? Her thoughts baulked. She had never thought of her grandmother acquiring another partner.

These thoughts led to her husband, and Will's question. She did not know whether Hugh would be at their farmhouse home. She did not know where he would be. She had not minded before. The lack of contact was a price they paid for doing what they wanted. And they had both been successful in their endeavours.

She had once given up the job offer of her dreams to keep Rossington Manor in the family, but now she'd got a similar, probably better, job and worked pretty much on her own terms. She was taking part in the Elowen Garden restoration, albeit a small part, but one that enabled her to fulfil her newly discovered interest in training and developing disadvantaged young people.

But suddenly she wondered about the success of her marriage. It seemed so modern, so relaxed, but really, she and Hugh never saw each other, never did things together, hardly communicated about anything important. Maybe, she thought uneasily, she wasn't cut out for marriage, maybe she'd be better on her own.

TWO

The cobbled yard of Carne Farm was slick and slippery after the overnight rain. Anna surveyed it for a moment as she stood beside her car and was relieved she'd worn jeans and her walking shoes. The same music appeared to be thumping away in the house, the same voices raised above it. Did the household go to bed, she wondered as she walked to the path through the garden, or was this their general waking mode?

A loud barking greeted her approach, and a couple of collies tore around the corner of the end barn. A lurcher shot out of the barn to join them, and a Jack Russell came speeding out behind him. The four dogs came to a halt in front of Anna, still barking.

She hesitated. The collies were wagging their tails as well as barking. But the lurcher and terrier were not. Maybe it was just that the collies were bright enough to do two things at once. But maybe they were suspicious of her too.

As Anna dithered, a girl appeared in the barn's doorway. 'Mo, Bel, come here,' she shouted in a surprisingly authoritative tone for her ten or eleven years. She gestured vigorously and the lurcher and terrier peeled silently away from the pack and trotted towards her. 'Fly and Tip will take you to the door,' the girl called. 'Go on, they won't hurt you.'

Anna stepped forward resolutely and Fly and Tip paced beside her, silent now, but tails still wagging. They escorted her to the door at the side of the farmhouse, which was obviously the one in daily use. There was a narrow way through the jumble in the porch to the door itself. The collies sat outside, one on either side of the porch, as Anna picked her way through the tangled heap of boots and shoes, riding hats, wet suits, surfboards, balls, and racquets.

She scanned the doorway. There was no bell, no knocker, and she wondered how she was supposed to let Martha know she was there. A high voice from beside her hip startled her, and she glanced down to see another small girl, straw-coloured hair tied up in pigtails, hands grasping a basket of eggs.

'Are you here for Martha?' she demanded, pushing past Anna.

The girl lifted the back-door latch before Anna could reply or move to help her. 'Martha,' the girl's voice was raised to a shrill penetrating yell.

It was as if an echo answered. A rolling echo, sending the girl's voice back from different directions.

Anna was rooted to the spot as the echoes got louder. Both amused and startled she saw the source of the noise was solid enough as three small Labrador puppies came bolting towards the open door at the far end of the hall. They seemed to come from different directions, collided in the doorway and struggled for a second until their fat little bodies popped through and they came thundering towards Anna in a squealing excited mass.

'Don't let them out!' the girl yelled, disappearing into a room off the corridor.

Anna stepped forward quickly, slamming the back door behind her. She had just time to turn before the puppies were on her. There was one of each colour, black, red and yellow. She could tell that much, but each one of them seemed to be every-where. They jumped up, their paws scrabbling against her jeans, they wriggled round her ankles, they rolled over onto their backs between her feet.

The yellow one began to nibble at her shoelaces, and when Anna bent to push it away the puppy tightened its hold, pulling back with its trophy, growling ferociously. The black one popped up between Anna's knees and licked her chin enthusiastically. At the same time the brown one bounced up on all fours in front of her face and managed to lick one of her ears.

'Off!' A firm voice distracted the puppies and they turned around, tails wagging eagerly. 'Down!' the voice commanded, and the puppies flattened themselves happily on the floor with three synchronised thumps. 'Jenny, come and take the puppies.' A woman walked quickly down the corridor, pausing to give each of the puppies a titbit. 'Take them to the scullery,' she said to the little girl who had reappeared in the doorway along the corridor.

The child ran off, calling the puppies, who leaped enthusiastically after her.

'Sorry about that, Anna,' the woman said. 'I didn't hear the gong.'

'Hi, Martha,' Anna said, her words ringing in her ears in the silence left by the puppies. Even the thud of music seemed only a gentle background hum now. 'What gong?'

'Our front doorbell,' Martha said. She frowned. 'It should be just inside the porch. I hope nobody's moved it. It's the only way we hear if there's a new visitor.'

'I didn't have much time to look,' Anna said. 'Jenny let me in almost as soon as I arrived.'

'Right.' Martha's frown cleared. 'Well, let me give you a quick tour and then we'll go through to the kitchen and we can have coffee while we talk about these studios of yours.'

'How many dogs do you have?' Anna asked. 'I met four more outside.'

'It's like the kids, I'm not always sure,' Martha said. 'There are more arriving all the time. Toby, my eldest son, brought the puppies home. He's in the throes of being a gun dog trainer, although he's still at college at the moment, so we end up looking after them most of the time. God knows if the idea will last, but at least he seems to have thought it through, so it may work out.'

Martha led the way through one of the other doors that lined the corridor. 'Most of this part of the house is my working area, out of bounds to the kids. If there's a problem, they can speak to me from the door, but otherwise they don't come in here,' she explained. 'Tony opened all these rooms into one for my work.'

Anna was staring around, fascinated. One end of the room was lined with sinks, shelves were fitted against the walls and held a range of bottles of different dyes as well as labelled boxes of dried leaves, flowers and roots. Wooden clothes airers hung from the ceiling in the middle of the room, draped with skeins of wool in rainbow colours. A tall spindle stood beside a wooden chair at one window, a large basket of fleece beside it. Against the other end wall stood two large knitting machines, which Anna walked over to, drawn by the pattern on one that was growing in bronzes, coppers and greens, with occasional threads of mulberry, red and silver. There was no obvious pattern, but what she saw made her think of autumn leaves and berries, lichened trees.

Martha gave her a couple of minutes to look round before she spoke. 'This room says it all, really.' She waved towards the boxes and dyes. 'I make my own plant-based dyes.' She pointed back to the spindle. 'I spin my own alpaca wool.' She gestured to the machines. 'I design my own patterns. At the moment, I chiefly make jumpers, scarves, the standard things. But Tony has built me a loom in the old cart barn on the far side of the yard, beyond our farm shop, and I'm experimenting with larger things, rugs, bedspreads.' She smiled suddenly. 'That's my relaxation. I get right away from the crowd in the house and nobody bothers me there. There's the threat of severe reprisals if they do, but they're glad to have me out of their hair for a bit, so the privacy idea works.'

Anna was still staring at the work on the knitting machine. 'This is beautiful,' she said. 'Gareth told me about the jumper you made for him, but I haven't seen it yet.'

'It was right for him,' Martha said. 'Right colours, right design. It was easy to do. Okay,' she turned briskly to the door, 'let's have that coffee and talk. If we can agree, I'll come over and look at the studios this afternoon.'

She led the way out into the corridor and paused in front of another door on the far side. 'This is the Soap Room, also out of bounds to the kids unless they're working with me. I make herbal soaps, salves, potions, mainly from the herbs and flowers that my sister, Esther, grows in the old garden. She's a beekeeper and her bees love it there, so we get wonderful honey from the hives. Come again later in the year and I'll show you around outside.' She opened the door so Anna could see inside the room.

A wave of scent, faint, insidious, appealing, wafted out to Anna, who was staring again at rows of sinks and shelving laden with bottles and cartons. Anna saw an old apothecary's cabinet whose glass-fronted drawers seemed to be filled with rose petals in different colours. Bunches of dried leaves and flower heads hung from the clothes airers in here, reminding Anna with a sudden pang of nostalgia of the kitchen at Rossington Manor where she had spent so many happy times with Lucy and her family.

'I have a special linctus which is in demand during the winter, it deals with coughs, colds, most of the seasonal ills. That's what Esther has been preparing more of recently, as my usual supply has run out,' Martha said, pulling the door shut. 'And I have a remedy for chilblains which even brings in Shona Trago. She gets them badly, working with her horses in all weathers, so she's constantly over here for fresh supplies. Although you mustn't tell anyone she comes here, she doesn't want her husband to know she's in touch with the enemy.' She moved on, saying over her shoulder, 'I won't show you around in there, it's not what I want one of your studios for. I sell the stuff through our farm shop, where it goes well enough, so we're extending our opening hours and Lissa, a young friend who works with me, is setting up a website to sell it online. I've got more time for my own work now,' Martha added, 'as the woman from the village who cleans the house is doing more hours, God help her. I wasn't sure it would work in the first place, this place is so chaotic, but she's been coming here for years and she seems happy enough.'

The hum of noise ahead grew louder and burst in full strength on Anna's ears when Martha opened the door at the end of the corridor. She led the way into the kitchen, a large room that seemed crowded with people.

Most of the noise came from two youths of about fifteen who seemed to be shouting at each other, outdoing the jazz blasting from the radio. Anna looked from one to the other of the stocky, sandy-haired figures, realising they were clearly brothers, wondering if they were twins. Even the furious expressions on their faces looked the same.

A man, wiry, dark, was at the cluttered table in the centre of the room, the paraphernalia of a dismembered clock laid out on a newspaper in front of him. From the crutch propped at his side, Anna guessed this was Tony Zennor. He seemed oblivious to the mayhem around him, concentrating totally on the machinery in front of him.

A little boy sat on the floor, playing tug with the Labrador puppies, a baby murmured from its walker as it rolled across the floor, ricocheting happily off the furniture.

Anna remembered what Gareth had said about the family. He was certainly right about its size. And he had been right about the food too. A huge pan on the Aga was full of a simmering stew, the scent wafting over to Anna. She guessed from the size of the pan that it would feed at least twenty. She looked around again, wondering how many of the children were Martha's, how many were part of the extended family that Gareth had mentioned.

Well, Anna was sure the young man leaning over the back of a chair beside the Aga was Martha's son. He was very blond, unlike his mother, whose hair was coal-black, but the facial resemblance was strong.

Anna was not so sure about the girl in the chair, working on her laptop with a fierce expression of concentration. She looked to be about eighteen, probably the same age as the boy, but was darker, with long brown hair scooped back from a rounded face and tied in a ponytail.

Martha's appearance with Anna had gone unremarked at first. It was the puppies who first noticed them and broke off their play to rush over in excited greeting.

'Nat, take them away,' Martha said above their yelping. 'I told Jenny to put them in the scullery.'

'She did,' the young man said, straightening up and striding over to scoop up the puppies. 'Silas let them out because they were howling.' He took them back to the little boy. 'They'll be okay with him.'

'Make sure they are,' Martha said.

'Martha,' the two youths turned to her, saying in unison, 'one of our boards is missing. He lost it.' Each pointed to the other.

'What kind of idiot loses his surfboard?' one added.

'Matt, Luke, enough.' Martha held up a hand, stemming any protest. 'It won't be lost,' she said. 'Go and look for it. Nat,' she turned to the young man, who was leaning over the chair again, commenting on something he saw on the screen, 'leave Lissa to get on. The fencing in the higher cliff meadow needs repairing. I can't think how it got damaged, but one section is down. Get it back up and see if there's more down anywhere. I want to get the alpacas in there this week, so it needs to be secure.'

'Don't want walkers cutting through either,' Tony said, his voice unexpectedly deep.

The noise of voices in the kitchen had diminished, and now the jazz was more noticeable. 'Tony,' Martha said as she went to the Aga and lifted a kettle onto one of the plates, 'turn it down. Anna and I want to hear each other speak.'

One of Tony's hands went out and turned a knob on the radio, reducing the noise slightly.

'Tony,' Martha spoke again, 'this is Anna Evesleigh. About the Elowen studio.'

Tony looked up, his eyes clear blue in his weathered face. 'Hello, Anna Evesleigh. You've taken on a big job there.' He spoke evenly, with a distinct local burr.

'I know,' Anna replied. 'Are you coming with Martha to the

local tour tomorrow?'

'What's this?' Tony looked across at his wife, who had gone to a door beyond the Aga.

She glanced back. 'You are. I told you last week. Anna sit down, Tony will clear some space on the table.'

As both Anna and Tony obeyed, Martha turned away, opening the door and calling through it, 'Esther, I'm making coffee.' She switched on the coffee grinder, briefly drowning out the sound of the radio.

'That's good,' Anna said to Tony when the grinder stopped. 'I'll be interested to see what you think of the work that's been done. And I'd love to know if you, either of you,' she glanced between them, 'know anything about Elowen, the place or the people. I want to set up an archive room there, history, local stories, folklore, all those kinds of things.'

'Seems to me you shouldn't add to your workload,' Martha said, spooning ground coffee into the largest pot Anna had ever seen.

'You're a fine one to talk,' Tony said. He turned to Anna, 'She and Lissa,' he gestured to the silent girl absorbed in her work by the Aga, 'are trying to generate more sales. That means more work.'

'My choice,' Martha said. She glanced at Anna. 'Lissa helps me, chiefly with the textiles – she has a fine eye for colour and design. That's why we can expand the business.'

Tony did not look up from his mechanics. 'Has she told her father what she's doing here yet?' he asked.

Nobody answered in the sudden silence that fell.

He went on as if he had not expected them to. 'Martha's the person you want, if it's stories you're after.'

It took Anna a second to realise he was talking to her. 'Of course.' She turned to Martha. 'I heard you at the Storytelling in the village last week. It was an amazing event. So many of you had stories to tell.'

Martha smiled as she poured water from the kettle into the

pot. 'That's us, all wanting to talk, tell the things we know from our parents and grandparents. An archive is a grand idea, if you've time for it, it'll save the old stories from getting lost.'

'Who's going to put it together?' Tony asked, as Martha brought the coffee pot to the table.

'I don't know,' Anna admitted. 'I only had the idea recently, when I was talking to Edward. He was telling me another story when I called in to their place yesterday.'

'Edward,' Martha said, a note of tolerance in her voice as she put down a tray of mugs. 'I'd take his stories with a pinch of salt. He knows some of the old ones well enough but can't resist embroidering here and there to make the stories "better".' She picked up the pot and began to pour the coffee out. 'We don't do that. It's the stories as they're handed down that we like to tell.'

'Visit there a lot, do you?' Tony asked.

Again, it took Anna a second to realise that he was talking to her, and then another second to realise he was talking about Edward.

'Quite a bit,' she said, accepting a mug of coffee with a smile of thanks, 'now that Mike's up at Soldiers' Meadow so much. Edward and Gareth always provide a welcome break if I'm walking up from Elowen.'

'He's started work up there already,' Tony said, looking up as he took his mug from Martha. 'It'll be interesting to see what he finds.'

Anna realised she was getting the hang of his conversational style when she knew at once that Tony was talking about Mike.

'Might put some stories to rest,' Martha said, offering her a jug of steaming milk. 'We know it's a burial site. There's enough proof of that, and of other events. But most of the other stories are nonsense.'

'Like what?' Anna asked curiously, passing the jug to Tony, leaving her own coffee a richly satisfying dark colour.

'Oh,' Martha shrugged impatiently. 'It was the local militia's practice site. True. It was where a soldier going off to war met his lover for the last time. Likely to be true. But it's the stories about treasure from the Spanish wreck that really catch people's attention. And that's probably all nonsense. I hope this dig of Mike's will put those particular stories to rest.' She pulled a face. 'I don't expect it will though. We'll still have people coming to poke around there.'

'The militia is true enough,' Tony agreed. 'And the lovers' story is, too. Lovers have met at that rock seat on the clifftop or down on the beach for generations.' He glanced at his wife. 'You should know that.'

Martha was back at the side door, calling, 'Esther, do you want your coffee?'

A voice could be heard faintly in the room. 'In a minute, coming.'

Martha came back to the table. 'Esther is a good cook, she makes our own meals and the "farmhouse" meals to sell in the yard shop here. Tony turned the old back kitchen into a commercial one, so she prepares them there, and they're selling so well we're thinking of opening a small shop in Corrington.' She poured milk into one of the mugs as a woman came out of the back kitchen.

Esther's face was so similar to her sister's that Anna was startled, then she realised that they were probably twins, that twins clearly ran in the family. After the initial shock, she saw that where Martha was well-built, flushed with a healthy glow, black hair springing vigorously around her shoulders, Esther was slenderer, even fragile, the black hair tied around her head in a coil was thinner and turning grey. Anna wondered if she had been ill, or if she was naturally a paler version of Martha, more shadowy than her vibrant twin.

'Esther, Anna's come about the Elowen studio,' Martha said, handing the mug to her sister, breaking into Anna's speculations.

Esther smiled at Anna as she walked across to the far side of the room. She handed over the bag she was carrying to a little woman Anna had not noticed, who sat on a stool in the corner, her hands wrapped round a coffee mug, coughing softly as her sharp dark eyes watched the people in the room. 'Here you are, Rosa,' Esther said, 'I've put in a few of the new recipes Lissa and I have been testing this week.'

Rosa's face was tight and wrinkled, just like a walnut, Anna though irrepressibly. The woman merely glanced at Esther as she took the bag, without responding, her eyes turning back to the room.

Esther turned back to the table, saying across it, 'Nat, I've just finished some sticky toffee pudding, I've left the bowl if you want to sample it.'

Finally, she sat down, turning to Anna, putting her mug down on the table in front of her. 'The studios sound a good idea, an outlet for the craft community,' she said, her voice softer than her sister's, almost gentle. 'You've got so much done at the garden; you must have been working very hard.'

'A lot of people have been involved,' Anna said. 'That's made it all so much easier.' She added, 'I've been saying to Martha and Tony that I'd like to set up an archive, with recorded stories from the Storytellings, and from people's memories, so do tell me if you think of anything to include.'

Esther looked surprised, holding her coffee cup just below her mouth as she glanced at her sister. 'What do you think, Martha?'

'I think it'll be a lot of extra work,' Martha said, 'and who's to do it?'

'You'd have to be careful,' Esther said slowly, 'people might not want some stories kept for posterity.'

'We wouldn't include those,' Anna said quickly. 'It's not gossip or recent scandal I'm interested in, but how people lived.'

'How do you separate the scandal and how people live?' Esther asked.

Before Anna could reply, somebody else spoke. 'I'll help with the archive.' It was a light voice, Lissa's, startling Anna who had forgotten the girl was there. 'I like the old stories, and people know me, they'll talk to me.' She looked over at Anna, her curious silvery grey eyes alight with interest. 'They don't really know you yet.'

'See what your father says,' Tony said, looking over at her.

'It's nothing to do with him,' she said, without heat. 'He does-n't care what I do anyway, as long as I don't get in their way.'

'He may care fast enough if it means you're more involved with us. You be careful.'

Anna was puzzled, and Tony saw it. 'One of those back stories that shouldn't go in your archive,' he said. 'Lissa's father owns the farm beyond Soldiers' Meadow. He says he owns that too, but I know he doesn't. He has one of those embroidered stories, like Edward's, one that suits him, but he's got no proof. That doesn't make any difference to Andrew Trago, he likes to get his own way. He got used to it while he was away making money. I reckon he'll be working on a way to get what he wants this time. And he won't want his daughter getting involved with us. You bear that in mind, Lissa.'

The girl shrugged, glancing at Nat, who grinned back at her.

Tony bent his head, beginning to put the clock back together again. 'Land has always caused trouble,' he said. 'That's what war has often been about. The urge to have someone else's land.'

Later that morning, Anna stood on the edge of the restored South Lawn in Elowen Garden while Ben snuffled around the foot of the trees in front of them. Behind them, ivy was richly green on the tumbled walls of the ruined house, and alive with the rustling of sparrows. Overhead, rooks flew steadily backwards and forwards, already busy repairing their nests in the lime trees of the front avenue.

All the busy thoughts in Anna's mind, racing around, forming into patterns, gradually quietened down. She began to feel the mild warmth of the spring sun on her face, hear the bird song around her, notice the emerging haze of green in the shrubs and trees as buds began to open. A rustling near her feet brought her gaze down to watch a blackbird busily rooting among the leaf mould, tossing it briskly over his shoulder. She spotted the robin perched on a nearby branch, one beady eye fixed on her, and reached into her coat pocket for the small bag of mealworms she always carried when she was in the garden.

She had just scattered some when she was startled to hear voices, drawing closer, approaching from the fogou, the underground chamber that had been restored in the arboretum. She was annoyed when the robin flew away in alarm and she knew that her moments of quiet were at an end. Frowning, she waited to see who was coming. She had not known there would be anybody working near this part of the garden today.

Ben was suddenly alert, his face intent, his ears pricked, and gradually his tail began to swish backwards and forwards. Anna's frown disappeared as she too recognised Hugh's voice and she stepped forward to meet him as he emerged from the trees to the collie's ecstatic welcome. 'Hugh,' she called out happily. 'I didn't know you were back. I'm so glad you've made it.'

She reached him, hugged him tightly as she kissed him on both cheeks, while the collie skittered happily around them. Hugh was an old friend, one she had known before he met his wife Lucy, who was an even older friend of Anna's from her childhood. She turned from him to greet Lucy and was visibly taken aback to find another woman waiting just behind Hugh.

'Anna,' Hugh said quickly, 'this is Laney Scholz. She's a fellow photographer, a very famous one. Laney, Anna Evesleigh is the driving force behind the garden restoration.'

The women exchanged greetings and studied each other. 'You've sure got a big job on here,' Laney said easily. 'But it's an amazing place. I can't wait to take some shots.'

A tiny frown grew between Anna's eyebrows as she glanced at Hugh. Surely he had not brought this woman here to take photographs of the place without discussing it with the rest of the garden committee. Alright, Hugh had not been at the meeting when the others made the decision to control access to press photographers, but she had sent him the minutes so that he would know what was happening.

'We've only just got here,' Hugh said, meeting Anna's glance with a bland look of his own, before bending to stroke the eager dog, 'and Laney wanted to see around before we got ourselves sorted out. We're just heading up to the restored studios.'

'So am I,' Anna said, deciding at once to find out more about what Hugh was up to. 'I've got two potential studio tenants coming up this afternoon, so I want to make sure everything there is okay.'

'Hugh was telling me about the studios. It sounds a great commercial idea,' Laney said as they followed Ben along the path beside the wall edging the eastern side of the garden. They were screened from the house now by the towering shape of the magnolia grandiflora with its stately ivory flowers. It was so thickly flanked by camellias and rhododendrons, that there was no hint of the house beyond.

Anna paused by the holm oak that arched over the green door in the wall, wondering just how much Hugh had told Laney. She was strangely reluctant to take her companions through into the walled gardens beyond.

'How are the plans coming along?' Hugh enquired, before Anna could begin to ask the questions he knew were on the tip of her tongue.

She glanced at him in surprise as Ben came back to her side. 'Haven't you read my emails?'

'Of course I have,' he lied, not willing to admit they ranked too low in importance in the many he received every day for him to bother any more. 'I just wondered how things are progressing.' He knew he sounded pompous and resented feeling wrong-footed.

Laney saved him. 'What have you got planned? I know there's a party, Hugh's invited me to that. Is there more on?'

Anna's lips tightened imperceptibly. Hugh had invited Laney? The invitation list to the launch party had been strictly vetted to keep the numbers within their agreed limit. Presumably he had forgotten or not bothered. Suddenly she doubted that he had read her emails. Really, he wasn't any longer the man she had once known.

Anna realised Laney was waiting for an answer. 'Yes, there's the official launch party next Saturday afternoon, and the numbers for that have been rigorously controlled. But we've invited local people to come on a tour tomorrow afternoon and have tea in the studio yard, so you'd best come to that.'

Hugh just stopped his exclamation of surprise. He had not known that. He really had better start reading Anna's emails.

Hurriedly he pushed open the green door under its curtain of scented clematis, ushering the women through into the walled gardens.

With Ben beside her Anna led the way into a wide courtyard, with a row of single storey granite buildings on three sides. The far end was lined with glass houses flanked on each side with a door, closed now, that led into the main gardens.

'Wow,' Laney said, looking at the tables and chairs filling the courtyard. 'You are expecting crowds, aren't you?'

'Not really,' Anna said sweetly, 'we've had to strictly limit the numbers.' Before she could say any more, a man appeared in the doorway of the end studio.

He was probably around eighty, his grey hair still thick and tidily brushed. His pale eyes were bright with interest in a tanned and lined face adorned with a luxurious curly grey handle-bar moustache and Anna was relieved to see him. 'Aaron,' she said quickly, 'Hugh's made it back for tomorrow's tour after all.'

'That's good,' Aaron said, raising one hand in greeting to Hugh, and using the other to stroke the collie, who was pushing his head expectantly against the man's leg. A woman came out of the studio behind Aaron, brushing impatiently past him and the dog.

'Anna,' Aaron straightened up as he spoke, 'Kerenza came up from the village with me. She wanted to talk to you about her B & B.'

'Yes, that's right.' The woman's voice was brisk. 'You probably don't know me yet. Kerenza Pascoe. I run the B&B in the village. I want to have a look round the garden, see if I can recommend it to my guests and if it's worth leaving my brochures with you.' She looked displeased as she added, 'Aaron wanted me to talk to you before going around, so, now that I have, I'll go and see what you've been up to.'

'Not today,' Anna said firmly. 'The garden isn't open to the public yet and we can't allow anyone to go around on their own until it is.'

Kerenza tutted in annoyance. 'Then you'd better take me around now. I don't have time to come back later.'

'Not today,' Anna repeated. 'I don't have the time either.'

'Come to the tour tomorrow, Kerenza,' Aaron said. 'You'll see much more that way. And you'll maybe hear more about Anna's plans for the local archive she wants to set up here.' He turned to Anna and said, before Kerenza could answer, 'Kerenza is the person to talk to about the Storytelling. It was her grandmother who set it up, and Kerenza has carried on with running it since her mother died.'

'It's just formalised what had already happened for generations,' Kerenza said, briefly diverted. 'And took it out of the pub, amalgamated the men's stories with those the women told among themselves.'

'There's no local story Kerenza doesn't know,' Aaron said, adding slyly, 'though she doesn't tell them all.'

'I don't hold with gossip,' Kerenza said firmly. 'I've always tried to encourage my children to keep to facts. Other people should do the same.'

'Kerenza set up the local playgroup. She must have seen four generations of local kids grow up, so you can imagine what she knows,' Aaron said.

'Wow, that sounds really fascinating,' Laney broke up the exchange. As they turned to look at her, she said to Kerenza, 'You do B&B, right? That sounds just what I need. Do you have a room for me?'

'Laney,' Hugh interposed, looking surprised, 'you know you're welcome to stay with us at Withern.'

'Sure, Hugh, but you and Lucy are just back from trips. You won't want me bugging you. And this sounds as though it'll be fun.'

'I rent two rooms, one is free at the moment. It's the bigger of them, it depends if that's what you want.' Kerenza was looking at Laney curiously. 'You look familiar. Have you been here before?'

'I've never been to this part of the world,' Laney said. 'I guess I just have a familiar-looking face. People always think they've seen me.'

'As Anna is so busy, I'll take you to my house now and you can make up your mind.' Kerenza looked austerely across at Anna. 'I'll see you tomorrow.' She turned her eyes to Hugh. 'You can pick your friend up from my house in the village when you've finished here.'

Anna was not sure whether Kerenza had very slightly emphasised the word *friend*. Before she could say anything more Kerenza turned and walked out of the walled garden. With an amused shrug for Hugh, Laney followed obediently.

'Phew,' Anna said to Aaron as the footsteps of the two women died away.

'Sorry,' he was apologetic. 'I couldn't stop her waiting for you. She's alright really, just convinced what she wants to do is more important than anything else. And you won't get a better source for your archive if you get her on your side. There's nothing that has happened here, and is happening here for that matter, that Kerenza Pascoe doesn't know about. She could certainly correct a lot of the local family trees. It's a mercy she is discreet, otherwise she could cause a lot of trouble.'

Anna had finished her inspection of the garden studios and was satisfied. The work on them had been finished ahead of schedule and the rooms were ready to be used. She felt more relaxed now, although Hugh's behaviour still stuck in her thoughts, especially as he had left after Laney and Kerenza without saying anything beyond goodbye.

She went over to the stone building beside the gate that was her office, pausing to enjoy the scent of the lilies that had been planted in pots throughout this part of the walled garden. Lilium regale, she reminded herself.

With a slight sigh, she pushed open the office door, planning to have a coffee while she thought about its furnishings. At the moment, she looked round ruefully as she entered the old potting shed, where her desk was a plank stretched over two columns of bricks, and her chair was an old plastic one that had been one of the village-hall rejects. She knew she would have to be careful, they would soon have to make a door through to the building next door to increase the office size for the staff she would have to employ. She was only just finding enough time and skills to deal with the garden's affairs and had already made that plain to the Trust committee. But she'd like what she had now to be a bit more attractive, even if it was only for a while. Anna switched on the kettle, glad she was able to make real coffee. She certainly felt she needed it.

A few minutes later, she almost groaned at the sound of more voices. Ben had settled on his bed beside the desk, where she had just sat down, drawing a large notepad and pencil towards her, her freshly-made coffee close to hand. She leaned forward to peer out of the window as Ben sprang up, his tail lashing furiously. Her frown eased and she stood up quickly, walking to the door to call out, 'Isobel!'

The older woman turned, smiling with pleasure, stooping to greet the excited collie. 'Anna. My dear, I wasn't sure if you'd be here or not. I know how busy you are.'

Anna had reached her, and the two women embraced warmly. 'I didn't know you were back yet,' Anna exclaimed. 'I'm so glad to see you.'

'We all met up late yesterday afternoon at the airport,' Isobel said. 'It was quite unplanned, but it became a Rossington family reunion. Will and Niri were there first, then Lucy, then we arrived shortly afterwards.' She turned to the man who stood just behind her. 'Anna, this is a very dear friend, Fabio, who is staying with me. I hope it will be alright if he comes to the party next weekend.'

'Of course it will,' Anna said, smiling brightly at Fabio as she wondered how many more unexpected people would be coming to the launch party.

'It is most kind of you,' Fabio said pleasantly, as he shook her proffered hand. 'I am very interested in what you are doing here. Isobel has offered to show me around a little when it is convenient.'

'Will that be alright, Anna?' Isobel asked. She smiled at her. 'I don't know all that much about it, but I know you'll be too busy, and I'm sure Lucy will be, too.'

'It depends,' Anna said. 'All the plans are under control at the moment, but there's likely to be a last-minute crisis. There always is. We've got the tour for local people tomorrow, so that's my main concern at the moment. It may be good to give you a feel for the place, if you'd like to come on it,' she glanced at Fabio. 'Then later on I can tell you more about whatever you're especially interested in.'

'That sounds very good,' Fabio said. 'I am here for ten days, so I will hope you have time to talk to me.'

'Perhaps we can all fit in lunch or dinner when you're not too busy,' Isobel said. 'We have so much catching up to do.'

Fabio was looking at his watch. 'And I have to start my catching up now.' He smiled at Anna. 'I know the area a little from long ago, when an old friend lived here. I will visit his son soon, but now I will see my own son's old nanny. She lives in your village here. It has been many years since we met, but she has always kept in touch and was very good to my Guido. We are to have lunch in the pub. I very much like English pubs.'

'Phew,' Anna said to Aaron again after they had left and he

emerged from the studio he had retreated into. 'I wasn't expecting it to be so busy today. I guess Lucy will be over soon, and probably Will and Niri too.'

She looked thoughtfully after Isobel and Fabio. 'I wonder if they'll bump into Hugh and that woman. Hugh's probably going to take her to the pub too.' She had noticed that Isobel had not mentioned Hugh at all. It may not have been significant, though. She suspected that Hugh had not been in touch with any of them recently, and so perhaps Isobel did not know that he was here. Anna's eyes narrowed as an earlier suspicion popped up in her mind. She had not really thought he was coming, she admitted now, and she wondered suddenly why he had.

'I expect they will,' Aaron said.

Anna stared at him blankly, and he explained, 'Meet up. I couldn't help hearing what you were all talking about.' He rubbed absentmindedly at a smear of paint on one hand as he continued, 'I remember Fabio from a long time ago, he and his wife stayed quite often with David Trago, but I don't think he's been back since she died suddenly some years ago, quite a bit before David did. She was a lovely lady, and he was devoted to her.'

Aaron looked up from his hand. 'It will be Andy Trago he's going to visit, and he'll get a shock when he sees what's happened to the house. But Shona will be pleased to see Fabio, if she finds out he's got a title, a count or something, I think he is.' He smiled at Anna's look of surprise. 'But now I expect it's Kerenza that Fabio's going to see. She was a nanny for some time when she was much younger, and looked after Andy Trago for a short while. That's how she and Fabio met, and she went off to look after his son in Italy. She's always been good with children.'

Anna's mind boggled. 'Strict, I guess.'

'Perhaps,' Aaron agreed, 'but she enjoys their company, and they always recognise that. They like to know where they stand too, and there's never any doubt about that with Kerenza. A shame really that she didn't have children of her own. Lissa Trago is almost like a daughter to her, though. Kerenza pretty much brought her up after her mum died. Just as well, Andrew Trago wasn't much of a father for a young child, still isn't for that matter. Too busy with his other interests.'

Anna's mobile phone bleeped, startling her. She was so used to not having reception in the main garden that she still had not got used to having it here in the walled garden. She scrolled down to look at the message.

'Lucy,' she said. 'I thought she might be here too. Oh Lord,' Anna groaned. 'She wants to meet for lunch in the pub at Genarren. Will and Niri are coming too.' She looked at her watch. 'They're on their way now. I can make it, I suppose, although I've got to be back here for two-thirty to show Gareth around, and Martha's coming afterwards, about three o'clock.'

'I'll be here,' Aaron said. 'I can show them around if you're late, and then you can talk business when you get here.'

'Thanks, Aaron,' Anna said gratefully. 'I don't think it's going to be a lunch I'll want to prolong.' She looked thoughtful. 'I wonder if I can get Mike over.' She bit her lip. 'No, maybe that's not a good idea.'

Anna drove her newish red Jimny into Genarren. It was not a particularly large or attractive village. Cottages of different shapes and sizes lined its main street, all fronting directly onto it, generally in their bare granite state, which even in bright sunlight had a faintly gloomy effect. Yet their small front gardens were bright with tulips and crocus, primroses flowered in drifts across the tiny lawns, while pots full of daffodils stood on steps. Trees formed a backdrop behind the cottages on both sides, their branches just greening with emerging leaves.

She stopped the Jimny in front of a short row of grey stone cottages. The pub was the middle one, identified by a faded signboard swinging heavily from a post in front of it.

She switched off the engine, sitting still for a minute to steel herself for the meetings she was sure were about to happen. At least it would be quicker to leave from here than from the small car park at the back of the pub. She had a tight schedule, she knew she would need to leave in good time. She grimaced. And she was pretty sure she would want to leave as soon as she could.

She had passed Isobel's Mini parked on the other side of the street, parked, Anna guessed, outside Kerenza's cottage. Hugh's Audi was nowhere to be seen. Were he and that woman already inside the pub? Anna glanced towards the car park even though she knew she could not see into it from the main road. Lucy might park there, she thought, so if she saw Hugh's car, she would know he was here. Well, Anna braced her shoulders. There was only one way to find out. Better get this over with.

She swung her legs out of the car door and stood up. Before she could move, a voice hailed her. She turned in surprise, not recognising it.

A yellow sportscar had just pulled to a halt ahead of her. It had not pulled in, just stopped in the road. A blonde woman got out languidly, seeming all legs in sleek jodhpurs. 'You are Anna, aren't you?' she demanded. She went on without waiting for an answer. 'I thought I'd have seen you before now. I want to talk to you about Elowen Garden and how we're going to publicise it. It's very important that we get it right, get the right people on our side.'

Anna stared at her. 'Have you been in touch with us about it?'

'I can't stop now,' the woman said briskly. 'Ring me later and we'll get it sorted out.' She slipped back into the car and it roared away.

Anna felt bemused. She brushed her hair back from her face and turned towards the pub, when her name was called again. Another car pulled up, this time parking neatly by the pavement. This one Anna recognised. It was Lucy's old Fiesta.

Lucy got out, stretching. 'I'm still stiff from the flight,' she confessed as Anna reached her and pulled her into a hug. 'Oh, it's so good to see you.'

Lucy stepped back and studied her friend. 'You're looking

very good. I thought this would be peak stress time.'

'It's been fine, but the stress may be setting in today,' Anna said, returning the survey.

Lucy, always slender, looked thinner than ever, very finely drawn, her cheekbones sharp in her small pointed face, and her chestnut hair cut much shorter than usual, fitting like a slightly ruffled cap. 'Did you see the woman in the sportscar?' Anna demanded.

Lucy looked puzzled. 'The flash yellow job that was shooting off? No, I didn't see the driver. Was she a problem?'

'I don't know,' Anna said slowly. 'I don't even know who she is.'

'Well, let's get inside and see if anybody else knows. That car must be pretty well known locally,' Lucy said practically. 'It's much too cold to stand around out here anyway.'

Anna stared at her. The weather was chilly, even though the sun was out, but still it was warmer than it often was in March. Primroses and violets had been flowering beside the lanes for some weeks, and buds had already appeared on the roses that covered the walls of the cottage where she lived with Mike.

Lucy recognised Anna's surprise and her gamine grin flashed out. 'It's a bit warmer than this in Peru,' she said, pushing open the door into the pub. 'I haven't acclimatised back to English weather yet.'

There was a hum of voices as they stood in the small lobby, taking off their coats and hanging them on an already crowded rack. The hum grew louder as they opened the door into the main bar.

A few people were at the bar counter as the women came in, heads turned, greetings were exchanged. Lucy, in particular, got a warm welcome from several locals, and the barman enquired, 'Home again? How were foreign parts this time?'

'Warm,' Lucy said, smiling ruefully, surprisingly pleased to see his familiar face, used now to the nose studs and the frequent changes of hair colour, although the gelled spikes were always retained. 'Are you still doing mulled wine, Jed? I'm feeling the cold here at the moment.'

'Mulled wine coming up,' he said cheerfully. 'Anna?'

'Orange and lemonade, please,' she said ruefully. 'It's been one of those days already, I definitely need to keep a clear head this afternoon.'

'Rough going at Elowen?' Jed asked.

'A bit,' she said, 'but it's mainly first-night nerves.'

'Is tomorrow's tour still on?' he asked. 'Everyone's talking about it, there's quite a crowd planning to go.'

'The tour's fine,' she said. She leaned forward over the counter to take her glass. 'Thanks. Do you know a blonde woman in a yellow sportscar? She stopped to talk to me as if I know her, and I'm sure I've never met her.'

Jed grinned as he passed over Lucy's drink. 'That's our Lady of the Manor.' He sniffed disparagingly. 'She thinks.' He saw Anna's puzzlement. 'Shona Trago, from *Trago Place*. It was a farm, but she doesn't like it being called that, not after all the work they've done modernising it. Calls it an *estate* now.' He sniffed again. 'Only been in the area eighteen months and thinks she runs it. Then, she thought that as soon as she arrived, and nobody and nothing has changed her mind. Yet.'

He leaned closer to Anna, jerking his head towards the far corner. A tall, well-fed man, tending towards bulk, was standing in the centre of a group by the fireplace. 'That's her husband, Andy Trago. Sorry,' Jed grinned, 'I forget, he's Andrew these days. Sounds a bit grander, I expect. He brings his business colleagues in here from time to time. Likes to show them some local colour. But he doesn't like it when the locals call him Andy. Seems we're too simple to remember his *proper* name.'

'What does he do?' Anna asked curiously, remembering Mike's exchanges with the man.

Jed shrugged. 'Property developer, investor. Nobody's quite sure, but he's got a finger in a lot of pies. And he seems to make money, that's for sure. He's a local bloke, not that you'd think so now. He's done up the old farm like one of those modern American ranches. Probably for her. He'll do almost anything to keep the peace, they haven't been married that long yet. She's his third wife, or maybe she's the fourth.' He shrugged. 'I wonder if *Andy* loses count too.' Jed turned away to serve another customer, saying over his shoulder, 'Your Grandma's already here, Lucy, in the other bar. Are you joining her or Hugh?'

Lucy blinked. 'I didn't know Hugh was here,' she said carefully.

'Oh, he called by the garden early, with that woman photographer who's visiting,' Anna said, aware that Jed was listening to them while he poured drinks for his other customers. 'I expect they're talking business. And Isobel and Fabio are lunching with his son's old nanny.' Anna held her hand out, stopping the questions she was sure Lucy was about to ask. 'Don't go there. Let's not get involved with either of them, we've got so much to catch up on.'

She turned and led the way to her favourite table tucked into the corner beside the lobby, relieved to find it empty. She put her drink down and waved Lucy into a seat on the settle. 'Stay there. I'll see what today's special is. I'll have to have something quick, I've got to get back to see some potential studio tenants.'

She turned back to the bar as Lucy said, 'I'll have the chilli, if it's still on the menu.'

Anna got to the counter and glanced at the blackboard listing the day's meals. 'Hmm, spinach tortilla sounds good,' she said to Jed. 'I'll have that, please. Lucy'd like the chilli.'

A thin elderly woman sitting on one of the bar stools, nursing her half-pint glass in her hands, was watching her. 'You're the woman from Elowen,' she stated, her voice rasping. 'I heard you up at the Zennors' place. You need to come and talk to me.'

Not another one, Anna thought in astonishment. She had no time to answer as Jed said, 'Getting in on the act, Rosa?'

He grinned at Anna. 'Word's got around about this archive you're planning. Rosa's got a fund of stories, haven't you, love?

Picks them up from all over, but especially when she's out in other people's houses. Even the grand lady of the village won't be spared, now that Rosa's working for her. We'll look forward to hearing about her parties.'

Rosa frowned at him. 'I know enough about you, Jed, to wipe that smile off your face. Aye, and about plenty of others here too.' She leaned forward, saying to Anna in a piercing whisper, 'You'll get stories from me that you won't hear anywhere else.'

'Oh,' Anna was rather nonplussed, although she recognised the woman now, the hunched posture, the sharp black eyes, from the kitchen at Carne Farm. This was awkward, she did not want to rake up local scandals, just get the traditional stories. For the first time, she realised how difficult it might be for people to distinguish between them.

An arm snaked round Anna's shoulder and Edward's voice spoke in her ear. It was lowered, but still loud enough for Rosa to hear. 'We used to think she was a witch when we were kids. Watched her house at full moon to see if she flew off on a broomstick.'

Rosa glared at him, her eyes narrowed, and Anna had to stifle a giggle. She did look she might cast a spell on Edward at that particular moment.

'You can mock, Edward,' Rosa said in her hoarse rasp. 'Think you're a local, don't you?' She sniggered. 'The stories you don't know go back centuries. Yours are just gossip. And,' she leaned forward, one arm jabbing towards him, 'I know what you and your crowd were up to all those years ago. Those that laugh last, laugh longest. You remember that.'

'Oooh, I will,' he said, throwing up his hands in mock terror. He reached out suddenly, grabbing the man who was just going past. 'Andy, did you hear, Rosa's going to record all our childish pranks for posterity.'

Andrew Trago had to halt, but his expression was neither friendly nor amused. 'I'm sure we'll survive her revelations.' He did not look at Rosa. 'At least, I'm sure I will.' He picked

Edward's hand off his arm and dropped it. 'That suggestion of yours for a "get-together." No, I'm not planning any childish reunions, Edward. The issue between us is business, no point thinking otherwise.'

'Oooh, how unfriendly,' Edward mocked. 'Maybe I should speak to Shona, she might be more amenable.'

Andrew's face darkened, but Anna was distracted by the sight of Hugh and Laney coming through from the small back bar at the side of the pub.

She took a step forward to intercept him, but she did not reach him before he spotted Lucy. Anna noticed the slight hesitation before he branched off to her table.

Laney let him go and walked on to join Anna. 'I guess she's Lucy, I thought they might like a few moments together,' she said. She looked appreciatively around the pub. 'Hugh said this place was pretty genuine, and it's just what I think an English pub should be. He reckons there's another good one down on a place called Roscombe Quay? Do you know it?'

'She should do,' Edward said, one eye on Andrew who was lingering, listening to the conversation. 'She lives near there, so it's her other local. You remember it, don't you, Andy? The Lobster Pot. I expect it's too rural for you now, but we used to have some good times there.'

'A long time ago,' Andrew Trago said with finality. He nodded to Anna. 'If you'll excuse me.' He walked away, unhurried, but with purpose.

'You'd never think he was such a wild youth, would you? He's really become a bore now,' Edward said mournfully.

'Did you grow up together?' Laney asked. 'I should have said, I'm Laney Scholz. I just came down with Hugh Carey and I really want to see around the place.'

That's done it, Anna thought crossly as she saw Edward's eyes brighten as he glanced over to the corner table where Hugh stood, talking to Lucy. Edward will add that item to the gossip mill and it'll be around the village before teatime.

'I'm Edward,' he said confidingly to Laney. 'You must come and see me and my partner, Gareth. We've a place up on the cliffs where he makes the most amazing pots. You'd better come soon,' Edward glanced with theatrical alarm at the door that had closed behind Andrew Trago, 'before Andy takes the ground from under our feet. Literally, I mean.'

'He's not a friend of yours, then? Andrew Trago, is that his name?' Laney said.

Edward laughed. 'Oh, he's a friend in a way. There was a group of us grew up together, and now that Andy has come back to the family homestead we're all here again. But as Andy says so bluntly, time moves on. Some of us get rich, some of us don't.' His eyes flickered to the corner table. 'Ah, it looks as though Hugh is joining us. And dear Lucy is staying where she is.'

'We're having lunch, and catching up on the garden news,' Anna said, suddenly aware that Rosa sat silently on her stool nearby, her back to them, her eyes bent on her glass. She had no doubt that Rosa was mentally recording everything she heard. That seemed to be another side to storytelling that she had not thought of, becoming part of a story herself.

'All the Rossingtons together,' Edward commented, watching Laney move over to meet Hugh and then step over to Lucy. 'Isobel's in the other bar too. I wonder if she and Hugh had a chat. But no,' he said with a sharp smile, 'the Rossingtons aren't all together, are they?'

'Hugh isn't a Rossington,' Anna said, mentally kicking herself for rising to Edward's bait. 'But Will isn't here. He will be soon though.' Shut up, she told herself.

The door banged, and she looked round hopefully. Then she blinked. Oh yes, it was Will, arriving right in the nick of time. But goodness, Will had grown up. He was drawing Niri in with him, and goodness, it could not be clearer that they were a couple.

'Sorry, Edward,' she said mendaciously. 'I'd better join the others before Isobel gets here too.'

As she turned, she met Jed carrying the plates of food she and

Lucy had ordered. 'Getting a bit congested, isn't it?' he murmured conspiratorially. 'Rosa would be worth a bit of time, though, if you can cut through the scandal to the old stories. She knows as much as any of the Storytellers, probably more, although she doesn't belong to the group.'

THREE

Anna looked round the crowds in the walled garden as the couple she had been talking to moved away to greet friends. There were more people here than she had anticipated, even though the day was a little chilly. Thankfully it was sunny too, and had been for some days, so the tour would show the few areas that had been cleared for public access at their best. The sun meant that the wild windflowers would be open in the patches where they had pushed through the woodland floor after decades of scrubby growth had been removed. The cowslips edging the lawn behind the house had already elicited praise from arriving guests, much to Anna's satisfaction. She had spent a long time on her knees planting them last autumn.

The size of the walled garden itself had stunned people who had not been in the many volunteer crews that had been working on it. The section they were in now was the only part to be restored and in use so far. But people were able to look through one of the gates on either side of the glasshouses to see the sheer size of the main walled garden. It was stripped bare of all the shrubbery and undergrowth that had colonised it, leaving only a few of the original fruit trees standing on bare ground, gnarled reminders of the garden's heyday. There were four square beds of newly turned soil waiting for the vegetable seedlings growing in the glasshouses. By the autumn more of this garden would be fully restored to its original purpose, producing fruit and vegetables to supply the café now rather than the old house.

Anna felt a twinge of disbelief when she remembered how she had first seen the hidden doorway leading into this very part of the walled garden. It had lost its door, the entrance was half hidden by brambles and thick grass and further screened by the branches of the overhanging holm oak that had rooted in the bank. All that Anna had been able to see of the interior that first time was a thicket of spindly bushes, interlaced with honeysuckle and clematis. Blue periwinkle flowers had wound through the long grass, draped like strands of fallen stars. Hidden birds had flitted through the branches, betrayed by a fluttering of wings and squawking alarm calls as they took startled flight, unused to human intrusion in their seclusion.

Now massive volunteer efforts had revealed the hidden secrets of all the sections within the walls, restored the old stone garden buildings here and in the end section beyond the main central part. Of course there were more beds to be dug, fertilised and filled with vegetables and flowers for cutting. And more tenants to be found for the far studios. But they had already achieved more than any of the trustees had believed possible.

This first courtyard was the current focal point and was where the initial efforts had been concentrated. The main offices were here, and three larger studios, and the tables and chairs they were using for tea later were part of the nascent café in the middle of the glasshouses.

Anna took a sip of her sparkling water and surveyed the crowd of people in front of her. Lucy was chatting happily to Aaron Tregonan, they were old friends and very fond of each other. I wonder, Anna mused, whether Lucy intends to get one of his doll's houses. She bit her lip quickly, realising this might be a subject to avoid since Lucy couldn't have children and Hugh wouldn't consider adoption.

A slight frown touched her forehead. Hugh was here, talking to the photographer from the local paper. Here in body at least,

Anna thought crossly as she saw his eyes flicker around the garden. His mind definitely seems elsewhere. He's probably wondering where that Laney is. I hope she's not wandering around taking photographs. She felt her annoyance with Hugh returning as she scanned the crowd. She could hear Mike in the far corner and see his flailing arms as he made a point for some-body beyond the main crowd.

Her gaze moved on. There was Kerenza, the centre of a small group, which included Isobel and her Italian friend. Anna searched her memory and was triumphant. Fabio. Interesting that, Isobel and Fabio seem very comfortable together, she thought, momentarily side-tracked. I wonder what Lucy makes of it. Her wandering eyes came back to Lucy and Aaron, who had been joined by Martha and Gareth. At least, Anna reflected, their inspection of the studios had gone well yesterday, they had each agreed to take one of the larger studios, here in this courtyard. That was the three main ones spoken for now and they would all be occupied for the public opening at Easter, she thought happily.

Anna's thoughts jumped from Martha to Tony Zennor. Was he here? Ah yes, she spotted him in the group around Mike, appar-ently without his crutch. No doubt that was why Mike was so stimulated, she thought, expounding on his favourite subject. She recognised the woman who came to join them, conspicuous in her working dungarees, oblivious to the chatter around her as she began talking to Mike. She was a spare, bronzed woman, her tight curls bound with a turquoise and white striped bandana. Melanie, Mike's most recent partner in the new archaeological company he had set up. Anna wondered if she had come to see the garden but suspected there was something else she was discussing with Mike. Probably work as Mike's enthusiasm was unabated. The two younger people who had been on the fringes of the group were now becoming absorbed in the conversation, Martha's son and Andrew Trago's daughter, so Anna was sure they were talking about the dig.

Nat and Lissa, that was it, she remembered their names. Anna

was surprised to see them move on to join the group around
Kerenza, until she recalled somebody telling her that Kerenza had
run the local playgroup. No doubt the young people had gone to
it some years ago. Now, she thought, who had told her. Was it
Edward? No, it was Aaron, yesterday morning.

As she looked over the faces in the crowd Anna wondered
idly if Gareth had told Edward about the studio yet. Probably, as
Gareth knew as well as she did how quickly gossip spread locally,
and it was possible one of the garden volunteers had seen him
going round the studio with her yesterday. Rumour was likely to
be circulating already. And Edward missed very little that was
going on around him.

Her forehead wrinkled again as she looked around. Edward
was not here. Oh yes, there he was, just coming into the garden.
With Andrew Trago, who was looking very grumpy, and much
as if he wanted to be somewhere else. That Canadian woman was
with them, Anna saw, her annoyance returning. And she was
carrying a large camera. Anna's irritation grew as she saw Hugh
break away from the local photographer he had been chatting to
and move through the crowds towards Laney, who looked as
though she was dressed for work in cargo pants and a thick cotton
jacket with many pockets.

But somebody was there before him. The thin little woman
who worked for Martha. Rosa, that was it, Anna remembered.
She clearly wanted to talk to Edward, and the sound of her rasping voice cut through the people between her and Anna, even
though the words were unclear.

Anna heard a note of anger in Rosa's voice, saw Andrew
Trago seize his chance to leave while Edward playfully raised his
hands to Rosa in mock apology. He only served to aggravate her
more, and her voice became louder. Gareth had moved to join
them, but rather than dislodging Rosa he seemed to be drawn into
her diatribe.

Anna began to edge towards them through the crowd, saw
Hugh reach them, and withdraw Laney from the group. She was

watching the two of them move away and was about to follow them when a voice called her name.

She turned, half recognising the voice, then realised that it was Esther as the woman came towards her, a paper carrier bag in one hand. 'Anna, I know that you'll be busy today, so I've brought you one of my meals for tonight, it'll save you cooking. Let me know what you think. It's one of my new recipes, using up the last of the mutton.' Esther glanced over her shoulder. 'Don't mention it to Martha, she doesn't approve of giving things away. She believes in bartering for something in exchange.'

'Thank you,' Anna said gratefully, taking the bag that Esther proffered. 'I'll put it out of the way in my office.' She turned and opened the door behind her, fending off the excited collie who was keen to join her, and putting Esther's meal on a high shelf. 'I'm so glad you were able to come, Esther. Carne Farm's household has certainly turned out in force.' She looked over at Nat and Lissa. 'I'm glad they were interested enough to come.'

'Lissa is,' Esther agreed, 'but Nat perhaps not so much. He came with me, as we're on our way home to the cottage, and he came in because he knew Lissa would be here and he wouldn't just be stuck with a lot of old people. You know what they're like at that age.'

She saw that Anna looked a little puzzled, and explained, 'We don't live at the farm, although we're there most of the time. It's good to have your own space.' She smiled suddenly. 'Martha can be overpowering, she's got so much energy. She can always find something for anyone at the farm to do. You remember that.' Esther sighed a little. 'And Nat needs some quiet time, away from his cousins, to study. He's a bright boy, he'll do more than farming.'

Anna felt her head spin and saw Esther recognise her confusion. 'Nat is *my* son,' Esther said softly. 'Not Martha's, although everyone thinks so and she never bothers to say otherwise. Her own eldest son, Toby, is a year older and away at college.'

Anna did not know what to reply, but there was no need to

do so. She saw Esther's eyes widen a little as she looked past Anna, then she lifted her hand in farewell to her and faded into the crowd.

Anna stood rooted to the spot, staring after Esther. She suddenly felt a firm hand on her arm, holding her in place. She turned an outraged stare on the woman who had detained her.

'You didn't ring,' Shona Trago said sharply. 'I know I'm too busy to pick up the phone, but you could have left a message. I'm astonished that it's taken you so long to get in touch.' She glanced around. 'We're going to have to do better than this,' she said. 'I'll hold a big fundraiser at our house, I've got superb caterers. It'll be much more impressive than this.'

She looked at Anna, who was staring in fascination at the other woman's immaculate make-up, rigorously groomed blonde hair and tightly fitted dress. 'I'll look at my diary and give you some dates.' Shona's expression grew more noticeably displeased. 'We haven't had our invitation to the press event next weekend. You should always check how your staff are doing things, they're never reliable. And you use volunteers, I gather. You just can't trust them to get things right. A lot of other important people may have been missed out too.'

She paused at last for breath and Anna cut in quickly. 'Our volunteers are doing a splendid job,' she said frostily. 'Your invitation was for today, that's why you're here now. Next week is mainly for the press, so we're not duplicating the attendees.'

'If you had only ...' Shona began crossly, when she was interrupted.

'Anna, I'm so sorry,' Will Rossington said unrepentantly, his eyes wide with suppressed amusement, 'but you're needed.'

Clearly, Anna realised, Will had noticed her sharp tone, unusual when she was normally so equable. I must be careful, Anna thought, I don't easily get rattled, but there's something about Shona that really gets to me.

'Lucy thought you should do your introduction,' Will said to Anna. 'They want to get on with the tour.' He took her arm, with a bright smile to Shona. 'I'm afraid Anna is the linchpin of the whole affair, we can't do without her, so I'll have to drag her away. But,' he said, struck by a sudden brainwave, 'there's a famous photographer here. She came in with your husband just now. Why don't you talk to her about your wonderful house?'

He firmly led Anna towards the far side of the walled garden. She was staring at him with fascinated approval.

'Actually,' Will grinned at her, 'Lucy thought you needed rescuing.'

'That was brilliant, Will,' Anna said. 'Evil, but brilliant. How do you know so much about the woman?'

'Aaron told Lucy, she told me,' he said succinctly, glancing at his watch. 'We should be getting on with the tour, it's nearly two-thirty now. So that'll give us an hour to go around as you planned, with tea back here at three-thirty.'

'I don't know,' Anna said, as they reached the steps outside her office. She picked up the microphone but did not switch it on. 'I'm not sure the timing will work, Will. There are more people than I was expecting, so it may take longer.'

'No, it won't,' he said firmly. 'We're dividing them up into five groups. Here,' he handed her a sheet of paper. 'I got Niri to run it off. See, it shows five different routes, so there'll be plenty of space for them to go around. Make sure you take general questions when they get back for tea.'

'But,' Anna was anxious, 'I don't want people to go around on their own.'

'They won't be,' Will said. 'There are five leaders, you, Lucy, Mike,' he grinned at her expression. 'I know, I had to tear him away from that Melanie, but he's happy enough to take a tour and says he knows enough to tell them what they're looking at. Niri and I will take a party each too, we can bluff as well as Mike. And,' he added hastily, seeing she was about to expostulate, 'we went around with you and Lucy yesterday after lunch, we can remember what you said. Just tell people you'll take general questions when you're back in the garden.'

'Can't Hugh take one of the groups?' Anna asked, glancing round for him.

'I asked him,' Will said, his voice hardening. 'He says he hasn't seen enough of the garden recently to be useful. That does seem to be true, doesn't it?' He put his hand on Anna's arm, holding her back for a moment. 'Who is this American woman he's brought down? I know she's a famous photographer, Lucy told me that too, but I thought invitations for the events were strictly controlled, and yet he's invited her.'

'They are strictly controlled,' Anna said, pulling her arm away and mounting the steps. She glanced back at Will. 'I don't know who she is, or why Hugh's brought her here. I think she's Canadian, but I'm not sure why. Let's talk about her later.'

Lucy led her group down the restored stone steps and paused in the glade, admiring the wood anemones that spread out underneath the bare oaks. Another focus of attention was the eighteenth-century statue of Aphrodite, gleaming white now that the encrustations of centuries had been cleaned off her form. She showed at her best at this time of year, against a backdrop of the scarlet rhododendron whose colour Anna loved. Rhododendron cinnabarium's swags of red bell-like flowers hung in decorative swags, one strand just draping itself over the statue's shoulder. Around the statue's plinth were the nodding heads of primula sikkimensis, the Himalayan cowslip whose subtle scent was filling the air.

On either side of the group, a path wound through the thickets of rhododendrons and camellias. To their left, the thicket opened to give a glimpse of a copse of Himalayan birches, their slender trunks varying from pure snowy white to red flecked with silver. Slightly ahead, to their right beyond Aphrodite, was a grove of stumpy tree ferns. They grew up from an irregular shaped hollow, once part of a surface tin mine, and their branches hung over the path like parasols waiting to shelter the guests. Beyond them, a sombre green bank of towering rhododendrons was brightened by a flower palette of pale yellows and creams. Some of the other rhododendrons held a promise of stronger colour, their buds just tinted now with purple. They partly concealed the lake below, visible only as glimpses of gleaming water, and the small temple glinting white on a height above the garden.

Lucy could not see it but knew that beyond the rhododendrons there was a grotto squatting in a damp hollow near the lake. She would take her party to see it, although the interior was not yet restored so they would have to peer in over the safety barrier. But now that that her group was wandering around the glade Lucy had time to relax her attention and consider them. They were interested and complimentary about what they were seeing, and in many cases knowledgeable about the garden, its history and its plants. She was glad Aaron had joined them. He knew the garden well and was totally unflappable. He would be a good man to have on her side if there was a problem. Now, she wondered suddenly, why did I think that?

There was a movement nearby as a tall slender man came up to her. Usually dressed in a suit, Rob Elliot was today noticeably casual in jeans and a jumper under a thick donkey coat. Rob Elliot, or Inspector Elliot, depending on how they encountered each other. That's why I'm thinking of problems, Lucy thought suddenly. I normally only see Rob when we're in difficulties of some kind. He's somebody else to rely on.

'You seem to have most of the locals on your side now,' he said without preamble.

Lucy wondered if he was referring to the problems they had encountered when the project first started. She decided not to ask. The afternoon was going too well to revive bad memories.

'How are you, Rob?' she asked instead. 'It's been a while since I've seen you.'

'Much the same,' he said. 'Crime never stops, but it's been a bit quieter while you've been away.'

Her gamine smile flashed out suddenly, lighting her small pointed face. 'Anyone listening to you would think I was a persistent criminal.'

He smiled too, his rather serious blue eyes lighting up with amusement. 'Perhaps. But when the four of you are together you seem to act as a catalyst. I know Anna and Mike are in the area permanently, but you and Hugh travel away much more, so I'm hoping you're not going to bring me any more trouble as a trio.'

'I hate to worry you,' she said lightly, 'but Hugh is here too. Though I don't expect he'll be around for long.'

Rob glanced at her searchingly. Before he could say anything, a small girl ran up to him, grabbing his hand and pressing against his legs as she stared up at Lucy.

'Lucy,' Rob said, looking down at the child, 'this is my daughter, Carrie. I usually go up to see her for a weekend when I can, but now she's staying with me for a while.' He touched the child's head with his free hand, 'Carrie, this is Lucy, she's one of the people who are bringing the garden alive again.'

'Is it magic?' Carrie asked eagerly. 'Daddy said the garden's been sleeping for a long time.'

'It is a kind of magic,' Lucy said. 'It's a special one called Nature, but Nature needs helps sometimes, and that's what we're doing, giving her some help.'

The child stared up at her, eyes wide. 'Can I learn that kind of magic too?' she asked, almost in a whisper.

'Of course you can.' Lucy glanced at Rob. 'If you're staying here for a while your daddy can bring you over and I'll show you how to start.'

'I'm going to be here for a long time, for ever probably,' Carrie said gravely. 'My mummy's ill. My granny says she's going to die and I'll have to live with my daddy always.'

Lucy glanced quickly at Rob, seeing his shocked expression. Carrie looked up at him too. 'I shan't mind,' she said in a friendly tone. 'I like living with you. And granny has mummy all the time now, so I don't see her anyway. She can't play with me now or read stories.'

Carrie's face suddenly crumpled, and Lucy said quickly, 'I'll tell you a story about the garden, how it was secret and hidden away, and we can write it down so you can send it to your mummy. Then you can still share a story with her.' Lucy looked round apologetically. 'If you don't mind, Rob.' She glanced at her watch as she spoke, drawing in her breath sharply as she saw the time.

'I'd better move my group on, we've to get down to the lake and back up to the walled garden. The path isn't open to the public all the way round yet, so we're only going down to the grotto and back.' Before she turned away, she said, 'I've got just one more major trip to make for the Seed Bank, to Ecuador, then I'm going to be here for longer spells now to get things ready for the autumn. Call in if you're passing, Rob, and bring Carrie if you want. I've got the office next to Anna's in the walled garden. I'm going to be here most days for the next month.'

She beckoned her other group members, and they began to move forward, as she added to Rob, 'It would be good to talk more, and I'd like to let you know how the rehabilitation training is going. I'm planning to start the first course at the same time as the apprenticeships. You supported the idea right from the start, and your contacts in the local prison and the probation service have been very helpful and encouraging.'

Lucy's party drew together as she moved, and Rob and his daughter fell in with them as they followed her towards the path. She was surprised to hear voices ahead of her and wondered if she'd delayed so long that she was about to bump into one of the other groups.

As she turned the corner, she saw three people emerging from the grotto. Frowning, she paused. The only one she recognised was the woman Hugh had brought down from London, the photographer, Laney, although the men seemed vaguely familiar. But none of them should be wandering around here. And where was Hugh? She had expected him to join Laney in Will's group.

'Are you lost?' she asked, walking towards them as they paused. 'Has Will's group gone on?'

'Yes, Lucy, darling,' a light voice said, and she remembered. Edward, some kind of poet. So the other man who looked faintly familiar to her was probably Gareth, the potter he lived with.

'Will was so overwhelming with his details that we slipped away for a little light relief. The grotto is so pretty we wanted to show Laney, she's keen to get some good pictures, but of course the light is too bad now, so she'll have to come back.'

'If they're for commercial purposes you'll need to speak to Anna,' Lucy said as politely as she could to Laney. Really, she thought, Hugh should have made that clear. 'And the grotto isn't really safe to enter yet, that's why the barrier is there.'

'Oh dear,' Edward said with mock humility. 'We've all been naughty children.'

Aaron was beside Lucy, forestalling her and Rob Elliot as he moved the barrier back into place. 'Nothing much has changed then, Edward,' he said. 'You'd best all come with me, I'll take you on to Will's group. He's likely wondering where you all are and holding up the others for you.'

Anna led her party back across the lawn to the walled garden. A surreptitious glance at her watch showed her that it was just after three-fifteen, so she had kept to the timetable well. She felt pleased with herself. And, she acknowledged, grateful that Shona had not been in her group. She felt a bubble of laughter rising in her chest as she remembered that Shona had latched onto Mike's group at the last minute. Relief tinged her amusement as she recalled that Shona's husband had gone off with Hugh. Andy alias Andrew had clearly thought Hugh was the most important person there. Or the most useful.

Anna frowned slightly as she reached the gate. She did not recall the two men joining any of the other tour groups. So much, Anna thought tartly, for Andy's judgment. And really, she thought, her temper rising, Hugh could at least have gone on a tour around the garden he had just told Will he did not know enough about.

With an effort she controlled herself, turning back to wait for her group, straggling slowly along behind her. The view of the ruined house of Elowen soothed her. The late afternoon sun cast a shadow over the south front. Without its summer drapery of wisteria and roses the ivy-covered grey stone walls could look sad, the house showing its deserted state. But Anna had dragooned Mike into stringing strands of white lights through the thick stems that seemed to hold up the stone. Aaron had volunteered to help, and the two men had spent a couple of hours on the job. Mike had struggled and cursed as the strands slipped and refused to be wound where he wanted. But Aaron had kept his usual calm, and somehow the job had been done and she had timed her return strategically from a task well out of hearing to find them both standing back, looking at the result with mutual satisfaction.

And now she was enjoying the result too, as the white lights were already glimmering against the house and through the bushes that surrounded the lawn. The overgrown meadow that she and Mike had first encountered on their exploratory trespass through the deserted estate was long gone. It would be a while until the reseeded lawn looked really good, but it was already a lot better than it had been when it had first been cut last year, the warm wet winter had clearly helped with that. And it had helped to establish the trees and shrubs that had been planted around the edge of the lawn, replacing the original ones that had died. A fringe of pink cyclamen edged the shrubs, which began at one side of the grass with the impressive magnolia grandiflora, and a magnolia campbellii at the far side, already holding out rose-purple flower. As she ran through the names, pleased that she could remember them, more little lights began to twinkle among the branches. That's lovely, she thought, entranced. I hadn't expected Mike and Aaron to do so much. It's quite as pretty as it must have been in its heyday.

For a moment her thoughts drifted, and shadows passed across the scene in front of her. Women strolled over the lawn, elaborately coiffed, wearing wide feathered hats, their long embroidered coats concealing the flowing skirts that swept over the grass. Men walked beside them, thickly coated against the chill. It was strange, Anna thought, how she always pictured the Edwardians here, but at least her imagination, her vision, she didn't quite know what it was, seemed to be keeping pace with the seasons.

'Anna, it's beautiful.' Isobel Rossington spoke quietly, but still Anna started. 'I'm sorry, I didn't mean to startle you.'

'It's alright,' Anna said, 'I was just imagining how it must have been once. Rather like this, if you pretend the ruins of the old house aren't so obvious.'

'Indeed,' Fabio agreed, joining them in time to hear this. 'We are following in the footsteps of many others here, where you are recreating the beauty they enjoyed.' He turned to his silent companion. 'What do you think, Kerenza, you who could always make a story out of the slightest event, isn't this one of the best stories you could have?'

Anna hoped she concealed her surprise. Kerenza and imagination, somehow that seemed an unlikely combination. Kerenza the oral historian seemed possible, repeating stories she had learned as a child, but the dream-weaver seemed, well, fantastic.

'It could be,' Kerenza replied. 'But,' she turned to Anna, 'whatever story you make out of this now, I can tell you many about its past. That's what you want, isn't it?'

'Yes, very much,' Anna said, smiling at the others of the group as they followed Isobel and Fabio into the walled garden. She was relieved to see them gather up Rosa, who had been lingering nearby. The woman had been a pest, the only real difficulty in Anna's group, constantly trying to talk to Kerenza, who kept brushing her off and moving away.

Anna stood beside Kerenza now, idly wondering what Rosa had been so agitated about. Kerenza had been genuinely interested in the garden as Anna's group went around, and flatteringly surprised at what had been achieved. She seemed to be in a different mood this evening, far more amiable than when they first met.

The two women gazed for a while across the garden until Kerenza roused herself with an effort. 'You should be with the others,' she said briskly. As she turned, she looked directly at Anna. 'I was sharp with you yesterday. I'm sorry.' Her mouth tightened for a second before she spoke again. 'I'd had a difficult morning, Shona Trago had been to see me before I came up here. She's interviewing for staff again, she can never keep them for more than a couple of months. One to find out what working there is like, one to work their notice – if they do. Now she's having to get them from further afield, so she's got to put them up somewhere before she sees them, and it wouldn't be in her precious palace up on the cliff. Oh no. But my humble hovel will do, they can't expect anything better. And of course, I'll be so grateful to have them that I'll give her a bargain rate. Huh!'

Anna gurgled with laughter. 'She can't possibly have said that,' she demurred.

'Not exactly,' Kerenza agreed, 'but that's what she meant. And, can you believe it, the wretched woman turned up again this morning to inspect the rooms. I virtually had to turn her out. And then I had to watch her out in the street interrogating one of my guests, for question after question doesn't make a conversation to my mind.'

'Oh?' Anna queried encouragingly. 'Who was she bothering?'

'That Canadian woman who came with Hugh,' Kerenza said. 'Laney something. A photographer, she says, and she has all the gear, cameras, lenses, tripods, you name it, she's got it. Powerfully interested in people too, so maybe she's going to take pictures of us all. I must have seen one of her somewhere, because I'm sure I know her. I never forget a face.'

She's not taking pictures here in the garden, Anna thought furiously, without committee agreement.

'She walked up here with me,' Kerenza went on. 'I haven't seen her for a while, although she set off with Will's tour. But we bumped into Edward when we arrived, and he cornered her. A new person, of course he couldn't resist trying to find out about her. I think he promised to show her hidden corners of the garden, off the beaten track, and she seemed interested in that. I wasn't really listening, but if I didn't know better, I'd suspect his motives. He does have a wonderful capacity for causing trouble of any kind and he was with Andy Trago, who looked as though he'd rather be somewhere else. Most people feel like that after a few minutes with Edward, so I wonder how Laney got on. At least,' Kerenza added with satisfaction, harking back to Shona's iniquities, 'I've got no spare room for any other guests now. I've only got the three and I always keep one free for Lissa if she wants to stop over. Laney says she's staying indefinitely. And Melanie will be with me until she finds her own place, although I don't know if she means to rent or buy. I never see her, that woman's got so much energy, she never lets her dodgy heart stop her from doing anything. If she's not working, she's out walking on the cliffs or swimming.'

'How does Melanie get on with Laney?' Anna asked curiously.

Kerenza shrugged. 'They've only seen each other at breakfast, but they were talking happily enough. It sounds as though Laney knows some of the archaeological sites Melanie worked on in South America, and the places she was talking about in Canada.'

Kerenza grasped Anna's arm and tugged. 'Come on, you've got to get in there and circulate. And I want another word with Lissa.' A worried frown wrinkled her forehead as she let her hand drop from Anna's arm. 'She's found some old letters from her aunt to her mother, and Lissa wants to know more about Laurie. She can't trace the aunt, there's no address on any of the letters, and they're just signed, *your loving sister,* no actual name. So now Lissa's asking me about Laurie. It's difficult, it's always difficult, to know how much to tell anybody about someone else's life. And especially when it's telling a child about her mother.'

'Did she die?' Anna asked cautiously, not sure how much Kerenza might want to tell her.

Kerenza nodded. 'An accident, when Lissa was a baby. Laurie fell on the cliffs, went over close to the place where Jeremy, her small son fell to his death. Lissa doesn't remember her at all and hasn't asked about her for years. It's difficult to know how much she's heard elsewhere or guessed.' Her frown deepened, and she sighed heavily. 'Laurie, her mother, had just got over post-natal depression, she suffered from it after the birth of both her children. But she was finding life with Andy difficult, she couldn't manage his endless affairs, and took to wandering along the cliffs, remembering Jeremy, and in the wet weather she went too close to the edge and fell.' Kerenza shook her head in disbelief. 'Andy's still at it now, anything in a skirt and he tries it on. You watch your step.'

Anna laughed. 'Just let him try,' she said. 'And,' she went on, 'Lissa is old enough to know what he's like, so that won't surprise her. Shona's his third or fourth wife, isn't she?'

'Fourth, they've been married about three years, I think. And she seems to have him under her thumb, more than the others ever have, anyway. Maybe you're right about Lissa too,' Kerenza agreed. 'I sometimes forget how grown up she is now. She's taken to Melanie's stories of archaeology, Melanie's been all over the world, it seems. Next thing Lissa will be wanting to do the same. And Nat will likely be off with her. I'm never sure which one of that pair leads the other.' She seemed to shrug the worry off. 'Anna, enough of my problems, they'll all be wondering where you are. Come on.'

Anna bit her lip, realising with resignation that she was going to have to go back and deal with her own problems. Like Laney. And Hugh? Garden restoration seemed to be very trying on her temper. And on her friendships, she wondered uneasily? But no, the thought rose as she brushed back her hair and pinned a bright smile on her lips. The troubles with Hugh were nothing to do with the garden.

The other tour groups were already back so the walled garden was humming with noise when Anna entered it with Kerenza. More fairy lights sparkled around the edge of the walls and Anna caught a faint waft of the winter heliotrope that Lucy had insisted should be planted throughout the garden. Tea was being served, and most people already had a mug and piece of cake. Some had found seats at the little metal tables dotted around the courtyard, others stood in small groups, but all were in animated conversation.

As Anna looked round she felt that the afternoon had been a success. Then her gaze fell on a few people near the studios. Edward was talking to Martha and seemed high with excitement, his words tumbling out, his arms waving. He was clearly enjoying himself. Gareth, standing just beyond him, had been cornered by Rosa, who was talking, bent forward like a small bird concentrating on the worm it intended to land. Gareth's expression was darker than Lucy had ever seen it, and when he made an abrupt movement, as if to brush past Rosa, the woman grabbed his arm, talking even more urgently.

And, Anna saw with a pang of concern, that woman was still there, Laney, the photographer, observing them all. She seemed to be half-listening to what Edward was saying, but her eyes were on the little scene playing out before her. Until Lissa approached her, when she turned and fell into conversation with her. They were obviously discussing Laney's cameras, because she swung one off her shoulder and held it out to Lissa. To one side of them, Kerenza had come to an abrupt halt, staring at the scene with an odd expression, perhaps surprise, on her face.

Anna wondered suddenly how much she minded the girl she had brought up becoming so much more independent, spending time with the Zennors and now introducing herself to the famous photographer.

Her gaze was brought back to Martha and Edward by a sudden movement. Martha had clearly had enough of Edward's company, and with an abrupt word she was pushing past him. He put out a hand to stop her, and she thrust him away forcefully enough to attract the attention of the people around them. When he would have persisted, Gareth caught him roughly by the arm, holding him back.

Shona Trago had one hand tucked possessively into her

husband's arm, holding him beside her as they chatted to Hugh. She tugged Andrew's arm, nodding her head towards the disturbance, and said something with a brittle laugh. At the sound of it, Tony Zennor turned around, cutting off his talk with Mike and Laney. He saw Martha stalking away towards the studios and with a quick word to Hugh he followed her, moving with a slight limp.

'Phew,' Anna said, sinking back onto one of the metal benches in the courtyard with Ben curled up beside her, glad to be released from confinement in her office. 'It was a success, don't you think? But stressful.'

'Right as always,' Mike said, pushing a glass of Prosecco into her hand, watching Ben settle his head across her feet. 'Here, I've got Will opening the bottles, but I think you've earned the first glass.'

'I think we've all earned our drinks tonight,' Anna said, taking a grateful sip as Mike sat down next to her with his bottle of beer.

The walled garden was oddly silent now that the visitors had left. The fairy lights were points of brightness in the early evening darkness, and Niri brought out a tray of candles, handing the matches to Anna as she returned to the tearoom.

'I was surprised to see Melanie,' Anna said idly. 'I didn't have chance to talk to her, but it was nice of her to come.'

'She doesn't care about the garden,' he said, putting an arm around Anna. 'She thinks she's found something interesting in the dig she's supervising.'

'What?' Anna asked.

He looked down at her as she rested her head against his shoulder. 'They've been finding Mesolithic flints, which we had expected, and exposing Iron Age field boundaries. But they've just uncovered a stash of axes. It may be an isolated find, but we always live in hope there'll be more. Keep it to yourself,' he added as an afterthought. 'I'll have to be over there more than I'd planned as we'll have to get the area excavated more quickly, or the nighthawks will invade us. We may have to keep a guard overnight if there's much there.'

'It sounds exciting,' Anna commented. 'Can I come and see them when you've got it all out of the ground?'

'You'll be better seeing them when they've been cleaned and conserved,' Mike said. 'But come over with me if you want to see it on site.'

Anna nodded, her eyes wandering around the courtyard. 'Where's Hugh?' she demanded suddenly, sitting up straighter so that Mike's arm slipped off her shoulders. Ben shifted his head, curling up with his nose under his tail.

Mike shrugged. 'God knows,' he said impatiently. 'Gone with Laney, I suppose.' He glanced at Anna. 'What's going on there?'

'I don't know,' she said, striking a match and leaning forward to light the candles. Frowning a little, she tried to hush him as Will approached.

'It's alright,' Will said. 'I'd like to know that myself.' He plonked the bottles he was carrying down on the table and sat on a chair as he leaned forward to pour more Prosecco into the glasses Mike had put out. 'I know I've been away for a while, and Lucy and I aren't great communicators. But she and Hugh don't seem to be much of a couple anymore. I've asked Gran,' he added, 'but she doesn't seem to know what's going on either. Or she isn't saying.'

'Well,' Anna said slowly, 'they both seem happy with things as they are.' She glanced over to where Lucy sat with Isobel, both clearly engrossed in their conversation. But then, Anna thought suddenly, I don't think Lucy's had much contact with Isobel either so she must have a lot to discuss with her grandmother.

'You think Lucy's happy to have Hugh arrive here with this woman?' Mike demanded incredulously.

'Well,' again Anna spoke carefully, 'it could just be a business arrangement. After all, I'm not suspicious every time you turn up with another woman. And you spend enough hours with that new partner of yours.'

'Oh,' Will asked, 'is the partner a woman then?'

'Melanie,' Anna said. 'You spoke to her, Will, when she was talking to Mike before the tours.'

'Oh yeah, that's right,' he nodded. 'I guess you've nothing to worry about there.'

'She's a damned good archaeologist.' Mike said. 'She's worked on a number of international excavations, and we're lucky she wanted to join our partnership. Especially as we're getting so much work.' He caught Anna's eye as he was about to expand on his favourite topic and changed tack. 'One woman at a time is quite enough for me,' he said gruffly. 'And if things with Hugh are all so straightforward, why isn't he here with us tonight?'

Will had been sitting there, a beer clasped in his hands. 'I think I'll have a word with Hugh.'

Niri had arrived in time to hear this. She put down two bowls of crisps and looked at Will. 'That wouldn't be a good idea,' she said. 'Lucy won't thank you for interfering. She's quite capable of sorting out her own life.'

'But is she?' Will demanded. 'I don't think she's happy,' he said stubbornly.

'No,' said Niri, sitting down at the table and accepting a glass of Prosecco. 'I don't think she is. But maybe she hasn't fully realised that yet.'

'What about Hugh?' Mike demanded. 'Do you think he's happy?'

'I don't know,' Anna admitted. 'But what we've all got to remember is that they're both doing what they want. Maybe they're happy with a different kind of relationship.'

She looked questioningly at Will and then Niri, 'And what about Fabio? I hadn't heard about him, and he seems to be a feature in Isobel's life. Come on, you two, you've been to stay with her in Florence, you must know all about him.'

Will looked reluctant to change the conversation, but Niri picked up on Anna's question. 'He's very nice, and he's enjoying being here. He knows the area from way back,' she said. 'He and Isobel are really happy doing things together.'

'Okay,' Mike said. 'We can see that. But who is he? What does he do? He seems to know a lot about the garden.'

'He's …' Will said, breaking off to revert to the subject on his mind. 'Look, Anna,' he said abruptly, 'can't you have a word with Lucy and Hugh?'

'I don't think so,' Anna said. 'I might try to say something to Lucy, but these days she doesn't open up much about anything other than work or the garden. And Hugh, well, I don't think Hugh would welcome my interference. But' she weakened at the look of worry on Will's face, 'I will speak to them if I get chance.'

'Which means,' Mike translated, banging down his beer bottle on the table, 'she will interfere as soon as she can.'

Hugh was not even on the edge of Lucy's thoughts as she sat with Isobel at a table further down the courtyard. Grandmother and granddaughter had always talked freely, and now Lucy had a lot to tell her, and perhaps even more to discuss.

Tales of plant hunting and seed conservation in South America were finished. Pictures of Isobel's latest creations had been flicked through on her iPad. Lucy sat back, a half-full glass of wine in her hand and was about to ask about Fabio.

Before she could say anything, Isobel spoke first. 'You and Hugh seem to be doing a lot of travelling now,' she said.

Lucy glanced at her. 'Yes,' she said soberly. 'Anna has mentioned that too.'

'It suits some couples,' Isobel said. 'Does it suit you?'

Lucy was silent, obviously considering. 'I like the travel,' she said, then added half seriously, 'perhaps it's in the family genes. After all, Will is likely to be in India as much as he's here, as far as I can see.'

'Perhaps,' Isobel conceded. 'But it's you I'm concerned about.'

'There's no need,' Lucy said quickly.

'Perhaps not,' Isobel said, 'but I am. And I'd like to see you happy. Are you?'

'I'm not unhappy,' Lucy said, finishing the last of her wine.

'Alright,' she went on, 'I'm in a muddle. You can see that, Anna can too, but Hugh doesn't. And it's Hugh I'm in a muddle about. I can't see why we stay married, and I don't think I want to be anymore. All that I once was, all that I wanted, it's changed. And I think that's true of Hugh too.'

Isobel nodded. 'I was afraid that was it. Well,' she said, leaning forward to touch Lucy's hand, 'make up your mind and sort it out, talk to Hugh. You'll be ill if you go on like this. You're far too thin. And,' she added, 'you must talk to Anna about Ben.'

'Ben,' Lucy repeated, startled. 'What about Ben?'

'Lucy,' Isobel said patiently, 'it isn't fair to either Ben or Anna for you to reclaim him after your trips away. You're away more than you're here, and that's not going to change much now. Ben's become Anna's dog. You should make that a permanent arrangement.'

Lucy was frowning. 'You kept Juno, even though she was boarded in Roscombe while you were away. Why is it different?'

'Juno was very old when I began living in Italy. If she'd been younger she'd have travelled with me. She was perfectly happy in Roscombe with Gina and her visits to me became just that, visits to an old and dear friend, but not to her home. Ben is young, active, he'll bond with the person doing things with him.'

'I'll think about it,' Lucy said. 'I don't want to give him up.'

'Watch him,' Isobel advised. 'See how he behaves around you and Anna. See who he goes with, who he sits with. That will tell you what you have to do. In fact, who is he sitting with now?' She glanced across the courtyard to where the collie lay with his head on Anna's feet.

'Maybe I should apply the same advice to Hugh,' Lucy said dryly.

Hugh Carey was standing by the gate posts at the entrance of the lime avenue that led to the main front of Elowen house. The area to the right of the avenue had been turned into a small car park. Most of the visitors had driven, sharing their cars to minimise the number to be parked. Some had walked up from the village as the early afternoon had been chilly, but pleasant.

Kerenza and Laney had been among the latter, and he had intended to drive them back to Kerenza's cottage in the village. Many people had stayed on long after the official end of the tour, only drifting away in dribs and drabs from the walled garden during the early evening.

The main exodus began before Hugh had realised that Kerenza and Laney were part of it, so he had set off some way behind them through the slow-moving crowd. He had walked as quickly as possible through the straggling groups of villagers meandering back down the lime avenue, aware that he was barely acknowledging greetings from people he knew in his haste to catch up with the two women. He reached the car park in time to see them getting into Isobel's Mini with Fabio.

Hugh felt both annoyance and relief as he watched Fabio drive away. Annoyance to have wasted his time, relief that he did not have to spend more time with Laney. She was an interesting woman, but he was beginning to find that her intense concentration on the people she met was wearing.

And, Hugh admitted to himself, standing alone in the car park, he felt alienated from Lucy and his friends here. He did not feel part of this life anymore. He was not sure how it had happened, but his focus had for some time now been centred more on his own life, his own activities.

He had his car here and could easily drive off now to Withern. God knows, he thought, it was some time since he had spent more than a couple of nights there, in the place he called home. Perhaps, his thoughts went on, it was time to change that, to amend his relationship with his wife – and his friends, the rueful thought intruded.

Hugh was pretty sure that the others would still be in the walled garden. Perhaps they were talking over the afternoon. Almost certainly they would be eating and drinking. They all had a lot to catch up on, apart from the garden news itself. Hugh turned back to face the house, lit eerily by the nearly full moon.

The sky was clear enough to make it easy to find his way back along the avenue, empty now of villagers, and he found that his feet took the route through the tree shadows without conscious thought.

It seemed barely any time since he had come here first, that was in the evening too, but a warmer May evening, to enjoy a picnic in the grounds that Anna and Mike had discovered. It had been a happy time, he realised with surprise.

Anna and Mike. Hugh pondered the relationship that had developed between them. He still could not quite believe it. His thoughts were disturbed by a slight movement in the shadows. It was low down, in the darker shadows at the base of one of the trees. A fox perhaps, or a badger, going early about their nightly business.

Hugh paused, peering into the darkness. Whatever it was had frozen, no doubt waiting for him to move on. He waited, suddenly keen to see what was there watching him from the gloom. It was a long time since he had stood quietly observing the local wildlife.

After a few minutes Hugh gave up and stepped forward. Just as he did so, there was a rustle of movement, something heavy moved away in the dark shadows and although he paused to peer after it, Hugh saw no trace of what it was. Then there was another movement, closer, under the tree. A faint glimmer of white showed now, moving feebly.

Hugh strode forward, feeling in his pocket for his mobile phone and pulling it out, pressing the button to switch on its light. The bright beam fell on the bloodied face of the man who lay on the ground, the faint flicker of movement in his arm stilling as Hugh stared down at him.

At that moment Hugh was aware of a light moving behind him and soft footsteps approaching. He spun round quickly, wondering who was coming down the avenue towards him, and was blinded by a beam of light.

Ben raised his head, suddenly alert. 'What is it?' Anna asked idly, her hand on the dog's head. He stood up, his posture stiff, and she watched him, suddenly concerned. He moved, his speed taking her by surprise, and was racing out of the walled garden before she could speak again.

'Mike, quick,' she said, leaping to her feet, hastily putting her half-full glass of Prosecco onto the table. 'Something's wrong.'

Will had reacted swiftly too, he was at her side as she ran out onto the lawn. 'There,' he said, pointing at the house as Lucy caught up with them.

The fairy lights still twinkled in the trees and on the ruined house, but it was the moonlight that allowed them to glimpse Ben as he disappeared on the track under the arch on the right that led to the lime avenue.

Will, Lucy and Anna followed him, running hard, and could hear Mike behind them, shouting loud questions. They paused as they reached the avenue where the tree shadows lay like bars over the surface. Mike thundered up behind them, almost knocking Anna over.

'Ssh,' she hissed, grabbing at him to keep her balance.

In the sudden silence, marred only by Mike's heavy breathing, they could hear it. A voice, Hugh's voice shouting. Then they saw the beam of light further along the drive.

'Here,' Hugh shouted. 'Be quick.'

Will set off again, into the shadow of the nearest tree, thudding immediately into another figure. He recoiled, as Anna flashed the beam of her mobile over them.

'Fabio,' she said in startled disbelief, aware of Mike's heavy breathing down her neck. 'What's going on?'

'Anna,' he said, his Italian accent suddenly noticeable, 'I couldn't find the light on my phone, and I left my torch with Hugh. Come quickly, there's an injured man back there.' He gestured behind him with one arm. 'Isobel is with you, Anna? She is safe?' he asked urgently.

'I'm here, don't worry about me,' Isobel said quickly from behind the others, as Will raced off again.

Will was the first to reach Hugh, Anna was close behind,

again almost unbalanced as Ben flung himself at her, relieved she had come to join him.

'I don't know who he is,' Hugh said, turning the light onto the fallen man just as Mike and Lucy reached them, with Niri close behind. 'But he's badly hurt. There's still no mobile reception here in the avenue, so I'd better get over to Anna's office. There's reception there, isn't there?'

'Yes,' Lucy agreed, 'or mine. That's probably best. I'll come with you, the keys are in my bag there.'

Anna had knelt by the man, feeling for a pulse. Her fingers probed behind his ear, flinching slightly as they felt the stickiness of the blood that flowed thickly down from his head. She shook her head. 'I can't find a pulse,' she said grimly. 'Wait, there, just very faintly. Mike,' she did not turn, but spoke urgently, 'get down to the car and fetch up the blankets. We must keep him warm.'

'Here,' Fabio pulled off his jacket, 'have this for now.'

She took it, and the jumper Will offered, and spread them across the man. 'I need something to staunch the blood, quick,' she instructed. 'Anything you've got that is clean. He's bleeding very heavily.'

It was Isobel who supplied the clean handkerchief that Anna pressed down on the wound, and Niri who handed over a light scarf to bind the handkerchief down.

Anna scrambled to her feet, aided by Will. 'He's been brutally attacked,' she said sombrely, staring down at the fallen man. 'It looks as though he's got at least a broken arm and leg, and his head wound is very nasty. His pulse is very faint, almost not there, so there's probably more wrong that I can't see. He's going to be very lucky if he pulls through this.'

'Who is he?' Will demanded. 'I don't recognise him.'

'It's the potter,' Fabio said quietly. 'I was talking to him earlier.'

'Yes,' Anna agreed, 'it's Gareth.' She glanced round. 'I wonder where Edward is. They came together this afternoon.

FOUR

'I wish I'd kept my mouth shut,' Rob Elliot said wryly to Lucy.

'So do I,' she said sombrely. 'But you didn't make this happen, any more than we did.'

He nodded absently, watching his police team waiting to get to work while arc lights were put in place.

'Ah,' he glanced up at the sound of a siren, 'here's the ambulance at last. I don't expect it will be long before the locals arrive either. Our sirens will have alerted them, so I'm sure they're already on their way.'

The ambulance came to an abrupt halt in the middle of the lime avenue and the inspector moved towards it. 'Over here, under the tree,' he said as the paramedics scrambled out.

By now Gareth's form was lit by the arc lights, and the medical team moved swiftly over to him. The onlookers were silent, waiting as the paramedics worked. One of them looked up. 'He's in a very bad state. We'll get him back to the hospital at once.' He stood up and began to unfold the stretcher he had laid nearby.

He and his colleague had just moved Gareth onto it when the sound of hasty footsteps reached them, coming down the avenue from the gates.

Elliot moved swiftly, turning to block the view of the victim. 'How the hell did you get here?' he demanded as a man came into sight, puffing slightly with the speed of his approach. Beyond him there were more footsteps, and a uniformed officer appeared, calling out breathlessly, 'Sorry sir, he gave us the slip.'

'You mustn't blame them, they did their best, but of course I know a side way in, and couldn't resist. We heard the sirens in the village, and were so concerned,' Edward said rapidly, his breath coming rather fast. His eyes rested on the ambulance. 'Do tell me, who is it? Is it somebody I know? I'm so worried about Anna, she stayed behind with her friends. Such a trouble-prone lady, she makes a habit of finding bodies, you know, but I expect you do.' Edward's gaze had been searching the group behind the inspector, 'I see she's safe and sound. Such a relief.' He laid a hand theatrically on his brow.

'You must leave now,' the inspector said coldly. 'You really shouldn't be here, and there's no excuse for your intrusion.' He nodded to the uniformed constable who had come to a halt behind Edward. 'See this man out.'

'Actually, Rob,' Anna stepped up to him, saying quietly, 'this is Gareth's partner, Edward. They live together on an old farm site near the cliffs.'

The inspector's lips tightened. 'Just what I need,' he muttered. More loudly, he said, 'Wait a minute, sir. I gather you may know the injured man.'

At that moment the paramedics moved past them on their way to the ambulance. Edward craned his neck to see who they were carrying and gave a gasp of horror.

'No, no,' he cried, pushing past the inspector with unusual force. 'I don't believe it, it can't be.' He stopped abruptly by the stretcher and stared down at Gareth, whose face was almost completely hidden behind an oxygen mask, his dark hair visibly matted with blood.

'Move,' one of the paramedics snapped. 'Every minute counts for him.'

Anna put her arm through Edward's, pulling him back. 'Come on, Edward, we'll take you to the hospital.' She looked over her shoulder. 'Mike, let's get your car.'

She saw him mutter, but he moved quickly to Edward's other side. 'Come on, let's get going.'

Edward was staring at the ambulance, apparently oblivious to their presence. 'He'll pay for this,' he said in a venomous whisper. 'I'll make sure he pays.'

'Interesting,' Rob Elliot commented to Lucy, watching Anna and Mike escort Edward down the avenue, the constable staying close behind them like an eager sheepdog. Ben, the actual sheepdog, was also keeping close to them as they passed in and out of the tree shadows, that were now pitch black as the moon rose high in the night sky.

'I wonder who he means,' the inspector went on.

'And I wonder if he knew his partner was here,' Hugh commented. 'He got here very quickly, it would be interesting to know if he came back alone. I haven't seen anyone else yet, but plenty of people will be coming to investigate.'

The inspector glanced at him, saying, 'They'll be stopped at the gates. At least,' he added ominously, 'they had better be.' Elliott's face was gloomy. 'We'll have to look into Edward's movements. He has to be a possibility. But,' he sighed, 'nothing is ever simple when you lot are concerned with it.'

'Rob,' Will said, glancing round at the investigators starting their minute search of the surroundings, 'can we go home soon? We are,' he gestured towards a silent Niri, sitting on a log just beyond the avenue, and including himself in the movement, 'still a bit jetlagged and would like to get some sleep. You know where to find us tomorrow, we'll probably be at home most of the day.'

'Just a few questions now, then you can all leave,' Elliot said. 'Do any more of you know the injured man or his partner?'

Will shook his head. 'I saw them both here at the event this afternoon. The other one, the partner, Edward, was definitely on my tour, he wanted to be the centre of attention, so I couldn't miss him. I think Gareth was there too. But I didn't speak to either of them, in fact they disappeared halfway round. I can't be sure it was Gareth as I've never, as far as I know, met or seen him before. And I couldn't identify him now.' He grimaced suddenly. 'I'm surprised Anna could.'

'She knows him better,' Niri said quietly, getting up to stand beside him. She looked at Inspector Elliot. 'I haven't met them or seen them before. But I talked to the injured one, Gareth, briefly this afternoon when I was with Isobel and Fabio.'

'Yes, that is so,' Fabio confirmed, his arm around Isobel. He glanced at her as he went on, 'Isobel was talking to him about some pottery she wanted to commission for a photo shoot she's has arranged for some magazine. I also, I wanted to discuss a commission with Gareth, so we arranged I should visit him at his pottery. Edward wasn't there when I talked to his friend, and I didn't speak to him at any time.'

'Did any of you,' Elliot included them all in the question, 'see anything suspicious during the event? Anything at all, whether it involved Gareth or not.'

Will glanced at Niri, then at Lucy, who nodded slightly. It was Lucy who answered. 'We were discussing this just now, before Hugh gave the alarm. Not suspicious things, we didn't see anything like that. Nothing to make us think something so awful would happen,' she clarified. 'We were just aware of stresses, undercurrents, among some of the guests.' She looked apologetically at Elliot. 'No more than that.'

'Tell me,' he said.

She took a deep breath, trying to pinpoint a starting place. 'It seemed to focus on Edward, Gareth's partner, who's just gone to the hospital with Anna and Mike. I don't know his surname. Or maybe it started with the woman from the village, a little elderly lady, I don't know her name at all.' She glanced enquiringly at Will and Niri, who both shook their heads. She did not think to check with Hugh, sure he did not know the woman.

'This little woman,' Lucy went on, 'clearly wanted to speak to Edward, who seemed to be in a very excitable state, talking to a number of other people rather wildly. Most of them clearly couldn't get away fast enough. But this woman kept cornering Edward. He laughed her off whenever she did, and brushed her off quite rudely in the end, which made her angrier. Eventually she got hold of Gareth, who didn't look very happy about it.'

'I did see Gareth as people started to leave the walled garden,' Niri said, suddenly remembering. 'I think it was him, anyway, with Edward. Gareth didn't look very happy then, and Edward seemed to be trying to soothe him.'

'Did you think they had argued?' Elliot asked.

Niri thought for a moment. 'Not argued, no,' she said slowly, 'but I think Gareth was angry with Edward. Whether that was his normal state, I don't know. Nor do I know whether Edward's behaviour was normal for him. It just seemed as though there was some kind of atmosphere between them.' She lifted both hands and let them fall again. 'I'm not sure, I'm sorry.'

'It wasn't just them,' Lucy said. 'Other people seemed to be uncomfortable, annoyed, too, but I really don't know their names. Anna would, a couple of the people I know she's seen recently, farmers, I think. Edward seemed to have annoyed the wife, I saw her walk off at one point. Anna said that she's taking one of the studios. And,' a shadow of her gamine smile touched her lips in the glare of the arc lights, 'Anna was greeting nearly everybody by name, so she's really the person to tell you more.' She glanced round at the others, to see them all nodding agreement.

Elliot looked at them, standing silently waiting for his next question. 'You're all singing the same unhelpful tune,' he said resignedly, catching Will's grin. 'Names and faces unknown.'

Hugh's lips twisted into a sardonic smile. 'I didn't know any of the suspects, Elliot. I haven't been here much.'

'Names and faces unknown,' Will said ruefully. 'I'm afraid so. Sorry, Rob, I was only here for Lucy. And I guess the same is true for Niri.'

'Yes,' she agreed. 'But what Lucy says is right. Anna can put names to faces and then I'm sure we could be more useful.'

'Thank you,' Elliot said. 'If I can provide photographs of the guests will you be able to describe more of what you saw? If,' he added ruefully, 'Anna can put names to them it will certainly make things easier. She must at least have a guest list she can give us.'

'Of course,' Lucy said, and the others murmured agreement. 'Do you want us to come to the police station tomorrow?' She frowned suddenly. 'I expect Anna's going to want to be here to keep an eye on what's going on and field questions from the press. Would that be alright?'

She saw him hesitate, and went on, 'The public launch is next weekend, and there's still such a lot to do, without the extra work this incident is going to cause. We could,' she suggested tentatively, 'all meet up here in the morning to look at the photos. That way you won't have to visit us separately or trek over to the station.'

'Not here,' the inspector said at once. 'This is a crime scene, and I can't be sure we'll be finished by then. But a joint session with the photographs is a good idea. I'll see what we gather in tomorrow morning and send them over to you all by email. We can meet in the back bar at the pub tomorrow, at midday, for a discussion. I'll get Jed to keep it out of bounds to other punters.'

'Can just Anna come into the garden?' Hugh asked. 'She can come in the back way without disturbing any of your people. Unless you think the walled garden is part of the crime scene.'

Elliot looked at him soberly. 'I don't know yet. No,' he said decisively, 'I'm afraid Anna can't come in until I do know, but I'll contact her about it as soon as I can.' He looked at Lucy. 'I'm sorry.'

'It's not going to make Anna happy,' Lucy said. 'She's put a lot of work into this.'

'It can't be helped,' Hugh said, turning away. He began to walk out into the parkland, carefully guided by a police officer in a fluorescent yellow jacket along the exit route outlined by police tape. Will and Niri walked rather wearily after him, with Isobel and Fabio close behind them, but Lucy hung back with Rob Elliot.

'I'm sorry this has happened now you've got Carrie with you,' she said. 'Where is she now?'

'An elderly neighbour comes to look after her when I'm out,' Rob said, running a hand over his ruffled hair. 'She's sleeping there tonight.'

'Well, if it helps, bring her over tomorrow, she can stay with me during the afternoon. I was going to be working here too, but obviously that's got to wait, so she and I can do something together. Only if you like,' she finished hastily.

'Thank you, Lucy, I'm sure Carrie would like that a lot. I know I would, she took to you in a big way.' He smiled suddenly. 'A magic garden, just what she's always dreamed of. You hit the nail on the head there.'

Rob looked at her in silence for a moment, and she could not make out his expression. 'We'll be out of here by the end of tomorrow,' he said, 'as long as nothing unexpected turns up. I'll let Anna know if it's okay for her to come in before that. And I'll be happy for the launch to go ahead next weekend. After all,' he added, 'I expect Anna's got the great and the good coming. You won't be able to get them all again for a long time, if at all. And,' he became more cheerful, 'perhaps it will give the press a different focus.'

'Thanks, Rob. I'd better get hold of Anna and discuss it all,' Lucy said. 'Hopefully we won't have to rearrange much.'

She was startled to hear Will calling her name. She looked round and saw he and the others standing with a bored-looking policewoman at the start of the exit path. 'I'd better go,' she said hastily. 'You've a lot to do.'

He walked with her over to the others, where she was greeted impatiently by her brother, who seemed to have forgotten his jet lag. 'Come on, Lucy, don't stand around gabbing. Strange as it seems, it's only just after eight. We're adjourning to The Lanyon Arms for something to eat. Anna and Mike can join us there, and we can talk through what to do about the press launch. Then Niri and I can get on home.'

'That sounds good,' Hugh agreed. His mind was uneasy. He wondered where Laney was and what she was doing. He mentally shook himself. Why should he be worried? She'd barely been down here more than a day, how likely was she to get into trouble? After all, Elliot was thinking this was a domestic dispute that got out of hand, and he was probably right. That meant there wasn't an unknown assailant buzzing around looking for victims.

'Can we bring something up for you, Rob?' Lucy asked, lingering as the others began to walk away.

'Thanks, but I'll be fine. There won't be time to eat it, anyway. Once we've got the scene totally secured, I'll need to get back to the station and check the operational set up.' He looked down at her, a glimmer of a smile on his face. 'At least I'm likely to be in the area more than I would have been. Maybe we can do that catch-up over lunch one day?'

She looked at him seriously, her eyes shadowed in her pointed face. 'Yes, I'd like that.'

'Well, this will certainly get the garden more publicity,' Hugh said frankly, putting down his glass after taking a sip of the local beer.

'But not the sort we want,' Anna said crossly.

'Any sort will bring in visitors,' Hugh said cynically. 'And the interest in this attack will soon wear off. There will be plenty more to absorb the ghouls.'

'But what if Gareth dies?' Anna agonised. 'Oh dear,' she shrugged one shoulder elegantly, 'how awful that sounds. The garden really doesn't matter as much as all that.'

'It's alright,' Will said. 'We know you wouldn't put the garden ahead of any of your friends. Not really.'

'Will,' Niri spoke quietly, but he turned at once, giving her his full attention, 'if we're going to do these press notices, we'd better get back to the manor. We want them to arrive with the media ahead of any other information about the incident.'

'Sure.' Will put down his own glass and pushed back his chair, getting to his feet at the same time.

'Umm, are you sure this is okay?' Anna asked. 'You're not too tired?'

'It's cool, Anna,' Will said breezily. 'We've got the agreed wording in the official format – we'll just bung the thing off from the office at the manor to the addresses you gave us. You know the internet connection is good there. Better than risking the one here, it can be dodgy.'

'We'll be fine,' Niri added reassuringly, 'but we should get on.'

With a cheerful smile around the table, Will turned and began to push his way through the crowd that had gathered in the main bar of The Lanyon Arms. Lucy saw him reach the doorway and go through, followed by Niri.

Other people in the bar watched them go too. She knew that news of the attack on Gareth had brought out many more people, hoping to hear what was going on. Even Kerenza had called in, thankfully without her guests. This means good business for Jed, Anna thought, seeing how hard-pressed the barman was by the unexpected influx.

Aaron appeared silently at their table. 'I've passed the word round,' he told them. 'Everyone that needs to know does. The launch is going ahead. It's good to keep going,' he told Anna, aware that she was torn between pressing ahead and postponing the event. 'The police will probably have arrested the culprit by then.'

'I know,' she said, 'it just doesn't feel quite right to go ahead with the launch, but I know we've got to.'

'Is there any news yet?' Aaron asked.

'About Gareth? No,' Anna shook her head. 'We left Edward at the hospital with him. He didn't want us to stay.'

Aaron studied her shrewdly. 'In a bit of a state, was he? Always did get worked up when he was a lad. Didn't like things not going his way.'

Anna gave an involuntary spurt of laughter. 'It's a bit more than that this time,' she pointed out. 'And no,' she went on, 'after an initial outburst he became very quiet, very concentrated on Gareth, as if he was willing him to live. He was,' she tried inadequately to explain, 'quite different to normal.'

'He puts on that light malicious manner,' Mike said unexpectedly. 'It's an act. Gets him noticed, he likes that.'

Aaron nodded. 'It's become a habit, started when he was in his late teens. He thought it was amusing because it irritated people, especially Andy Trago.'

'What's the general feeling in the bar?' Hugh asked. 'About the attack?'

The older man rubbed a finger over his curly moustache as he considered the question for a minute. He said slowly, 'Mixed, I suppose. Of course, Edward could have done it in a rage, but not many really think that. He's never shown any signs of being violent, he's more prone to subtle comments, nasty but not obvious, to pay back people who've upset him.'

'Probably doesn't like blood,' Mike said practically. 'Not everyone can cope with it.' He glanced meaningfully at Anna, whose skill at coping with injuries was renowned among her friends.

'And if it wasn't Edward,' Hugh pursued, in the persistent manner that had made him such a skilled barrister in an earlier stage of his life, 'what then?'

'There are all sorts of wild theories going around,' Aaron said dismissively. 'A publicity stunt seems to be the favourite.'

Mike glanced across at Anna and saw suddenly how pale she was. 'You're tired,' he said abruptly. 'Let's get home. We've got an early start tomorrow.'

Anna closed her eyes for a second, contemplating that. As she opened them again, she said, 'Not that early. Rob rang to say it'll be okay to go through the back gates to get into the walled garden, but he said mid-morning, after ten-thirty. It was nice of him to let me know so quickly,' she said.

She glanced at Mike as she added, 'We've got to come by the village after the early morning service. Kerenza spoke to me at the bar earlier, she offered to help clear the tables and chairs, and generally sort things out for next week's reception, so we can pick her up, and just take the one car up. There's only room for two in the back lane, and Lucy,' she smiled at her friend, 'will need the other space. And,' Anna added more gloomily, 'Rosa's coming with Kerenza. She seems to be glueing herself to somebody or other at the moment, and now it's Kerenza.'

'Went to school together, those two,' Aaron's comment was almost drowned out by Mike's explosive expletive. 'Rosa's older, but she relies on Kerenza when she's a bit out of sorts with the world.'

'What does that mean?' Anna asked.

'Well, Rosa's had a lot of problems in her life, and she doesn't have many friends. Her own fault,' Aaron said bluntly. 'She's nosy, pushing in where she's not always wanted, and she's indiscreet. She passes on things she's heard, things she shouldn't have been listening to, and certainly not repeating. You can't even be sure she's got them right. Sometimes,' he went on slowly, 'I think she's not above letting people know what she knows about them, exerting a bit of power, perhaps extracting small favours.' He paused, thinking of what he had said.

Hugh said abruptly, 'That sounds like blackmail.'

Aaron shook his head. 'It's only a bit of butter here from one farm, a punnet of fruit there, a pretty scarf, nothing much to it. She's had a hard time, it maybe helps her feel better, feel she belongs in a way.' He paused again, thinking of what he had said, trying to be fair. 'Rosa really has no one to support her, except Kerenza. She's always been there, helped her through the bad times, the death of her husband, even though some thought that was a relief to her. He was a heavy drinker, knocked her about at the end. Kerenza keeps the demons from the door for her, I suppose,' he summed up.

'Come on,' Mike said impatiently. He was already standing, poised to push through the people between him and the doorway. 'We don't need to have this bloody woman's life history.'

Anna smiled at Aaron as she stood up and began to edge out from behind the table. 'Thanks for telling me. It does help to cope if I know a bit about her. It won't be for long anyway, we'll have to be back here to see Rob by midday.'

'Just shove her off on some job that keeps her out of the way,' Mike advised, grabbing Anna's arm and pulling her away, Ben coming out from under the table to follow them.

Aaron moved off in their wake, leaving Lucy and Hugh alone at the table. Silence fell, each busy with their own thoughts. Lucy's heart was heavy as she watched the collie leave, realising that Isobel had been right, he was Anna's dog now. She sighed a little and felt no happier as she became aware of the constraint that had fallen between her and Hugh.

Hugh's thoughts were elsewhere, once again wondering where Laney was. All Kerenza had said when Hugh asked about Laney was that she had gone straight out when they had arrived back at the cottage.

He started. 'Sorry,' he apologised, looking across at his wife. 'I didn't hear you.'

'I'd like to go too,' Lucy said, getting to her feet. 'But you've got your car here, stay on for a bit if you want to.'

He hesitated before deciding. 'Yes, I will.'

Lucy passed him silently, leaving him regretting his decision. But not enough to change it, a small voice said inside his head.

Mike drew his battered Passat to a halt beside Kerenza who was waiting outside her cottage in the village street. Anna leaned forward, speaking across him as he opened his window. 'You weren't planning to walk there, were you?'

'Of course not,' Kerenza's tone was brisk again. 'But Rosa seems to have slept in. She was supposed to be at my house fifteen minutes ago, and when I passed her place on my way home from church all her curtains were still drawn. I'm just going along to see if she's up now.'

'Leave her in peace,' Mike said impatiently. 'We don't need her.'

'She'd like to take part,' Kerenza said firmly. 'You wait here, her place is only just there.' She gestured to a small row of cottages behind them.

Anna put her hand on Mike's arm. 'We'll wait,' she said, forestalling the comment that was about to burst out of his mouth.

They watched as Kerenza walked on a few paces and paused, the blustery wind blowing her scarf out behind her like a pennant. Rosa's little cottage was in the centre of a terrace of five low whitewashed buildings, whose thatched roofs stretched down over tiny upper windows. Their front gardens were narrow, but all were bright with spring flowers, daffodils at nodding distance from early tulips, daisies already spattering tiny patches of grass. The cottages looked small, but Anna knew that many of them had been extended into their long back gardens. She wondered idly if Rosa's cottage had been, but judging from the shabby walls and dilapidated thatch, she thought perhaps not.

Kerenza was looking up at the window over the front door. From Anna's viewpoint it was almost hidden under the straggling thatch, but Kerenza could see it directly. She began to hammer on the door, loudly enough for Anna and Mike to hear the noise in his car.

Anna felt uneasy. 'I'm going to see what's the matter,' she said, unfastening her seatbelt and opening the passenger door.

'For God's sake,' Mike groaned, 'the bloody woman's overslept. Leave her in peace, and let's get on. I want to get over to Melanie's site sometime today.' Behind him, Ben fidgeted in the back of the car.

But Anna had gone, her swift pace taking her to Kerenza's side before he had finished speaking. 'What's wrong?' Anna demanded, as Kerenza stopped hammering with the door knocker and stepped back to look up at the window again.

'I'm not sure.' Kerenza sounded strained. 'It just doesn't feel right.' She glanced at Anna. 'Rosa's always up early, it's the habit of a lifetime, you know how it is. And she really wanted to come today. I'm afraid she may be ill.'

'Wouldn't she ring you?' Anna asked practically.

Kerenza shook her head. 'Not if she can't get out of bed. She

won't have an upstairs extension, thinks it's a waste of money.'
She bit her lip. 'Look, I've got a key at home. I'll just nip back
and fetch it. I won't be more than a couple of minutes. You and
Mike go on. I can drive up later or come by this afternoon when
you've finished with Inspector Elliot.'

Anna hesitated. 'No,' she said, deciding quickly, 'we'll wait.
I'll just go and tell Mike.'

They walked quickly back up the street. Anna stopped by the
Passat while Kerenza went into her own cottage. Two faces looked
up at Anna, Mike glaring furiously, the collie fixing her with a
hopeful stare.

'Mike, Kerenza thinks something may be wrong, so we'll just
wait until she's got the spare key and gone in. I'm sure,' she saw
the scowl grow on his forehead and forestalled his comment, 'that
Rosa's overslept, but Kerenza is really worried about her. It'll only
take a few minutes to check.'

'For God's sake, Anna, you've been chuntering on about how
little time there is to get sorted before we're seeing Elliot,' Mike
snarled. 'And now you're going to hang around here.'

Kerenza was back, bending down to speak to Mike through
the window. 'Sorry,' she said briskly. 'But I've got the key, we can
just see that Rosa's okay, then we'll be back.'

She and Anna were gone before Mike could say any more. He
watched as Kerenza knocked again, waited, then inserted the key
and opened the front door.

She led Anna straight through the door into a small parlour,
neatly furnished, beige and dull at first to Anna's eyes, but
redeemed by splashes of colour from cushions and rugs. And by
the African violets that filled the tiny hearth with jewel-like shades.
A vase of early narcissi stood on a small table in the window,
which Anna guessed Rosa used as a dining table – and a vantage
point, with its view over the street. But the scent of the narcissi
was not obvious. Instead, there was a pervasive scent of something
both sweet and sour. Anna did not know what it was, but she did
know that she did not like it. It increased the sense of unease that

had crept over her.

A door at the back of the room opened into a tiny kitchen, but a steep narrow staircase led up on one side of the parlour and Kerenza was already mounting this. Anna hesitated, waiting until the woman had reached the room above. The main bedroom, possibly the only bedroom, Anna guessed, directly over the parlour. She heard Kerenza's footsteps tapping across the floor, and then Kerenza called out, 'Anna, come quickly.'

Anna's heart skipped with fear as she heard the distressed note in Kerenza's voice. She went quickly up the stairs into the bedroom, aware that the smell she did not like was growing stronger. Her heart skipped again when she saw the scene in front of her, the woman who lay motionless, half in and half out of the narrow bed near the window, the bed clothes twisted around her. Kerenza was trying to lift her, to turn her to see her face, but Rosa lay heavily inert.

Kerenza stepped back, her face white as she said, 'I think she's dead.' Her nose wrinkled and she clasped one hand to her mouth. She turned to the window, obviously going to open it.

'No,' Anna spoke sharply. 'Don't touch it. Don't touch anything.'

'Anna, the smell,' Kerenza said faintly.

'I know. Go outside. Tell Mike to call the police. And don't come back. I'll come down too.'

'And I'll get an ambulance. Maybe she's not dead yet,' Kerenza said, stumbling towards the door. 'She'll need an ambulance.'

'Just the police, tell them what's happened, they'll get an ambulance here.' Anna said firmly. 'It's too late to help her now, but they'll need it.' She bit her lip, afraid she had been too frank. After all, Kerenza had known Rosa for decades.

Kerenza gasped, stopping and half turning back, one hand raised to her chest.

Anna waved her away. 'Go and ring. And try not to let anybody else know about this yet. Use your house phone if Mike doesn't have reception here.'

Kerenza went, and Anna was left alone with the body, pulling up over her nose the scarf she had flung round her neck this morning, trying hard not to be overwhelmed herself by the smell. She looked around quickly, wanting to get out of the room as soon as she could. Rosa had an upturned glass on the small wicker table between the bed and the window. A small dark bottle in a puddle of water lay on its side, but its contents were still inside, held secure by the stopper.

Something had made Rosa ill, very ill, judging from the pools of vomit that stained the bed sheets and the floor. It looked as though she had been trying to get out of the bed when she had died, Anna thought bleakly. I wonder what's in that bottle? Oh, Lord, I wonder what she ate at the tour yesterday? Suppose she's died of food poisoning.

The church clock had chimed one, the note just sounding in the back bar of The Lanyon Arms. Anna pushed back her untouched lunch, resisting the sudden impulse to feed the chicken to Ben, who lay patiently beside her. She sat at a table by the window, glad that Jed had kept the room free for police use.

She had been watching Rosa's cottage, guarded now by a single constable standing stoically beside the police tape that screened it off. So many people had gone into the cottage, dressed in protection gear that looked so familiar from television programmes, that she wondered how they all fitted. Rob was still in there, and Kerenza. She hoped Kerenza would be able to leave soon.

Anna turned away from the window, looking round the room with its mismatched tables and chairs that normally gave it a quaint charm. Somehow, today, it too seemed crowded, although only her friends were there, and *that woman*. Maybe she was why the room felt oppressive, Anna thought. Fabio was here, too, with Isobel, but he was unobtrusive, calmly chatting to Isobel as they sat at one of the tables, waiting for Rob to arrive. But, Anna realised, if it felt crowded in here, it could be nothing compared to the crush in the main bar, judging from the hum of noise that penetrated the closed door. She shut her eyes wearily.

'Are you alright, Anna?' Lucy demanded anxiously from the bench beside her.

Mike frowned. 'Time you had a rest,' he said gruffly, as Ben raised his head, his tail waving a welcome. 'Let's get home, Elliot can see us there.'

Ben's tail wagged faster, he understood the word "home" very well. But Anna opened her eyes, and slowly shook her head. 'No,' she said, 'there's no point. I won't stop thinking about Rosa until we've got some idea of what's going on.'

'You didn't know her at all, Anna,' Mike said abruptly. 'You don't need to get involved.'

'One attack, one death,' Lucy said thoughtfully. 'They might be connected. I wonder how they could be.'

'We've got too little data to speculate usefully,' Hugh said bluntly. 'On the brighter side, at least next weekend's launch won't be affected by this death.'

'It doesn't make it any brighter for Rosa,' Anna said sharply. 'And the launch must be cancelled, or at least postponed, if there are more attacks or deaths.'

'Why should there be more?' Laney asked, from where she sprawled back further along the bench, a clutter of cameras laid out around her. 'And you don't know yet this woman was murdered, do you?'

'No, I suppose not,' Anna said, more sharply still. 'I suppose she could have died of food poisoning.' She threw Hugh a scathing look. 'That really would put paid to the launch.'

'Don't be stupid,' Mike growled. 'Nobody else is ill. And there's no reason to connect her to the attack on whatshisname. Rosa's death is just a coincidence,' he went on firmly. 'She probably had some health problem we don't know about, or she picked up a virus.'

'You didn't see her,' Anna said quietly.

Lucy put a hand on hers. 'Well, let's think about what we

know,' she said calmly. 'What seems to link Rosa's death with the attack on Gareth?'

'Gareth is Edward's partner,' Anna said immediately. 'Rosa was determined to talk to Edward yesterday at the garden.'

'Does that make Edward another potential victim, or a suspect?' Hugh asked.

Anna shrugged. 'How should I know?' She glanced at Laney, who was adjusting a lens on one of her cameras. 'You spent some time with Edward,' she said suddenly. 'Yesterday, in the garden. Did he say anything to you?'

Laney looked up, rather surprised. 'Not really, but then I'd only just met him, he wasn't going to say anything significant to me. He was just a bit of a gossip, keen to show me the "best bits" of the garden.' She frowned. 'I got the impression he likes to have a finger in as many pies as possible.'

'Two different methods were used,' Will pointed out. 'The attack on Gareth was surely opportunistic. But if this woman you found was poisoned as you think,' he glanced at Anna, 'that must have been planned.'

'That's a good point,' Hugh said.

'Two different murderers, that's stretching it,' Mike protested.

'Only one murder so far. You're forgetting,' Niri said, 'that Gareth is still alive.'

'But he's not likely to survive long, from the cagey way Elliot's talking about him,' Mike said gloomily. 'It will be two murders, right enough.'

'Talking of Rob,' Lucy said, 'I've had just had a text from him saying he's on his way. He's got more questions about Rosa's death, and he wants to discuss the tour photos with us. I think,' she glanced round, 'he sent copies to everyone this morning. Did you all get them? Rob seems to have gathered in a lot.'

'Photos?' Mike exploded. 'What photos? I haven't seen any bloody photos.'

'That's because you haven't checked your email,' Anna said, placing a restraining hand on his arm. Seeing his expression, she went on quickly, 'They're photos of the other people at yesterday's tour. We're the only ones who know who all the people were. It was hard for Lucy and the others to explain what they saw and heard to Rob last night while we were taking Edward to the hospital.'

'I thought he was bringing them here,' Mike snarled, scrolling down his mobile phone screen. He scowled as he stared at it. 'How many of these does he expect us to look at?'

'I haven't seen them either,' Laney said, sitting up and looking across expectantly.

Hugh picked up his mobile, but Lucy said swiftly, 'Rob only wants to discuss them with the garden committee, so we should leave it to him to show them to you later if he wants to. It was, after all, only us he asked to meet him for this discussion.'

'Sure,' Laney said easily. 'I'll shift my ass when he gets here. Unless he pleads with me to stay and view the gallery.'

Hugh hesitated, a slight frown on his face, then put his mobile back on the table.

'Here, Mike, look at the photos on my iPad. It'll be easier than using your phone,' Lucy said, getting to her feet as she passed it over. 'Rob should be nearly here. I'll see if he's in sight yet.' She walked towards the door to the main bar room.

'I'll have a beer,' Mike declared, putting the iPad down on a table and following her. 'I'll need it if I've got to go through thousands of photos of people I won't know.'

'Afterwards, perhaps,' Hugh said warningly. 'It'll be best to keep a clear head when we're talking to Elliot.'

Mike stopped dead, turning to stare at him in outrage. 'Beer's never yet affected my memory,' he snapped.

'Hugh's right, Mike.' Anna said. 'Let's get the meeting with Rob over, then we can relax over a drink.' I hope, she thought to herself.

Lucy opened the door and the full volume of several voices talking at once broke into the comparative silence of the back bar. The main bar of The Lanyon Arms was certainly packed. The noise died abruptly as people in the crowded room became aware of Lucy. All eyes swivelled to stare at her, and then at Mike who had reached her shoulder. They watched avidly as the pair moved into the room. Mike strode ahead, escorting Lucy to the porch door, little knots of people parting before him, dividing like the Red Sea to allow them to pass.

Inspector Elliot opened the outer door just as they arrived at the porch, so their parade grew by one, returning through the silent crowd to the back room. The inspector's face was grim, and a low murmur grew up in his wake. 'Sorry, Lucy,' he said quietly, 'I couldn't bring Carrie with this new incident, especially as it's a death.'

'I know, I didn't expect to see her,' Lucy said as she stepped into the back room again. 'We'll sort out something else when this is all over.'

'Are you OK?' Rob asked Anna, closing the door behind Mike, who had forgotten about his beer.

'Yes, of course,' she said, smiling faintly at him as he came over to her, bending to stroke the dog. 'It was rather horrid, though.'

He nodded. 'You did well,' he said. 'I wouldn't expect otherwise.' For a moment his expression lightened. 'With all your experience.'

His gaze sharpened as he saw Laney turn to look curiously at Anna. 'Ms Scholz,' he said politely, 'I'll have some questions for you later.' He stepped back to the door and opened it slightly.

Laney smiled, 'Sure, I'll be waiting.' She took her time to pick up her cameras and bestow them around her body. Slinging the strap of the largest one around her neck she walked over to the door. She was almost there, when Elliot moved slightly, stopping her. 'Just one thing, now. I recall that you didn't return to your B & B until long after midnight last night. In fact, I believe you weren't seen after leaving Elowen Garden in the early evening. Can you tell me where you were?'

'Oh, I was bashing that man around, for the sheer hell of it,' she said sardonically. 'Sorry.' Her face sobered. 'Seriously, I don't know the man, why would I want to hurt him?'

'Where were you?' the inspector repeated.

She shrugged. 'I was out walking. I like moonlight scenes.' She gestured at the cameras. 'I thought I might get some good shots.'

'Where did you walk?' he asked. 'You must have been out for six or more hours.'

'I wasn't watching the time,' Laney said. 'I went up to the cliffs, that's quite a way, and I wanted to see the house that woman was on about.'

'What woman?'

'I don't remember her name,' Laney admitted. 'Tarty sort of blonde in the walled garden.' Mike snorted, and she flicked a smile at him. 'You know who I mean then.' She turned back to the inspector. 'When you let me look at your photos I'll point her out. She cornered me at tea-time yesterday, wanting me to take photos of her and her fantastic house. Once I got to the cliffs I thought I'd just take a look at the place.'

'In the dark?' Elliot asked.

She laughed in his face. 'It was nearly full moon last night, almost as clear as day. It made the place look kind of spooky, but I'll see it in daylight before I decide whether it's worth my time.'

Hugh was frowning as she turned to look at him. 'Not really my kind of pictures, but she was pretty insistent.'

He nodded, looking across at Elliot. 'Shouldn't you be asking Ms Scholz these questions in private?'

'Sure, in for the attack, Hugh, that's the way,' Laney said approvingly. 'But, hey, I don't mind, I've nothing to hide.'

She looked at the inspector. 'Is that it?' When he nodded, opening the door wider for her, she lifted a hand in general farewell and strolled out.

Hugh was aware that the others in the room, with the exception of the inspector, were nearly all staring at him with varying degrees of hostility. Only Fabio was unconcerned, watching him curiously. Isobel was perhaps not hostile, more maintaining an air of neutrality. It was her attitude that struck Hugh most forcefully and he was cross with himself for so openly supporting Laney. He pushed his chair back a little and stretched his legs, not meeting any of the eyes fixed on him.

'We haven't heard anything about Gareth,' Anna said, breaking the silence as Rob sat down opposite her and she turned her gaze to him. 'Do you know how he is?'

The inspector had been considering the others, his gaze lingering briefly on Lucy as she sat down, but he turned to Anna, his lips tightening. 'There's been no real change. The main concern still seems to be the internal bleeding. He lost a great deal of blood, and they've removed his spleen, which was damaged beyond repair. He must,' the inspector's eyes were cold and hard, 'have been kicked repeatedly when he was down. And the head injuries are severe, again it looks as though his head was kicked or repeatedly thumped on the ground. If he does survive, there's no knowing how much lasting damage will have been done.'

'Surely there must have been considerable noise during the attack,' Hugh said. 'I must have been on the scene soon after it happened, and I heard nothing except for a rustle. It was the movement that attracted my attention.'

'I too heard nothing,' Fabio said quietly, 'and I wasn't far behind Hugh. I had just returned from driving Kerenza and Laney back to the village.'

I wonder, Hugh thought grimly, does he think he's providing me with an alibi? More soberly, another thought struck Hugh. Does he think I need one?

Elliot was shrugging. 'They'd have heard you coming and stopped before you got close. And we don't know how many people were attacking Gareth.'

Anna was aghast. 'So even if Gareth survives, he may never be the same again,' she said. 'That's what you mean, isn't it?'

'That's the gist of it,' Elliot agreed.

'How is Edward taking it?' she demanded.

Mike asked, 'Got over his prima donna act, has he?'

The inspector frowned. 'He seems to have done,' he said slowly. 'He has closed right down and is saying nothing much, knowing nothing at all.'

'But,' Mike said forcefully, 'when he arrived at the scene he said he knew who'd done it.'

A faint smile touched the inspector's lips. 'He says now that he was talking generally. He also says that Gareth was angry with him for telling his stories, and when Gareth is angry he goes walking. I gather,' Elliot said carefully, 'that Gareth sent Edward off with a lecture and planned to walk back to their place. Edward hung around a bit on the lane, wondering whether to go back and see if Gareth had changed his mind, before deciding to go down to the pub.'

'He was assuming it was a man though,' Hugh said. 'That's perhaps natural.'

'Surely with those injuries it would be,' Lucy said.

'Women can do just as much damage as men,' Hugh replied. 'It depends on the provocation.'

Elliot nodded. 'We can't rule out a female attacker. No matter what Edward thinks. Or,' he said grimly, 'is concealing.'

I wonder, Anna thought suddenly, whether Laney was seen on her walk. But, she realised, Rob will check that.

'Is the attack on Gareth connected with the death of this woman in the village?' Will asked, patently unconcerned about whether women could be as violent as men.

Elliot shrugged. 'We don't know yet.' He held up a restraining hand. 'And now I'd like to ask the questions. It is my job, after all.'

'Oh alright.' Will sat back with a resigned grin.

'Rob,' Lucy said, glancing quickly at Anna, 'can you at least tell us whether Rosa's death was an accident?'

He considered her for a moment. 'It wasn't,' he said quietly.

'Oh God,' Anna said urgently, 'was it food poisoning?'

His gaze turned to her. 'It was poisoning,' he said deliberately, 'but I don't think it will be food poisoning. Especially as nobody else at the Elowen tea party has been taken ill.' He smiled faintly. 'You didn't cause her death, Anna. We'll have to wait for the test results to know what killed her.'

'Thank you,' her tone was heartfelt. 'I was worried about that.'

'Everyone will know soon enough that she was poisoned,' Elliot said. His gaze moved to Hugh. 'But so far that information is confidential, not to be passed on to anybody not in this room now.'

They all nodded, Hugh slowly, his eyes on the inspector's.

'You've all seen the photos and sent commendably detailed replies,' Elliot said. 'All except for Mike.' He looked across at the archaeologist. 'Did you look at your emails this morning?'

'Some of them. I'll look at the photos now, it won't take me long on Lucy's iPad.' He picked it up as he spoke.

'Inevitably you all saw different things, but it's obvious there were some definite arguments or angry discussions among the visitors.' The inspector sighed, watching Mike skim through the photos on the iPad screen. 'This whole thing seems very complicated. It sounds as though many of the people there quarrelled with someone else.'

'Too damn right they did,' Mike snarled, his eyes still on the photos. 'Small communities, they're often full of hidden resentments. Always have been, all through history. Most of the local ones seemed to be surfacing yesterday afternoon. And I haven't a clue what they are,' he ended firmly.

Elliot regarded him with an air of surprise. 'I couldn't have put it better myself,' he commented blandly. He looked round the room at the others, who were all watching him closely. 'I've tried to pull together the interactions you've reported into some sort of coherent whole. Please let me know if I've got something wrong or have missed something. If Mike has anything to add, we'll slot it in.'

He picked up a sheet of paper, closely filled with printed lines. 'There were tensions right from the start in the walled garden, before you set off with the tours. Edward was late arriving, he came after Gareth, and was with Andrew, who was looking disgruntled. Laney had just met them on her way in with Kerenza, that's when Edward latched on to her.'

He looked down at the paper in his hand. 'Rosa went to talk to Edward after he appeared, she clearly wasn't happy about something. It's unclear whether it was something to do with him, or something else. He doesn't know she's dead, at least I hope he doesn't, so we may get more out of him when he does. One of my sergeants is at the hospital now, breaking the news.' Elliot held up a restraining hand as Will opened his mouth to speak. 'Questions and comments at the end, Will, or we'll never make any sense of this schedule.'

Will sank back in his chair and ostentatiously tapped his fingers together.

'Whatever the reason, Edward seemed to annoy Rosa even more, and Gareth joined them. He seemed to be drawn in too. Laney was there at first. She didn't follow what the discussion was about, it seemed to be about pranks Edward had played as a child, but she wasn't sure.'

Anna shot a swift glance at Hugh, who was watching the inspector intently.

'The next observed incident was in the garden, on Lucy's tour, when Edward and Gareth were found leaving the grotto, which was out-of-bounds, with Laney.' Hugh shifted slightly, irritably, on his seat, aware of Anna's second glance at him.

'Edward,' continued the inspector doggedly, 'had apparently thought Laney would like to see the interior, and Gareth had been interested too. Edward said the barrier was only for the general public, and it wouldn't matter if they ignored it.'

Anna felt an unusual spurt of anger. How very like Edward, she thought. He could never think of himself as a member of the general public, a small part of a larger mass. And, the thought suddenly lit her mind, Laney, it's always Laney there with them.

'Two other interactions were mentioned in the tour groups,'

the inspector went on, suppressing his amusement at the sudden glimmer of suspicion he detected on Anna's face. 'Shona Trago went with Mike's group and was primarily interested in becoming part of the garden committee. Her husband went off with Hugh and insisted on discussing land law, apparently not interested in the garden or whereabouts in it they were.' He glanced at Hugh. 'You didn't know where you were either.'

Mike leaned forward and Anna put her hand on his arm. 'Later,' she said urgently. 'Let Rob finish.'

'Afterwards,' the inspector went on, ignoring the byplay, 'when the groups were all back in the walled garden, Edward was once again in action, reportedly in a highly excitable state. This time he was talking to Martha, who clearly didn't want to hear and physically pushed him away. Gareth was nearby, seemingly cornered by Rosa and getting angry either with her or about something she was saying. Or with something else altogether.'

Elliot put down the piece of paper. 'One thing strikes me as immediately obvious from this summary. Edward and Rosa were, separately, clearly annoying a variety of their companions. Does anybody have the faintest inkling why?'

He looked slowly round the table, where the others were shaking their heads. 'I thought you wouldn't,' he remarked. 'That would make life far too easy.' He leaned back, picking up a pen and absently tapping the table-top with it.

'Alright, Will, what did you want to say?'

'I didn't remember before,' he said, 'but Shona was keen to get hold of Anna before the tours started. And then she pushed people out of the way to join Mike's tour.'

Anna was nodding. 'Yes, for some reason she's desperately keen to be involved in the garden restoration. Although I can't see why, she doesn't have any interest in the garden itself.'

'She thinks she'll get matey with the great and the good,' Mike said cynically. 'She kept on at me about it on the tour, but I wasn't listening. And she's almost certainly the woman who badgered that photographer, Hugh's friend, about her amazing house.'

'Jed did say Shona is very keen on running things,' Anna said thoughtfully. 'The barman here,' she explained, seeing Rob's interrogative look.

'The woman's just like her husband,' Mike said forcefully. 'She wants to get her own way just as much as he does.' He turned suddenly on Hugh. 'That's why Trago went off with you, isn't it?' he demanded. 'He wanted you to tell him how to get possession of Soldiers' Meadow.'

'Peace, Mike,' Hugh said. 'I didn't want to know about it, although that didn't stop him from giving me his account in a long-winded ramble. If it's of any interest to you, I can't see that he has the slightest chance of getting it.' He frowned. 'He didn't give me any idea of why he thought he should have it either, as far as I recall.' He smiled wryly. 'I wasn't really listening, I'm afraid.'

'Do any of you have anything else to add?' the inspector asked. He again saw a communal shaking of heads.

'I'm sorry, Rob,' Isobel said, 'neither Fabio nor I have been of much use to you.'

'It can't be helped,' he said. 'But if you do remember anything, however insignificant it seems, do tell me at once. Sometimes people outside of the main loop of events see more than they realise.'

Elliot looked round at the others in the room. 'I'll take this summary of events as accurate. For the time being, at least, but it gives us something to start with. The main dissensions include a small number of people, two of whom became victims, so we'll concentrate on them first.'

'Is Rosa's death connected to the attack on Gareth?' Lucy's quiet voice fell across the sudden silence. 'Because if it is, I can't see why it was Gareth who was attacked and not Edward. After all, from your summary, it was Rosa and Edward who seemed to be sowing discord. If that is connected, surely it should be the pair of them who were the victims.'

'We don't know,' Elliot said. 'But we can't discount a connection, so your point is valid, Lucy.'

'What does Edward say?' Anna asked. 'After all, he can tell you what he was talking about.'

'Childhood stories,' the inspector said. 'Just as Laney said. And,' he forestalled the question, 'Edward can't think why anybody should have been annoyed by them. They've been known about for a long time.' Elliot caught Hugh's eye. 'He's going to try to remember which ones he was telling. A difficult job apparently, there are so many of them.'

'Surely Martha can tell you what he was saying to her?' Anna demanded.

'She says she never listens to Edward if she can help it,' Elliot replied.

Mike gave a shout of laughter, and the buzz of noise outside the room died abruptly. 'I can believe that,' he said.

The inspector's mobile rang shrilly, and they all fell silent as he moved away to answer it. It was a short conversation, with clipped responses on his part.

As he ended the call, he turned round to face the group in the room. 'There's still a lot we don't know,' the inspector said, 'but we do at least know what killed Rosa. She took an overdose of digitalis, which had been added to her cough linctus.'

'An overdose,' Anna said quickly, feeling oddly uneasy. 'Do you mean she took it deliberately?'

Elliot shrugged. 'We don't know. But,' he said, 'I don't think so. There's no note,' he held up a hand, warding off Hugh's expected comment, making it himself, 'but that doesn't mean much. It's a locally made linctus, and Martha is the herbalist who makes it up. She says that Rosa hasn't had a refill recently. Apparently, Rosa always brought back the old bottle to have it filled again. Although,' Elliot sounded resigned, 'Rosa worked at the farm, and could just have helped herself. Martha is confident that isn't possible as she's sure Rosa wasn't a thief. Naturally,' the inspector's brows were in a straight line, 'Martha is emphatic that digitalis isn't one of the linctus ingredients and she doesn't use it in any of her other remedies. The bulk of her linctus is kept in a large container and has been tested. It's uncontaminated, so at the moment we don't know the source of the digitalis. Martha has also given us a list of other people she's supplied with the linctus in the last three months, and it seems to be a large proportion of the neighbourhood.' He sat down wearily in a chair. 'All of whom will have to be checked out.'

'So,' Will said, realising at once the importance of the inspector's earlier comments, 'somebody added it to Rosa's cough mixture specially. Somebody else? Or did she do it herself?'

'She might have done it herself and thrown away the poison container. Rosa's been complaining of a sore throat over the last few days and using her linctus a lot, so that she must have finished up her supply. We found the old bottle in the bin. The bottle she used last night was newly opened, and it contained the poison. So did the water in the glass by her bed, so it looks as though she tipped a little linctus into the full glass and drank from that.' Elliot sighed slightly. 'But we don't know where that bottle came from and we haven't found anything in Rosa's house that may have held the poison. It looks as if it was added to the linctus before last night.'

'You don't think she did it herself,' Hugh said quietly.

'No,' Elliot agreed grimly. 'I don't. Neither does Kerenza, who knew her well. I think she was murdered.'

FIVE

'Pass me that rod,' Mike instructed. 'I just want to measure the depth of this trench. The soil layers are interesting. See,' he took the measuring rod that Anna handed him, and pointed with it, 'here and here, these layers have been disturbed, mixed up.'

'Are you reaching the level of the bodies?' she asked, bending over the trench that Mike was surveying in Soldiers' Meadow, while Ben stood beside her, looking down in great interest. Really, Anna thought, it is lucky the weather was so good, otherwise these trenches would be full of water.

'Nowhere near.' Mike's voice was muffled as he bent over the bottom of the trench, peering at something embedded in the soil. 'Ah, that's interesting.'

'What?' she demanded, trying to peer round him. She shifted slightly, holding Ben's collar as the collie showed signs of going to investigate Mike's find.

'Some sort of metal object,' Mike said, feeling round it. 'I'll leave it for the field team to unearth, but it'll give us an idea of when this plot was disturbed.'

'What about thieves?' Anna demanded.

Mike grunted derisively as he stood up. 'It's probably a bit of broken ploughshare, nothing more exciting. Nighthawks will be looking for more than that. So,' he said derisively, 'will friend Andy.'

Anna straightened up. 'I think I'll go and visit Martha,' she said. 'I haven't really had much time to talk to her about the studio she wants.'

'Don't be all day,' Mike warned, still peering along the base of the trench. 'I'm only going to be here until midday, then I need to get over to Melanie's excavation. They extracted the axes yesterday.' He glowered. 'When you made it impossible for me to go over. Finding another body, was it really necessary? Anyway,' he did not wait for an answer, 'I want to have a close look at them. And I want to discuss an idea with her.'

He looked across the meadow beyond Anna, and she turned to see that he had opened a trial trench she had not noticed before. This one was at an odd angle to the others, almost on the edge of the meadow.

Mike noticed her gaze. 'I'm following a hunch,' he said, almost defensively. There was something odd in the aerial survey, and I just wonder ...' His voice tailed away as his gaze lifted to the outline of the ramparts on the headland beyond the meadow. 'This whole landscape is ancient, of course it is, but there's more to it than we're seeing. I'm sure of it.'

He looked back at Anna. 'I'll tell you more later. But get going if you want to see Martha.' He added gruffly, 'If you're not ready when I want to go, I'll leave you behind.'

'And love to you too, Mike,' Anna said sweetly to his back as he returned to his trench. 'I'm leaving Ben with you, make sure he doesn't come after me.'

She told Ben to stay and strolled off, leaving the collie looking anxious until Mike called him. Anna went out through the meadow gate, down past the higher Carne field and soon picked up the track that led down to the farm. It was a lovely day, the sun shining, the sound of the waves on the nearby shore a gentle continuous murmur, gulls calling overhead, and Anna felt insensibly soothed by the time she reached the farmhouse.

To her surprise an unusual stillness hovered over the yard when she entered it and there was none of the noise she had expected, no voices, no television no music. A slight frown touched her brow and she hesitated, wondering whether to go on.

Then she stepped forward, past the rickety gate that was propped to one side, onto the path leading to the back door. It stood ajar, and now she did hear voices, angry voices.

Anna hesitated again, but then she caught the words and her attention focused on them, so she stood still, listening.

'… mine,' Andrew Trago was shouting, 'and you should have told me. Even that little toad Edward knows the truth. And what about Tony, is he in on the secret too? Is it giving him a thrill to know what I don't, something I'm entitled to know?'

'You're getting Tony muddled with yourself,' Martha said, her own voice loud enough to drown out the angry man without having to shout. 'He knows what I know, and it's none of your business.'

'We'll see about that,' Andrew yelled. 'I won't let this go, Martha. I have rights.'

'It's not about your rights,' she said contemptuously, 'but if you want to make a fool of yourself, you go ahead.'

'I've been made a fool alright,' he said bitterly, 'for all these years.'

Martha laughed. 'You've been a fool without any help from us.'

There was the sound of a door slamming hard, then heavy footsteps coming heavily along the corridor. Hastily Anna moved back a few paces along the path and tried to compose her expression.

Andrew Trago yanked the back door fully open, striding straight out and down the path towards her. His expression was dark, his face contorted with anger, his eyes staring ahead, almost as if they saw something that Anna could not. He did not even seem to notice she was there.

She drew back off the path, tripping slightly over one of the large stones that edged it in places, convinced that Andrew would walk right over her if she fell. He strode on past her without a flicker, kicking the rickety gate as he passed it.

Phew, she thought, I hope he's not going up to the meadow. He's in just the right frame of mind to start a fight with Mike.

She saw with relief that he turned down the track. Looking past him, she saw the BMW that had been parked further down, completely blocking the way. It was the latest model BMW too, somebody had told her in the pub, but that didn't seem to concern Andrew. He revved the engine furiously, backing the car into one of the hedges, spinning it round and driving off at a speed that made Anna frown.

She turned back to the house, wondering whether to go in or not. As she stepped forward, a slight movement in the farmyard caught her eye, making her pause to watch. Tony Zennor was limping away from the back of the house towards the most distant barn, the old cart barn where he had built Martha's loom.

Had he been in the house with Andrew too, Anna wondered. From what she had overheard, she didn't think so. Tony's voice was normally quiet, but surely it would have been raised if he had been as angry as Martha and Andrew.

But no, she realised, he had not come out of the house, she would have noticed. He must already have been outside, perhaps in Esther's garden. But had he heard the row? Did he know what Andrew had found out?

Anna suddenly thought she should tell Mike about the overheard fragment of conversation. She saw Tony stop as somebody came across the yard behind him. He stood a little awkwardly, but without his crutch, Anna noticed, waiting for the newcomer. It was Laney again, Anna realised in disbelief, as she saw the photographer catch up with Tony and walk on with him. I wonder what that woman is up to, Anna thought grimly.

Suddenly determined, Anna walked quickly up the path and picked up the mallet to strike a hard blow to the gong that she spotted beyond the surfing boards. The noise reverberated round her head as she stepped through the back door and entered the corridor.

Martha stood in the doorway at the end, the strangely quiet kitchen behind her. Her taut expression relaxed when she saw Anna. 'Hi,' she said, 'come on in. I'm about to make some coffee.'

Anna smiled at her. 'That just what I need. I've left Mike up in the meadow, there's only so much interest I can express in empty trenches. Ben is more fascinated with them than I am, almost as fascinated as Mike himself.'

'I'm sure.' Martha was amused. 'But Lissa is dying to get up there to start excavating. I don't think she's any idea how mundane it's likely to be.'

'Mike will soon make that clear,' Anna said, adding almost incredulously, 'but most students don't seem to mind that at all. Or the crouching and bending or the dabbling in the mud and roasting in the sun. Anyway,' she went on deliberately, 'I was glad that Andrew Trago wasn't heading that way.'

'Oh, you saw him, did you?' Martha's back was to the room as she measured out coffee beans. 'God knows what he wanted to come here for. He must know we're not going to bother about him.'

'Was he here about Soldiers' Meadow again?' Anna asked bluntly.

Martha pressed the button of the coffee grinder, sending the beans whirring around. 'He rarely ever comes about anything else,' she replied, when the noise stopped. 'As well Tony wasn't here too,' she poured the ground coffee into the cafetiére, 'or things would have heated up into a first-rate row.'

She reached up to a shelf to fetch down a couple of mugs. Undoubtedly hand-painted, Anna thought, automatically assessing and approving them. Beautiful mingled greens and blues, they reminded her of the sea on a sunny day, seen in translucent clarity from the top of a cliff.

'I'd better see if Laney wants coffee too,' Martha said. 'I left her going through my workshop. She was fascinated by the processes. I suppose ....' She broke off, turning to the kettle and pouring boiling water into the cafetiére.

'I saw her going across the yard,' Anna said, watching Martha closely. 'She met Tony and they went off to the old cart barn.'

'He's taking her to see the large loom then, so I guess they've already been with Esther in her garden,' Martha said. She put back the third mug she had just reached down. 'She can have hers when they get back.'

Martha put the cafetiére and two mugs on the table. 'Sit down, I'll be glad to have a chat,' she said, waving a hand at a chair. 'So far, it's been one of those days you'd rather not have. It hasn't helped not having Rosa here. Poor soul, not her fault of course.'

Anna had just sat down and now stared across at Martha in surprise. 'Her death, do you mean?'

Martha gave a short laugh. 'In a way.' She frowned for a second, staring at the coffee mugs, then shook her head briskly. 'I'm afraid I'm being selfish. Rosa came to clean here four times a week and today was one of her days. I hadn't realised just how much she did, it'll be chaos after a couple of weeks without her. If you could stand her nosiness,' Martha said abruptly, 'she was a marvellous worker. You just had to remember not to leave out anything you wouldn't want her to see.'

'Really?' Anna queried, rather disapprovingly.

'Oh, she wasn't dishonest,' Martha said quickly. 'She just liked to know what was going on. There was no real harm in that,' she added, 'but you could never count on Rosa keeping quiet. It paid to keep her sweet with small presents, things she'd have had anyway.'

'Like Esther's meals,' Anna said, suddenly remembering the exchange she had seen.

Martha nodded as she reached over and began to pour coffee into the mugs. 'She'd be getting them anyway, Esther can never stop herself from giving things away. But Rosa liked to "earn" her treats. It gave her a reason for snooping. For example,' Martha gave a short laugh, 'Rosa had already found out about Laney's project, and it gave her a lot of pleasure to tell us about it long before Laney turned up. I can't see she'd have got any mileage from that morsel of information though.' Martha handed one of the mugs to Anna. 'Help yourself if you take milk or sugar. Milk in the fridge, sugar on the side over there.' She gestured towards one of the kitchen counters.

'No, I'm fine,' Anna said. 'What's this about Laney's project? I've been so busy with the garden recently I haven't had chance to catch up with anything else.'

'I'm sure you haven't,' Martha said, picking up her own mug and cradling it in her hands. 'Laney's keen to put together a portfolio of local activities, so she's been taking shots of my workroom and the soap room and, as I said, Tony's taken her to see the herb garden and the loom in the barn.'

'That sounds amazing,' Anna said carefully. 'What else is she interested in photographing?'

'I think she's been to Gareth's pottery, one of the children saw her there. I couldn't believe it, but I suppose Edward let her in. I should think,' Martha said thoughtfully, 'that Gareth will be furious when he finds out.' She looked across at Anna. 'Is there any more news about Gareth? I haven't seen Edward to ask. He wasn't at home when I walked over to see him last night.'

'No, I think Gareth's still the same,' Anna said. 'I haven't heard otherwise, so I guess the fact he's holding on is good news. I can't believe he'd want Laney to take photos of his work though, he's so reclusive.'

Martha gave another short laugh. 'Edward wouldn't be able to resist somebody famous. I gather Laney is. He's always persuasive, he'll get around Gareth, he usually does. And he's not the only one to be impressed by fame, Laney's going to Shona's place as well. In fact, I believe she was pressed to visit.'

'What for?' Anna asked in amazement.

Martha shrugged. 'The house, I believe. Anyway, Shona was cock-a-hoop about it when she came over earlier. I think it's more than made up for not getting herself onto your garden committee.' Martha smiled conspiratorially at Anna. 'For a while at least. It'll mean she won't pester you so much about it as she's got this bit of limelight to enjoy.'

'You don't like her,' Anna commented.

'I don't like her type,' Martha corrected. 'Self-important, pushing in where she isn't wanted.'

Anna could not help feeling Martha had described Shona well, from what she herself had seen. But she was more interested in Laney's project. 'I'm surprised Hugh hasn't mentioned what Laney's doing,' she said. 'I've seen him a few times, even if it has mainly been about the garden.' And deaths, she added mentally.

'Well,' Martha said slowly, 'I'm not sure she wants him to know. I've wondered if she might be treading on his toes. After all, he's a photographer too, isn't he?'

'Yes,' Anna agreed, 'but I don't know that he does much in that line now.'

Martha shrugged. 'Well, maybe she just doesn't want it to get around. She asked us not to tell anyone, said too many people would want to get in on the act and she wants to choose the right shots. For a magazine series, she said.'

And I wonder just what photos she's been taking in the garden, Anna thought grimly. And does Hugh know what she's up to?

'About time,' Mike said, striding down the track towards her as she waited outside the farmyard gate. Ben raced up to her, his tail waving furiously, as Mike went on crossly, 'I thought I'd have to come and drag you out. What were you doing for so long?'

'Well, I was a bit delayed,' Anna said, falling into step beside him. 'There was a row going on when I got there. Andrew Trago was having a go at Martha, and I didn't want to burst in on them, but I couldn't help overhearing.'

'What!' Mike came to a dead halt. 'The bloody man. He'll be making a fuss about the meadow ownership again.'

Anna had stopped a little further on. She turned back to face him. 'Come on, Mike,' she urged, as Ben hovered beside her. 'You want to get to see Melanie, remember.'

His face darkening, Mike strode forward. 'Well, wasn't he?' he demanded.

'It did sound like it,' Anna admitted reluctantly. 'But,' she said more cheerfully, 'Martha just laughed at him.'

'What a woman!' Mike sounded jubilant. His exuberance faded slightly as he asked, 'What about Tony? What did he say?'

'He wasn't in the house,' Anna said, a little frown appearing on her forehead as they reached the Passat tucked into its usual spot at the foot of the track. She opened the boot for Ben to jump in, then walked round to the passenger door and slid into the car, deftly avoiding the prickly bramble branches that sneaked out of the hedge at ankle height.

Mike pulled out of the track and braked so sharply that Anna jerked forward against her seatbelt, putting out one hand to brace herself against the dashboard. The Passat was nose-to-nose with a green Volvo that she recognised at once.

'It's Edward,' she said through the stream of Mike's swearing. She was undoing her seatbelt as she spoke. 'I wonder if he's got any news.'

Leaving Mike with his hands still clenched on the steering wheel she walked quickly over to the other car. As she approached, the driver's window was lowered. 'Oooh, I'm so glad you're with him, Anna, darling,' Edward said. 'Mike on his own would be terrifying. I expect he's very angry with me, isn't he? But,' he went on without waiting for a reply, 'another scratch or two wouldn't matter on his old banger, although thankfully we didn't get that close. I'd hate to have any dents on my old Angel. I do think cars like to have names, don't you, and this one has been an angel to keep running.'

Anna ignored his banter. 'Have you heard how Gareth is?' she asked.

Edward's eyes clouded. 'No better,' he said shortly. 'The doctor isn't very forthcoming, which I don't think bodes well.' His eyes brightened with malice, 'And your nice inspector friend doesn't seem to have got very far, does he? Perhaps he's too busy making up to Lucy.'

Anna's eyes flickered, but she did not respond to his needling. 'Let us know when there's any change to Gareth's condition,' she said, 'and if there's ever anything we can do.'

'Thank you, darling,' Edward said, his voice as sweet as usual. 'I'd better reverse to let Mike past. He's definitely not going to give way to me, and I want to get up to Martha to let her know the latest lack of news about Gareth.'

'She's having a busy day,' Anna said lightly, stepping back as he put the car into reverse. 'Andrew Trago was there before me. Laney was around too. It makes my schedule seem quite tame.'

'Well, Martha has always been popular,' Edward said, waving a hand. 'I just hope I'm in time for lunch, I'm sure she'll ask me to stay.'

She stood to one side as Mike drove the Passat past him, without exchanging a glance or a word. He pulled in to wait for Anna, his fingers drumming impatiently on the steering wheel.

'Really, Mike,' she reproved as she reached the car, 'don't be so unfriendly.'

'I don't like him,' Mike said unnecessarily. 'He's too nosy.'

'That seems to be a bit of a local trait,' Anna mused, opening the passenger door. 'Rosa had a reputation for nosiness too. Martha was mentioning it earlier, but like Aaron she wasn't bothered by it. Rosa was a good cleaner, and it seems that part of the price for having her to work for you was putting up with her nosiness.'

She stopped suddenly, one leg already in the car. 'For goodness' sake,' she exclaimed, pulling her foot out and straightening. 'I forgot to ask Martha when she wants her lease on the studio to start from. And that's what I went for in the first place.' She looked swiftly at her watch. 'Look, Mike, you've got fifteen minutes to spare, wait while I just sprint back and check with her. I really want to get the contract sorted out as soon as possible.'

He had barely started grumbling before she was gone, running down the lane to the farm track.

Anna had slowed to a quick walk by the time she was in sight of
the farmhouse. She saw a flicker of movement beyond it and
squinted against the sunlight to see what it was. Laney, she felt
she should have known it would be Laney. She was walking
steadily up the slope towards Soldiers' Meadow, and Anna
frowned, remembering what Martha had said about the project
she was working on. Surely she wasn't going to take photographs
of the dig. Mike would be furious at any trespass on his site. And
really, she thought practically, it can't be a scenic spot, just those
trenches in the ground.

Then her own artistic training came to the fore. It could be a
very atmospheric scene. The dark rectangles like open graves waiting for the bodies that were reputed to already lie there, set against
the green slope, the rolling white-capped waves of the ocean
beyond the cliff edge, the stone seat set against the backdrop of a
clear blue sky.

Sunset would be even better as a time for a photograph, Anna
mused, when the sky is streaked with pink and orange. Surely
Laney would know that, she's already been up here in the evening.
Maybe she's just prospecting for an angle. But, Anna thought, I
shan't mention it to Mike, and just hope he never finds out she's
been up there.

Edward's car was parked in the yard just beyond the house,
but there was no sign of him. There was no sound of voices either
when she turned into the garden and walked swiftly up the path.
She hesitated at the door, stepping back to look around the farmyard. And there they were, Martha and Edward, in the doorway
of the cart barn, their backs to the yard, looking at something in
the interior.

Anna was light-footed on the cobbled yard, soon drawing
near enough to call out to them. But then, once again, the sound
of a conversation made her pause.

Edward seemed unusually penitent. Martha on the other hand

was dismissive, her voice impatient. 'What does it matter?' she demanded. 'It's done, we'll just have to deal with it. But I do wish you could keep your poisonous tongue in your teeth for once in a while.'

'Don't be so crotchety,' Edward said. 'After all, I didn't actually give anything away. I think Rosa did that, keen to get in before me. She wasn't happy when I warned her that her "treats" weren't going to be as numerous. She always thought they were a just reward for her silence, even if the givers didn't realise they had secrets for her to keep hidden. Mind you,' he flicked a casual finger over his hair, 'I can't imagine she ever touched Andrew for a "treat", she probably thought Shona's cast-offs were on his behalf. But,' he mused, 'she did like making people aware that she knew something about them, even if her hints were sometimes rather obscure.' He went on sanctimoniously, 'You shouldn't have kept her out of the storytelling, she always minded that. It would have been a safe outlet for her stories.'

'What a shit you are,' Martha said dispassionately. 'The woman's dead.'

'And left you to face the music. Although,' Edward said maliciously, 'I expect you're getting some satisfaction at the thought of Shona without her cleaner too. She's not one to get her hands dirty, other than mucking out her horses.'

'Rosa was a decent woman,' Martha said sharply. 'And she didn't have much of a life.'

'Oooh, my heart bleeds,' Edward said, clasping his hands to his breast. 'I stand chastised. How I'd like to be one of your sons. The eldest of course, I could only be the most important.' He shifted slightly, and his voice changed, 'But I don't give a damn about Rosa, or why she killed herself. Unless I find she attacked Gareth, and I don't think that's likely, do you?' He did not wait for a reply. 'But I've got a good idea who did, and …'

A large goose had come out of Esther's garden, and had been pottering through the yard until it caught sight of Anna. Now it ran forward, neck stretched out, hissing furiously. It was instantly

joined by its companions, until there was a flock of a dozen of
more bearing down on her.

Anna paused, wondering whether to retreat, when a low call
from the farm shop detoured the birds in one sweeping movement.

'It's darling Anna,' Edward said, peering round Martha as the
geese strutted past the cart barn towards Lissa as she called again.
'Are you following me, darling? Or are you a spy? Or maybe
you're just getting into the personality of your next character. But,
darling,' he wagged a finger in her face as he sauntered across the
yard to join her, 'you really mustn't sneak around. You might get
hurt.'

Anna had just left the farmyard when she heard running footsteps
behind her. Turning quickly, she saw Lissa, and beyond Lissa was
Nat, walking rather than running.

Lissa came to an abrupt halt as she reached Anna. 'Sorry,' she
said breathlessly, 'but I wondered if you know how Kerenza is.
Nat,' she glanced sideways at him as he reached her, 'took me
down to her cottage this morning, but she wasn't in. We went
down yesterday as soon as we heard about Rosa, but the police
were still with her, and in the evening she wasn't answering her
phone or the door.' She looked at Anna appealingly. 'I don't want
her to be alone, she was close to Rosa.'

'You were there, too, weren't you?' Nat asked. 'When Kerenza
found the body.'

Anna nodded, but said nothing. She would prefer to think
and speak about that as little as possible.

'How was Kerenza then?' he asked. 'It must have been a terrible shock for her.'

'Of course it was,' Lissa said angrily. 'It would have been for
anyone.'

'She was upset,' Anna said carefully, 'but she coped very well.'

'She would,' Lissa said, 'she always copes, but for everyone
else, she never thinks about herself. She looked out for Rosa, she
does for me, she was always there after my mum died. She knows

what my dad is like, and she was there for my mum too before she died. I found letters from my aunt recently, they were in an old bag of my mum's that I found in the attic at home. Something,' she said bitterly, 'my dad must have overlooked when he threw all her things away. I've got nothing of hers, not even photos. I don't know much about her except what Kerenza's told me. Otherwise, all I know is that she died just after my little brother did, and I know that my dad always wishes it was me that died and not him. But the letters, they're so vivid, and my aunt was so concerned, my mum was so unhappy, but Kerenza was here and she helped her, she supported her.'

Lissa tugged frantically at her ponytail. 'I must see her, she's all the real family I've had. Although it's like coming to family here with Nat, and,' she added soberly, 'everything's out in the open here, there are no lurking secrets.'

I wonder, Anna thought. She said, 'How about your aunt? Are you in touch with her?'

Lissa shook her head. 'There's no address on her letters, and Mum's address book is long gone. I know they were both adopted by different families when they were children, and that Mum always kept in touch with her sister. Kerenza told me that. But I'll never know where to look for her, I don't even know her surname, because they both had new surnames, so there's no point even trying.'

'It doesn't matter,' Nat said. 'We've got our own lives, and we've got each other.'

She smiled at him. 'Yes, I know. It makes all the difference to me.'

Lord, Anna thought, startled, this is serious. I hope it's going to work out.

'Anna,' Lissa turned to her, 'can you try to get in touch with Kerenza and let me know she's alright. I'd really like to see her, but things are a bit hectic here and we can't leave again for a few hours.'

'We would if we could,' Nat said darkly. He muttered

something else, and Anna only just heard it. 'All these emotions washing around, we're staying out of it.'

Lucy sat in Anna's office at Elowen, her hands clasped round the mug of tea she had just made after the two women had shared a working lunch. 'I don't know,' she said thoughtfully. 'Almost anything seems suspicious in these circumstances, but I suppose it depends on the people.' She sipped her tea cautiously. 'You know them better than I do, so if you really think what you heard at the farm was important, you'd better tell Rob. After all, Edward said he knows who attacked Gareth.'

'He wasn't sure,' Anna corrected. She spread her hands out. 'I just don't know,' she said. 'I don't want to bother Rob unless I'm sure it's relevant to his enquiries. Edward is a little odd at all times, although Mike thinks it's all part of his pose.' She sighed. 'I don't really know Edward, any more than I know Martha. Our connections have all been quite superficial.'

Anna shrugged and reached for her own mug. 'I suppose I must tell Rob and let him decide if it's important,' she said ruefully. 'Even though I think it's probably just Edward being dramatic. And Edward will know I've told him. She sighed, then glanced at her friend. 'I was surprised to see Rob here for the garden tour. I didn't know he was interested.'

'Neither did I, but I've been talking to him about it and he turns out to be a gardener manqué. What he really enjoys is planning and planting. He'd like to have a proper garden of his own,' Lucy said. 'At the moment he's got a small terraced house with a tiny garden in Corrington but he's going to buy something bigger now that Carrie is living with him. He'd like her to be able to play safely outside.'

Anna's gaze sharpened. 'How do you know all this?'

Lucy smiled faintly. 'He told me,' she said. 'We've been in touch quite a bit recently. He's been very helpful about the structure of the young offenders' programme.'

'It's always useful to have official support,' Anna commented

wryly. 'What happened about his wife, do you know? I know they
were separated, are they getting a divorce now?'

'It's always sad when it comes to that if there's a child
involved, but sometimes divorce is the only way out,' Lucy said
reflectively. 'They were sorting it all out amicably enough. It
sounds as though they just grew apart. That happens easily
enough, especially with a job like Rob's.'

And a job like yours, and Hugh's, Anna thought uncomfortably. Did Lucy realise that?

'But,' Lucy sighed, 'they won't be divorcing.' She looked out
of the window at a blackbird busily pecking up moss from the
crevices in the courtyard paving. 'Rob's wife,' she continued, turning back to look at Anna, 'has terminal cancer and not long to
live. Her mother has moved in to care for her, and Carrie was sent
down to Rob. He's upset about his wife, of course, but he loves
having Carrie around.'

'How old is Carrie?'

'She's eight, nearly nine, an interesting child. I met her on the
garden tour.'

Ben had been sleeping on the floor between the two women but
now he raised his head, staring at the door. Lucy glanced out of the
window again and suddenly sat up straight. 'Here's Hugh,' she said,
her voice expressionless. 'And Laney. I wonder what they want.'

'I thought you'd be here, Anna,' Hugh said as he appeared at
the door of the office to an exuberant greeting from Ben. 'Ah,
hello, Lucy,' he added as he caught sight of his wife.

Laney appeared in the doorway behind him, her camera bag
slung over her back, making her look oddly bulky. Ben glanced
at her and moved away indifferently as she smiled round the room
in her usual self-contained way. 'Hi,' she said. 'I just bumped into
Hugh on the drive and dragooned him into pleading my case.'

'Oh?' Anna said, her tone unencouraging. She looked at Hugh,
her face unusually blank.

'Laney is keen to feature the garden restoration in a new project she's working on,' Hugh said. 'It will be fantastic publicity, so

it would be ideal if she can take photos while she's here, especially as the weather's good.'

So, Anna thought, he does know what she's doing. And he's kept it to himself until now.

Anna considered, amused that she was doing so instead of bursting into speech as she normally would. Hugh could be right about the publicity, he probably was, but he really couldn't be allowed to bypass the committee. Especially as he'd barely been involved with it recently.

'That sounds very interesting,' she said levelly. 'But,' she glanced at Laney, 'you'll have to put a proposal to the committee, we've had a number of similar requests and they'll all need to be considered.'

'Okay,' Laney said agreeably. 'I can do that. But there's nothing to stop me going around now and taking photos, is there?'

'I'm afraid there is,' Anna said, curbing her annoyance. 'The garden isn't open to the public yet.'

'Well, if Hugh comes around with me, that would make it okay, wouldn't it?'

'It wouldn't be a good idea for Hugh to pre-empt the committee decision,' Anna said. She turned to look at him. 'Don't you agree?' She knew him well enough to know that he was uncomfortable, and she found she was glad of that.

'I didn't know you'd had similar proposals,' he said.

'I expect you haven't had time to look at your emails,' she replied sweetly. Well, she thought, relieved, the proposals are fairly similar, so I'm not making it up.

'I'm sorry, Laney,' Hugh turned apologetically to the photographer, 'you'd better leave it for now. But,' he turned to Anna, his tone purposeful, 'I can contact all the committee with Laney's proposal and get their views.'

'Do,' Anna said, 'and do make sure to copy Lucy and me in. We'll look forward to it.' She was afraid her voice was becoming acerbic, and saw that Hugh was looking at her with a frown.

'That sounds great,' Laney said. 'It gives me a good reason to hang around for longer. I'm getting very interested in this part of the world, and that girl from the farm, Lissa, is shaping up to be a promising student. I'll be glad to spend more time with her.'

An uncomfortable silence fell in the office when she left. Hugh broke it. 'Well,' he said brusquely, 'I'll get on. Lucy, are you coming home soon? I may be late, I thought I'd go up to Soldiers' Meadow to see how Mike's getting on there.' He looked at Anna, one eyebrow raised. 'He will be there, won't he?'

Her usual bright smile broke out, banishing the constraint. 'He's out at another dig now, they seem to have found something amazing there, but I'm sure he'll be back at the meadow before it gets dark. You know what he's like when there's a dig on. Even if it hasn't officially started yet. The first volunteers arrive this week-end to stay over the Easter weeks.' She shivered dramatically. 'They'll be camping near the site, Tony Zennor has said they can use another of his fields and use the outdoor shower and loo at the farm. I don't envy them, it'll be really cold up there at night, and plodding down to the farmyard in the dark will not be a lot of fun.' At least, she thought suddenly, the geese will be locked up. And probably the dogs too.

'I don't know what time I'll be back, Hugh,' Lucy said, break-ing in on Anna's thoughts. 'I've got a lot to do here, and I'm expecting a couple of visitors.' She got up, taking her mug with her. 'Talking of which, I'd better get back to my desk.'

She strolled to the door, looking back as Anna called her name.

'Thanks for listening,' Anna said, putting out her hand to stroke Ben as he settled beside her. 'I will speak to Rob when I get home.'

Lucy shut the door carefully behind her. Anna looked away from it and found Hugh staring at her.

'What are you bothered about that Rob might need to know?' he demanded.

'Oh, just something I heard,' Anna temporised, looking out of the window. She stiffened. 'Hell, here come Shona. I bet she's looking for me.'

'I'm off,' Hugh said. 'Just get rid of her definitely, otherwise she'll be around making a nuisance of herself for months.'

'My friend,' Anna said sarcastically as he walked to the door.

He smiled, one eyebrow raised, and stood back, holding the door open.

Shona strode into the office, giving Hugh a bright smile. As he shut the door behind him, she sat down in the seat Lucy had just left, stretching long jodhpur-clad legs out. 'I've got to talk to you,' she said. 'I really want to be involved with this garden, and I can do a lot to help.'

Ben lowered his raised head to his paws with a small sigh, and Anna just stopped herself from sighing too. The respite Martha had predicted hadn't lasted long. 'What did you have in mind?' she asked.

Shona was silent, staring at her. Suddenly, she burst into speech. 'I know I get it wrong,' she said passionately. 'They all hate me round here.' Her hands, blunt fingered, with short carefully polished nails, clenched on the arms of the chair. 'I try to get involved with things, I want to make friends locally, but I try too hard, I know I do, but I can't help it. It makes me pushy, and everyone hates me for it. It's alright, you don't have to say anything.' She stood up and turned to leave. 'I'm alright with horses, but I've always been shit with people.'

'Wait a minute.' Anna was astounded to find she felt sorry for the woman. 'Look, sit down for a bit and let's talk about it.' She thought about offering coffee and decided not to, best not to prolong the conversation.

Shona sat down again, her blue eyes wide with surprise. Then they narrowed suspiciously. 'You don't have to feel sorry for me,' she said sharply. 'I've got my horses, I like them better than people anyway. I just wanted to be part of life down here, to make a difference.'

'We don't need more people on the committee,' Anna said, feeling it was best to be clear about that. 'But we do need people who can talk about the garden and what went on here.'

'I'd be no good at that,' Shona said at once. 'I don't give a shit about history, and I wouldn't know a,' she searched for a name, 'a magnolia from a rhododendron.' She smiled suddenly, baring white teeth. 'And that's even though I know we have both in our gardens. But the head gardener sees to them, he puts in what he wants, I don't care as long as it looks alright.'

'But you do know about horses,' Anna said, snatching at a straw. 'Horses were important then, for transport and working.' She gestured widely. 'That's the extent of my knowledge. You must know more, and that could be useful.'

'They were used for hunting and racing too,' Shona said slowly. 'I don't know a lot about it really, but I can find out. I'd like that.'

She sat back and stared at Anna again with those wide blue eyes. 'You're not just doing this because you're sorry for me, are you?' she demanded.

'You can't believe how much help we'll need to keep this place going,' Anna said. 'If you can be our horse expert, that would be very useful, it'll be another attraction we can offer. You know,' she said vaguely, 'have a session during a tour when you're around to talk about horses on the estate, and perhaps you might come in to talk to specialist groups. You'd be like one of the storytellers.' She stopped as she saw Shona's expression darken.

'Them,' the woman said explosively. 'Poisonous old bitches. Just spreading malicious stories all the time.' She saw Anna staring at her in surprise. 'I don't expect you've heard them all, they're probably careful with you, but they're constantly looking sly and dropping the odd hint about what Andrew got up to when he was a kid. It really pisses me off.' She frowned. 'And I had to put up with Rosa, who was a real expert at the venom-filled dart. But she was the only person who would come up regularly to clean. And now she's gone and let me down anyway.'

'Well, she couldn't help herself,' Anna pointed out, annoyed.

Shona stared at her, then smiled. 'Of course she couldn't. But it's a nuisance. Still,' her smile grew, 'there's some compensation about not belonging down here. At least they're not all discussing the dark secrets of my youth.'

Anna decided not to go into this. 'I'll have to talk to the committee about this idea if you're interested,' she said briskly, thinking of what she had just said to Hugh. 'But I'm sure there won't be a problem.'

'Okay,' Shona said, 'I'm interested, I'd be good at it.' She stood up and stared down at Anna, who rose to her feet as well, feeling at a disadvantage in her chair. Shona's face had brightened. 'This place must need money too. I'll get Andrew to cough up for something special.' She held up a hand, stopping Anna from speaking. 'Sorry, there I go again. I'm not trying to be bossy, honestly. But I will get him to put in a few thousand. Why not?' she said, going to the door. 'He's got plenty. And he owes me.'

The door closed behind her and Anna sat down again, feeling suddenly weary.

Dusk was falling as Hugh followed the footpath up the cliffside to Soldiers' Meadow. He had decided to walk up from Elowen but was now realising this may have been a foolish decision. If Mike wasn't here to give him a lift back to his own car, he would have to walk down again too.

Oh well, he thought, as he opened the meadow gate, I've had worse walks. And I doubt Lucy will notice if I'm late.

He had decided to walk to have time to think. Anna's obvious antagonism had startled him. He felt again that he was out of touch with life here, with the friends he had. The realisation was a shock. Anna obviously thought he had changed allegiance, putting Laney's interests above those of the garden.

That wasn't fair, though, Hugh argued to himself. Her proposal would benefit the garden. But, the little counter argument crept into his mind, that wasn't why you were interested in it. Anna was right about that.

He had felt there was more to her antagonism than that. He

knew that he should have been more involved with the garden, that was probably annoying her. She was right about that too. But even so...

Suddenly he stopped, just short of the first trenches stretching across the meadow. Surely she didn't think that his interest in Laney was personal?

His mind painted another picture. One where Will was off hand with him, where Isobel was polite but distant, where Mike was short with him and unusually reticent. Were they all thinking that?

Hugh felt the first niggle of annoyance. They really should know him better than that. Again, a counter argument popped up. But she isn't the first woman you've brought down here. They were all innocent relationships, he squashed the argument.

Suddenly, startling himself, he wondered what Lucy thought about Laney. Her appearance hadn't seemed to bother his wife. Hugh frowned, maybe that wasn't a good thing either.

His thoughts were unusually muddled, disturbing him. I'll clear this up, he thought decisively. I'll speak to Mike.

Hugh looked around, determined to do this at once. There was no sign of the archaeologist, but he might well be in one of the trenches. Hugh strode forward, almost unbalancing as he stepped unwarily close to the first trench. And there was Mike, crouching over something in the bottom of the trench.

'Mike,' Hugh said sharply.

There was no reply and Hugh leaned forward impatiently. Then his breath stilled, and he stared more carefully at the figure in the bottom of the trench. Mike was not working carefully over something in the soil. He was a hunched heap, face-downwards, eerily still under a thin layer of dust.

Hugh leaned over the edge of the trench, but it was too deep for him to reach Mike. Moving carefully, Hugh slid down into the trench and bent over the recumbent figure, gingerly touching one wrist, then the neck, feeling for a pulse. He could not find one.

'What the hell do you think you're doing?' Mike demanded, startling him.

Disconcerted, Hugh stared down at the body at his feet before realising the voice came from above the trench. And there was Mike, arms akimbo, roaring at him. 'Bloody hell, Hugh. What have you done?'

'Don't be an idiot,' Hugh retorted, holding up a hand stained with blood. 'I've just got here. I thought it was you.'

'Some idiot kids,' Mike said irritably. 'I've had them play tricks like this before. It was a skeleton on the last dig I ran. Just sling the thing up here. Unless it's one of them playing the fool, in which case he can stay there and freeze.'

'Mike,' Hugh cut into the diatribe, 'this is a real body, a dead body.'

The words Mike had been about to utter froze on his lips. He bent over the trench, peering down, trying to see. 'Who is it?'

Hugh lifted the face slightly from the earth. He and Mike stared down into the dead features of Andrew Trago, still recognisable despite the soil that coated them.

SIX

It was dark by the time Mike and Hugh drove away from Carne Farm. They left behind them the full panoply of a crime scene in Soldiers' Meadow – the suited scene of crime officers, the taped-off approach to the meadow, and Inspector Rob Elliot, who was now conducting his third investigation in the same area. The inspector had just finished interviewing Hugh and Mike and was moving on to talk to the entire Zennor household. The adults were quiet, almost reticent, but most of the younger members of the family were fascinated by what had happened, by being, as one of the children had said happily, 'in on a real murder'.

'What the hell is going on here?' Mike demanded, spinning his Passat sharply round a bend. 'Two deaths and a nearly fatal attack in such a short time, they have to be connected.'

'Mmm.' Hugh leaned forward, peering through the windscreen as the car sped past hedgerows. 'Are we going to the village?'

'We're going to the garden,' Mike said, turning to look at him and sending the car veering wildly towards a suddenly illuminated hedge. He jerked it back, and said, 'Anna texted instructions. She and Lucy think we should discuss what's going on. They'll bring fish and chips from the pub. Damn.' He groaned. 'I forgot to text when we left the farm. Send Lucy a message, Hugh, tell her we're on our way. And I want double chips.'

'Why the garden?' Hugh queried as he got his mobile out of his pocket. 'It's not going to be particularly comfortable there.'

Mike grunted. 'Private, I suppose. Your place and ours are just too far away, and the pub will be stuffed with villagers, all wanting to know what's going on.'

Hugh tapped out a short message to his wife. 'I suppose,' he said resignedly, 'we'll at least be in Anna's office. I don't fancy sitting outside mulling over the latest murder in the dark.'

'You're getting soft,' Mike said. 'We've done far worse.'

'Not by choice. But,' Hugh conceded, 'maybe I am spending too much time travelling and sitting in meetings.'

Mike ignored this. 'You do agree we're talking about murder, two murders and probably attempted murder?'

'Andrew Trago might have been good at making money,' Hugh said sardonically, 'but that wouldn't help him hit himself several times over the back of the head and then lay down on his face to die in one of your trenches. Nor could he do that by accident. Of course he was murdered.'

'He was obsessed with that bloody meadow,' Mike said. 'I wouldn't be surprised if he didn't die there on purpose to prevent the dig, even if,' he continued irrationally, 'he didn't kill himself to stop it.'

'Why was he so against the dig?' Hugh asked.

'God knows,' Mike said. 'I don't think Trago was against the dig, as such,' he went on slowly. 'I think it was more an issue of control. All I ever heard from him was that the meadow really belonged to him, but the land is all legally owned by Tony Zennor. I checked. I just don't know where Trago was coming from.'

'Hmm,' Hugh said again. 'It sounds odd. What does Tony Zennor say about it?'

'Not much,' Mike replied. 'I should think he's sicker of the subject than I am. It seems to have only cropped up after Trago returned to the area. But Tony's heard Trago on the subject for much longer than I have, so maybe he'd had enough. Especially if he found Trago in the meadow. But,' he went on, 'Tony doesn't seem at all the murderous type.' He saw Hugh raise a quizzical eyebrow and said grumpily, 'I know, that doesn't mean anything. And I've only been on the receiving end of Trago's ranting for a few months, but I'd already got to dread the sight of him. He couldn't talk about anything else, and if it had gone on much longer I might have got to the point where I couldn't stand another moment of it.'

He removed one hand from the wheel and clutched at his hair. 'And I expect the bloody man has managed to stop the dig. I'm expecting the team to arrive this coming weekend. What are the chances,' he glanced at Hugh and the car wavered across the lane, 'Elliot will have finished with the site by then? I don't expect I'll get such favourable treatment as Anna.'

Hugh was relieved that Mike righted the car as he finished speaking. He was even more relieved to see that they were not far from Elowen Garden. He had certainly forgotten how Mike drove. 'I've no idea,' he said. 'Would you say he favoured Anna?' He laid a slight emphasis on the name.

Mike was oblivious to it. 'Of course he does. He's always had a soft spot for her, probably admires her martial arts skills.'

'Hmm,' Hugh sounded noncommittal. 'Has he finished with the cottage in the village?'

'I couldn't tell you.' Mike swung the car into the car park beyond the Elowen gate posts. The beam of its lights illuminated the red Jimny parked on the far side. He cut the Passat engine and said angrily. 'That's Anna's car, she's here on her own. Without a thought of a mad murderer on the rampage, the woman goes wandering around a dark garden. Does she never learn that a black belt in judo won't save her every time?' He slammed the door and was striding off into the lime avenue as Hugh got out of the car to follow him.

Hugh was just feeling grateful there was a full moon to light the way into the garden when his phone pinged. It was a message from Lucy. 'On the way. Anna already at garden.' He hesitated, then decided to wait for her. He was sure the murderer was quite sane, but he was not sure why the deaths were happening and who else might be in the murderer's sights. And Lucy did not have a black belt in judo. At least, he did not think so. For all he knew she might have been learning since he was last at home.

Anna did not look in the least concerned when Mike burst into her office, almost tripping over the excited collie. 'Hello, Mike,' she said, looking up with a sparkling smile. 'I hear you've been in the thick of it.'

'What the hell do you think you're doing?' he roared, waving an arm so vigorously that one of the framed photographs on the wall slid sideways as if it was moving out of his reach. 'Sitting here on your own in the middle of a dark garden.'

'Catching up on paperwork,' she said ruefully as she shut down her laptop. 'I had no idea there'd be so much of it.' She slipped out of her chair and went up to hug him.

He seized her and pulled her close, as Ben lay down heavily by the desk. 'I wish you weren't such a bloody stupid woman.' His voice was muffled in her hair.

'One murder a day is likely to be enough,' she said lightly and freed herself a little to look up at him. 'I suppose Andy Trago was murdered?'

'Of course he was. He has to be difficult even in his dying,' Mike said glumly, releasing her and flinging himself into one of the chairs.

'You said he'd been found in one of the trenches you'd dug,' Anna commented, opening a cupboard door. She passed a bottle of beer to Mike, and brought out a bottle of wine and three glasses to put on her desk.

'He fitted in it as if I'd designed it for him,' Mike snarled. 'I'm beginning to really believe he's done it on purpose, got himself murdered there to stop my dig.'

'A bit drastic, though,' Anna said mildly as she poured herself some wine. She sat back with her glass and said more seriously, 'What does Rob think about it?'

'Elliot?' Mike grunted. 'I wouldn't know. You'd better ask him. I'm sure he'll be around to see you about it.'

'Why?' Anna asked in surprise. 'I wasn't there and I didn't know the man.'

Mike took a long swig of beer. 'But you've been to the farmhouse, and you heard Trago rowing with Martha. You know the set up too. I couldn't tell which of those kids belong there and which are visiting. If it comes to it, I couldn't really tell most of them apart.'

Anna's brows had drawn together. 'Why does it matter? I wouldn't know all the children either. But Martha can tell him if it's important.'

Mike shrugged. 'Don't ask me. But he seemed to be interested in the kids and whether any of them had been up to the dig. That was after they'd taken Shona away with screaming hysterics.' He shuddered. 'He's a better man than I am. She was really getting going when he took over and passed her to one of his blokes to deal with. A young bloke, new to CID by the looks of it. I've never seen a copper look so horrified.'

'Why on earth was Shona there at this time?' Anna demanded. 'I didn't think any of the Tragos were casual visitors to Carne Farm. Although,' she added as an afterthought, 'Andy's daughter is very involved with Martha's work and spends a lot of time there. Lissa. But I get the impression she and Shona don't get on well enough to do things together. Oh,' the memory popped into her mind, 'Shona does go there occasionally for salve for her chilblains.'

'Elliot was interested in Martha's work too,' Mike said, suddenly remembering. 'I don't know why. He kept hopping from subject to subject. It was difficult to follow his line of questioning, especially once Shona got going.'

He saw Anna open her mouth and said hastily, 'Martha rang her after Hugh and I got to her place and called the police. She thought she should know. That was a mistake. She's putting the woman up for the night now. You should have seen Tony Zennor's face when he heard Martha offer.'

It was mid-morning the next day when Anna pulled her Jimny into the yard beside Carne farmhouse. There were several cars in the yard, two of which she recognised rather ruefully. She had half expected to see Shona's yellow sports car still there, so she was prepared to meet the new widow. But Gareth's battered Landrover was a surprise, almost a shock, until Lucy realised that Edward must have driven it up here rather than use his own car.

The yard was quiet when Anna pushed the gate into the garden open. She kept a wary eye out for the geese and dogs as she approached the back door. The porch seemed no more littered than usual, but an uncanny silence hung over the house until Anna hit the gong.

Its reverberating echoes died away and silence fell again. Anna was just raising the mallet to strike again when the door opened. Martha stood there, her pale face lined with tiredness. Her expression lightened when she saw Anna. 'I thought you were going to be the police again,' she said, standing back to let Anna pass her. 'Go on through to the kitchen, it's warmer there. The weather suddenly seems to have turned colder.'

'I wondered if there's anything I can do to help,' Anna said as she settled herself into one of the basket chairs near the Aga. She realised with a sudden shiver that Rosa had been in this room when Anna first saw her, such a short time ago. She also realised that the room was strangely quiet, actually empty of other people this time.

'Thanks,' Martha said. 'I don't know. Tony's gone to see to Shona's horses. She's in such a state of shock that she doesn't feel up to it.' Martha's voice was very dry. 'He wanted her to go with him, thought it would help her to be among the horses, but no, she couldn't possibly go home, she'd be expecting to see Andy at any moment.'

'Oh,' Anna said inadequately. 'I realised that she was still here when I saw her car.'

'Oh no,' Martha said, 'she's not here now. She couldn't go

with Tony to see to her own horses, but Edward was a different matter. He felt it would do her good to go for a walk, so she went up on the cliffs with him to get a breath of fresh air. Took a flask of coffee too, so they won't be back that soon.' She glanced at Anna. 'Have you heard about Gareth?'

'No,' Anna said with a feeling of dread. 'What?'

'He died early this morning.' Martha gave her a faint shrug. 'I thought he'd come around when I saw Edward at the door, I'd heard he'd briefly regained consciousness in the night. But it was the last flicker of life, that's how Edward described it. The hospital summoned Edward, so there was possibly chance for them to say goodbye but I don't know if he got there in time. He didn't say. The police were able to speak to Gareth though, after all there was a constable by his bed, but whether Gareth said anything useful, who knows?' She shrugged again. 'I don't know any more than that. Edward didn't want to come in, said he wanted to get out in the open on the cliffs.'

She passed Anna a mug of coffee and sat down opposite her. 'They won't be able to pin that one on me.' She was watching Anna closely as she spoke. 'That inspector's a friend of yours, isn't he?' She did not wait for Anna to answer. 'He thinks I killed Rosa. I expect he'll think I killed Andrew too. There are times when I would have liked to.'

'Killed Andrew?' Anna queried carefully.

'Oh definitely,' Martha said vehemently. 'All this nonsense over the meadow. And now,' she paused, considering Anna, before she went on deliberately, 'now, there's this business of Nat. Gareth seems to have spoken about that before he died.'

'Nat?' Anna sounded as lost as she felt. 'What about Nat?'

'My son.' It was Esther who spoke, from the doorway to the back kitchen. 'Andy Trago's son.'

She glanced at Martha and said quietly, 'It doesn't matter now.'

'No,' Martha said. She sighed impatiently. 'It's an old story,' she said to Anna, 'one the family all know, including Nat, and now Lissa as well.' She paused, looking across at her sister as Esther poured herself some coffee. The eyes of the two women met, and Anna saw the sudden connection, the glimpse of a shared past.

Esther sat down in the other basket chair and cradled her mug. 'Once upon a time,' she said softly, 'that's how it should start, isn't it? Well, once upon a time Andy was quite different, he was lively, full of fun.' She shook her head disbelievingly. 'No one would have guessed how he'd turn out.'

'And very good-looking,' Martha said dryly. 'Don't forget that. And he knew it too, don't forget that either.'

'Martha never liked him,' Esther said quietly. 'And that seemed to attract him. He couldn't believe he wouldn't win her over. But he couldn't.' She glanced at her sister, 'Nobody and nothing ever wins Martha over if she's decided against them.'

Martha stayed quiet, her expression controlled, as she watched her sister.

'But,' Esther went on calmly, 'we were twins, and I liked him. I liked him a lot, and I used to meet him up at the rock seat on the cliff near Soldiers' Meadow. It wasn't until later that I realised for Andy it was a way of getting at Martha. In some obscure way, I think he thought I was Martha because we look alike. He thought it was as good as having Martha, nearly as good.'

Anna saw Martha grip her hands tightly together in her lap, but it was still Esther who spoke. 'It was only a brief affair, and Andy never knew that I fell pregnant. I could have stayed here, brought Nat up, or given him to Martha for another son. But Nat was mine, all mine, so I went away and had him and loved him and kept him, all by myself.'

She paused to sip her coffee and went on, 'But it was hard on my own. And I missed being here so much. I missed Martha.'

Martha's head was bent over her hands, and Anna could not see her expression.

'So I came home, and I've never been sorry. Nat has grown to love this area as much as I do, it's in his blood, and I haven't deprived him of the chance to grow up here.'

Martha looked up. 'And we were so glad you came home. You belong here as much as I do, and it's Nat's place as much as it's any of my children's.'

Again, the sisters' eyes met and an acknowledgment passed silently between them.

Martha carried on with the story. 'We had to decide what to tell the family about Nat.' She smiled faintly at Anna. 'We decided to tell them the truth. Nat has always known it, he grew up with it. It was so much easier than spinning a web of lies. It's always been left to Nat to tell Andy if he wanted to and he never has. He told Lissa though, a couple of years ago, and they're enchanted with the idea of being brother and sister. Nat grew up with his cousins, but although Lissa knows she had a little brother who died, she's pretty much grown up as an only child.'

'And then somebody told Andy that Nat was his son,' Anna said quietly. 'That's what he was shouting about when I was here yesterday. Was it Gareth who told him?'

Esther shrugged. 'I don't know. He couldn't know, unless Edward told him and … well, why would Edward?' She looked puzzled, but shook her head slightly and carried on, 'Andy was full of it, he had another son in place of the one he lost.' She saw Anna's expression, and explained, 'The boy who fell over the cliff, years back. Lissa's full brother. Andy never really got over his death.' She bit her lip. 'The boys were about the same age. I fell pregnant shortly after Laurie did.'

Martha's face was sombre. 'Laurie, Andy's first wife, was a friend of mine, a good friend, but she never settled here after her boy died. She was suffering postnatal depression after Lissa's birth, when the boy's accident happened. He'd gone out after his father on the cliffs, and got to the rock seat before Andy saw him. The boy began to run around, wanting his father to play chase, and he slipped,' Martha shook her head, 'right over the edge of the cliff before Andy could get to him. And that's where Laurie went over a few weeks after his poor battered body had been recovered and buried. I've never known if it was another accident, or whether she went over because she couldn't stand anymore.' Her expression hardened. 'But she loved her new baby to bits, and I can't believe Laurie would have left Lissa deliberately.' Martha sighed heavily. 'Andy was no help to her, there'd always been other women,' she pointedly did not glance at her sister, 'and he didn't make any effort to keep them secret. Laurie should have gone back to the States with Lissa, to her own family there. But I think she could never bear to leave her little boy alone in the cold Cornish earth.'

Anna remembered hearing something about these earlier tragedies, but now her thoughts were focused on the current ones. 'If it wasn't Gareth who told Andy that Nat is his son, his birth son at least, who did?' she asked.

Martha frowned. 'I can't quite understand that. It probably was Edward, he was one of the locals who knew or guessed. He told me he intended to use the knowledge if he had to as some kind of bargaining counter to stop Andy's plans to buy Potter's Yard. Andy was beginning to apply pressure in his inimitable fashion and Edward knew Gareth was worried enough to think about moving.'

'But Edward swears he didn't tell Andy,' Esther said. 'So that leaves Kerenza or Rosa. Kerenza wouldn't say, and why should Rosa? Edward warned her he was thinking of telling Andy, he could be malicious and he knew she'd think she would lose her treats from us. But she wouldn't have done, and surely she must have known that.'

'She certainly wouldn't have been getting treats from Andy for anything,' Martha said dryly. 'So what could she have gained? I know Edward thought she might have done it from spite, to get in before him and spoil his bargaining counter. But Rosa didn't really think like that.'

'How is Nat taking it?' Anna asked.

'Ok,' Esther said slowly. 'I think it's the finality of death that's affected him, and Lissa for that matter, not the fact that it's Andy who's died. Nat didn't have anything to do with Andy, and Lissa didn't like him. Andy never cared that she knew how little he thought of her.'

'Nat's one of us, part of the family,' Martha said quietly. 'Tony's the only real father he's ever known, and Tony loves him as his own.'

Martha glanced at her sister, who spoke tranquilly, 'I know that. I'm glad of it.'

Esther looked at Anna, her eyes clouding as she remembered the past. 'It was a different time, we were all so free and easy then, the whole group of us, you wouldn't believe the pairings we made up. The stories Martha could tell, but they're not stories for now, maybe for the future.'

'It's a shame,' Martha said thoughtfully, 'that Andy ever had to find out, and he obviously couldn't keep the news from Shona.' She laughed. 'I wonder how that went down. Shona certainly couldn't wait to pass that piece of news on to the police.'

She shook her head. 'Poor Andy. He was full of it. His new son. I think at first it trumped his interest in Soldiers' Meadow, but then he thought he'd get that too, that we'd gift the meadow to Nat and Nat would jump through Andy's hoops.' She laughed again. 'We couldn't believe it. We both thought he'd flipped. I knew Tony was angry, but he kept it together when I told the others Andy had been here, he had to, for Nat's sake.'

'Is that why you believe the police think you killed Andy?' Anna asked bluntly.

'Oh yes,' Martha said. 'They could see I would be the one to do something, if it had to be done. Nobody would ever think Tony could do something like that. But I could, and they knew it.'

'He's *my* son,' Esther said deliberately. 'Why wouldn't I be the one to stop Andy trying to take over his life?'

Martha smiled at her. 'Given a choice between me and you, nice quiet gentle you, who do you think the police are going to prefer?'

'But I don't see why the police think either of you killed Andy,'

Anna said slowly.

'They're not sure they do yet,' Martha said. 'But, you see, they don't think Rosa gave herself poison. They think I gave it to her to shut her up. And,' she glanced at her sister, 'that's my business, not yours.'

Esther's gentle smile appeared. 'I grow the herbs and plants you use. Do you really think they won't realise I know quite as much about what kills as you do? And I have as much access to it as you do.'

Anna did not know what to say. There was no time to speak though. The sound of the gong reverberated through the kitchen, making the pans rattle on the rack above the Aga.

Anna stood stunned at the farmhouse doorway, Inspector Elliot at her side as Martha Zennor and her sister, Esther Carne, were escorted down the path to the waiting police cars.

'I can't believe it,' Anna said. 'Martha said you suspect her of killing Rosa. And she thought you'd add Andy Trago into the indictment. What about Gareth?'

'Did Martha tell you she hadn't killed them?' he asked quickly.

Anna thought for a few seconds. 'No,' she said reluctantly, 'she didn't. But then,' Anna rallied, recalling the conversation, 'she didn't think she needed to. I don't believe for a moment that she did. And really, Rob, what proof have you got that she did?'

'You know I can't tell you that,' he said. 'But she's linked firmly to at least two of deaths, and she's physically powerful enough to inflict the damage on the men. She had the means, the opportunity, and she certainly had the motive'

'So, it seems, did Esther,' Anna pointed out.

Elliot ran a hand through his hair. 'Just what I need,' he said grimly. 'The case we're building could just as well apply to her. Twins too, not identical, but they look a lot alike, so how can we rely on identification?' He looked sharply at Anna. 'Can you tell them apart?'

'Of course,' Anna said confidently, then she hesitated. 'At

least, I can when they're together. I'm not sure I'd know which one it was if I saw one of them on their own.'

The inspector sighed, and she looked at him sympathetically. 'You haven't arrested them, though,' she said thoughtfully, 'just taken them in for questioning. So, you can't be sure yet that either of them is guilty, or you haven't got enough evidence.'

Elliot watched her, a faint smile on his face, as she went on, 'The means seem to be different, unless Gareth and Andy were poisoned too. It's the poison,' she said firmly, 'you think it came from the farm, or at least the bottle it was in. That's it, isn't it? Surely somebody else could have got at it?' She looked at the inspector interrogatively.

His smile widened slightly, but he said nothing. 'And you think there's motive,' Anna said, 'because of Nat.'

His brows rose in surprise. 'What do you know about him?'

'What the whole family know, and probably most of the neighbourhood guessed,' she replied cautiously.

'Which is?'

'Look, Rob, why don't you ask Martha and Esther,' Anna said. 'I don't want to tell tales.'

He nodded. 'Fair enough. But tell me this, are you talking about that boy's parentage?'

She looked at him a little suspiciously. 'Well, yes,' she said slowly.

'We've already been told he's Andy Trago's son. The widow couldn't wait to tell us that. Although there seems to be some confusion about his mother, one source saying that it's Martha, the widow saying it's Esther.'

'Of course,' Anna said, remembering the conversation in the farmhouse kitchen. 'Martha said Andy had told Shona about Nat. Well, as far as I know Esther is his mother. Won't his birth certificate say?'

Anna saw that Elliot's expression had changed slightly. 'The birth certificate says Esther, but the same problem arises – identical twins, who would know which was registering the baby. But you say the boy knew already about his father. Are you sure?'

'Well, Martha, or Esther, I can't remember which,' she saw the brief flicker of frustration on his face, 'sorry, Rob, but it doesn't really matter which. One of them told me they had agreed on total honesty when Esther came back here to live with Nat. He knew about his father, and he told Lissa she's his half-sister, so there are no hidden secrets there either. As far as I know, it's never bothered him, or Lissa. It's not as if Andy was a very good father to Lissa, the child he knew he had.'

The inspector moved suddenly. 'Thanks, Anna, that's very interesting. I'll see what the sisters say. But now I must go. There's a lot more to tie up.' He waved a hand and walked swiftly down the path to his own car.

Anna lingered in the porch, wondering what was best to do next. Should she go around to Trago Place to find Tony. But she couldn't know whether he was still looking after Shona's horses or was on his way back home. Presumably the police would tell him they had taken his wife and sister-in-law to the police station for questioning.

Anna was struck again by how quiet the farm was and noticed suddenly that all the surf boards had gone, leaving the porch strangely uncluttered. The children must be down on the beach, presumably there was a good tide coming in.

She made up her mind. She would walk along the cliff path. She knew Mike could not go to Soldiers' Meadow until Rob's officers had finished work there, but she also knew Mike would go up anyway, and glare at them from a distance. She could go and sit on the rock seat on the cliffs and try to think. Mike might see her there and join her. There was something just hovering on the edge of Anna's thoughts, but she could not grasp it and pull it into focus. A little peace might help. And she might come up with something helpful to say to Tony.

She thought he'd go to the police station, but he'd also need to get back to the farm as soon as he could to tell the children what was happening. She decided she could only stay a short time at the rock seat, then she'd have to come back to the farm or try to ring him.

The sky was a clear cloudless blue as she reached the cliff path, the sun was warm when Anna was sheltered behind a rocky bluff, but there was a chilly westerly wind blowing across the more open stretches of the path. Gorse bushes were thick with sulphur-yellow flowers, and there was a faint vanilla scent on the air around them. A constant low rumbling roar was the sound of the sea below, the tide coming steadily in. On a narrow stretch of path around a granite outcrop there was a gap in the bushes that allowed Anna to look down on the beach. There, as she had expected, were several small figures in wetsuits.

Out to sea, gannets dived, hitting the water with such force that each bird created a spout of crystal water. Gulls screamed as they approached the cliff, diving down suddenly out of sight to the ledges where they were nesting. A buzzard spiralled in a more leisurely fashion, circling over the nearby promontory where the hillfort ramparts and ditches were distinctly visible as shadows in the sunlight.

Anna was watching a robin on the blackthorn thicket between her and the cliff edge. The bird was watching her too, his head cocked, his manner expectant. She searched her pocket, relieved to find a small packet of biscuits that she had picked up some-where. She crumbled them onto the path, stepping away as the robin fluttered down to peck at the food.

After a while he flew away and Anna turned back to the path, hesitating there for a minute, wondering whether to go on or return to the farm. She didn't want to meet the children and maybe have to explain what had happened.

Anna saw a movement out of the corner of her eye and looked quickly further up the cliff path. Her heart skipped when she saw a figure coming swiftly towards her, only glimpsed in occasional gaps in the gorse. What could she say if it was Tony? No, she realised with a spurt of relief, Tony had driven over to Trago Place, he wouldn't be walking back.

The person emerged into the open stretch of path that Anna was lingering on, and she saw that it was a woman. An instant later she recognised Shona and her heart sank. Of course, Martha had said she'd gone out walking with Edward.

Anna looked quickly beyond Shona, feeling that dealing with Edward right now would be impossible. He might even believe that Martha had been responsible for the attack on Gareth.

Shona had seen her too and came on even faster. 'I've heard,' she said abruptly when she came into earshot. 'Tony rang me. I'm getting back to my car, I'll have to go home and finish seeing to the horses myself. He's driving to the farm to tell the children, then he'll go straight to Corrington. That's where they're holding them.'

Shona stopped in front of Anna. 'Were you there when they arrested them?'

'Yes, but ...' Anna said. Before she could say more, find the words to offer sympathy for Andrew's death, Shona put a firm hand on Anna's arm and turned her around. 'You'd better come too, then, and tell Tony what happened. He's in a state of shock.' She tugged Anna's arm. 'Come on.'

Reluctantly Anna fell into step beside her, watching her footing on the slippery shale of the path. Shona was setting an uncomfortably rapid pace.

'What about Edward?' Anna asked suddenly. 'Wasn't he with you?'

'He's another one in a state of shock. Really,' Shona said impatiently over her shoulder, 'some men fall to pieces so fast. Edward is totally cut up by Gareth's death, and I didn't dare tell him about Martha and Esther. I thought it would send him right over the edge. He was flitting between hysteria and morbidity when I left him at the rock seat, glooming and dooming all by himself.'

Anna felt uncomfortable. 'Should I go and check on him?' she asked.

'No need,' Shona said derisively. 'He'll only enjoy a good audience. Laney's going that way, she was at my place earlier, and said she'd walk out to the seat when she had finished. Apparently she likes the view. God knows why, it's just endless sea like everywhere else. And,' she added sneeringly, 'Edward's not going to jump off the cliff, if that's what you're worried about. He hasn't got the guts.'

'Have the police finished in Soldiers' Meadow?' Anna asked suddenly as they reached the farmyard. 'You'd have seen them if they were still there.'

'They were just packing up,' Shona said, going over to her car. 'I checked when we got there. I should think they'll be driving past here at any moment.'

'Tony isn't back yet,' Anna said, looking round the farmyard. 'I'll wait until he gets here, if you're sure he will really want to see me.'

'Of course he will,' Shona said, sliding into the driver's seat of her sports car. 'You can tell him exactly what the police said to Martha and Esther.' She slammed the door, lowering the window to shout, 'Make sure he gets them a good solicitor,' before she swung the car round in a tight circle and drove off at such speed that it bumped heavily over the ruts in the track.

Anna stood beside her own Jimny, looking after Shona. She felt even more uncomfortable. Something was very wrong, that errant thought was hovering ever more ominously on the edge of her mind, and she still could not work out what it was.

It was late afternoon, and dusk was beginning to dim the shapes of the buildings in the walled garden. Anna sat back wearily in her office chair and closed her eyes. Thank goodness, she thought, I'm on my own at last. At least, Lucy is next door, but she's too busy to come in here again.

Tony Zennor's stricken face lingered in her memory. He had arrived at Carne Farm before Shona had gone far down the track, so she had reversed, and got out of the car reluctantly to meet him with Anna.

He had been totally stunned by what had happened and did not utter a word as Anna told him what had taken place in his absence. She emphasised that the sisters had been taken to the police station for questioning, they had not been arrested. But she was not sure he had grasped the distinction.

Suddenly he had shaken his head vigorously, like a man emerging from deep water. 'No,' he said, 'no, they're wrong. I must tell them.' He turned back towards his own car, but Shona put out a hand to stop him. Anna saw her fingers tighten on his arm, forcing him to wait. She remembered how strong her grip was and was not at all surprised to see Tony's face darken with anger.

'Let go,' he had said softly. 'I'm not staying here.'

'You must wait for a while,' Shona had said firmly. 'You're not safe to drive, you're in a state of shock.'

'You should tell the children what's happened,' Anna had said quietly. 'They'll hear fast enough from somebody else if you don't get to them now.'

Tony had stood still, then shaken off Shona's hand and turned to walk with his awkward limp towards the path that led down to the sea from beyond the farmyard.

Shona had not lingered, and Anna had watched as she drove off again, dust flying into a cloud behind her sports car. Anna had suddenly felt that this had somehow become her role, acolyte to Shona, as she had watched Tony stumble uncertainly down towards the beach.

Then, later, Anna's much-needed lunch with Mike at The Lanyon Arms had been blighted by Hugh's arrival with Laney in tow. They had come, at whose instigation Anna was in no doubt, to pester Mike into taking Laney to the dig.

'The light is so good today, it'll be fantastic later on when the sun starts to set. That's when I want to take my shots,' Laney kept saying. She had been up on the cliff earlier, so Anna had felt she had had a narrow escape, they could so easily have bumped into each other. But Laney had seen the police team leaving, so she knew that the meadow was clear.

Mike, who had just been planning his own return to the meadow, had procrastinated, clearly not keen on the idea of taking Laney there. Eventually Anna had seen the realisation dawn that the woman would keep pestering, that he would be better getting it over with – if he didn't blast her firmly and for good. He had, surprisingly, decided to get it over with.

Anna glanced at her watch. Nearly four-thirty. Mike should be leaving by now, even if Laney and Hugh decided to linger. And Lucy would be meeting them at The Lanyon Arms in an hour. She began to pile her papers together and closed her laptop as she wondered if Mike had kept his temper.

Her mobile rang, and Ben lifted his head curiously as Anna picked it up. She glanced at the caller's name and was surprised to see it was Mike.

'Hi,' she said, relieved it was not a late work call. 'How did it go?'

'It didn't,' Mike said shortly. 'Edward was dead on the seat when we got there. That bloody woman had to find him. It'll be the end of this dig if people carry on dying all round it.'

'What!' Anna exclaimed. 'Are you sure?'

'Of course I'm bloody sure,' he said explosively. 'I've been stuck here with the police for the last couple of hours. But Elliot has agreed to the dig so far, as the scene of the crime, this time,' Mike said the last words with sarcastic emphasis, 'is far enough away.'

'No, Mike,' Anna said carefully, 'I meant are you sure Edward is dead?'

'Edward,' Mike said with deliberation, 'is definitely dead as a doornail. It looks as though he killed himself because of Gareth. There was one of those little brown medicine bottles on the ground near the bench.'

'Oh no,' Anna exclaimed. 'One of Martha's?'

'How the hell should I know?' Mike demanded. 'I'm sick of all this. Bodies all over the place, getting in my way. I thought Elliot had got the killer, that woman, what's her name?'

'Martha,' Anna said, thinking furiously. 'He's questioning her, and her sister, but I don't think either of them did it. And how could they have poisoned Edward? I know he called in at the farm-house to tell them about Gareth's death, but I don't think he went in, he was keen to get up on the cliffs.'

'God knows,' Mike said gloomily. 'But I want you where I can see you, so don't stay in the garden but get back down to the pub and stay there until I get there. I don't want you out on your own until this is all sorted out. If Elliot can't do it, I suppose we'll have to. Otherwise, you'll likely be the next candidate for dead body. And I'm not having that.'

'Mike,' Anna was torn between annoyance and laughter, 'I must speak to Rob, but really I'm not involved in this.'

'You always get involved,' Mike said. 'You can't seem to help it. And I'm NOT HAVING IT, do you understand, not again?'

Rob Elliot looked tired as he entered the back bar at The Lanyon Arms. Anna was sitting by a window, looking out onto the dark street, looking for his approach, but he had parked in the side lane and come through the rear door of the pub.

He looked around at the group waiting for him as the collie rushed over to greet him. 'I got your message,' he said to Anna, stroking Ben's smooth head. 'I can't be long, I've got a meeting in an hour back at the station. I hope this is important.'

Hugh raised an eyebrow as he looked at his watch. 'Overtime?' he asked.

'What do you expect?' Elliot said shortly as he sat down and stretched out his legs. 'Four deaths that are possibly, no probably, all murders. Can you imagine the pressure we're under to get results? At least I haven't had to get search parties out, but the demand on manpower is still huge.'

'You do think Edward was murdered then,' Anna exclaimed.

'Well, it can't have been Martha or Esther, Edward didn't go into the farmhouse. He just called to tell Martha about Gareth's death and then went out walking with Shona. There's no chance Martha or Esther could have given Edward anything with poison in it that Shona didn't see.'

'You were there, were you?' Rob asked. 'I haven't read your statement yet.'

'Well,' Anna bit her lip, 'not at the same time as Edward. But only a few minutes afterwards, and Martha told me all about it.'

The inspector's mouth tightened. 'You know better than that,' he chided. 'Martha told you …'

Anna flushed delicately. 'Well, I believe her,' she said stubbornly.

'I'd like to,' Elliot said ruefully. 'She tells a good story. But,' he said firmly, 'everything points to her or her sister. Motive – preventing Nat's birth father finding out about his son and making every effort to monopolize him themselves. Means – on at least two occasions it's likely to be in a potion that Martha makes. Opportunity – in every case.'

'And the points against her or Esther being the murderer?' Hugh enquired.

Elliot shrugged wearily. 'Their word. Anna's belief. Two different methods of murder, bludgeoning in one case, poison in two, both in Andrew's case, the fourth.' He looked across at Anna. 'Shona was there at the farmhouse when Edward arrived, and she agrees with you that he didn't eat or drink anything there. But,' he raised a hand as he saw Anna was about to speak, 'she also says that Martha provided her with a flask of coffee when she said she was going out walking. Shona didn't like to say she doesn't drink coffee, so she took the flask. Edward drank the contents. She left it with him when she walked back to the farmhouse when she heard about Martha's arrest. We've had the dregs analysed, and they contain digitalis.'

'There's no proof Martha, or Esther, put in the poison,' Hugh pointed out carefully.

'True,' Elliot conceded. 'Edward could have killed himself. That's certainly a possibility. His fingerprints are on the bottle, but at a slightly odd angle. Or Shona could have added the digitalis. If she did, which of course she denies, why would she want to kill Edward?'

'If Shona did it,' Hugh said, 'did she kill the others? Again, why would she?'

'God knows,' Elliot said. 'It doesn't hang together in a coherent pattern. Except for Martha's involvement. Or Esther's. And,' he grimaced, 'Shona's not much help, she's in a considerable state of shock. She thinks Martha meant to poison her.'

'Why?' Lucy demanded quickly.

'Shona doesn't know. The best she offers is that Martha is mad, or jealous.'

'Jealous of what or who?' Anna asked.

The inspector looked at her with a carefully blank face. 'She couldn't say. Not clearly, at any rate.'

'Well,' Mike broke in impatiently, 'who else could have done it if we count out Martha, Esther and Shona? It must be somebody who could get up there to leave the linctus bottle by the bench, however the poison got into the coffee.' He snorted derisively. 'I suppose you'll want my fingerprints next.'

Anna ignored this, saying reluctantly, 'I suppose there's Tony. Surely the same motive, means and opportunity apply to him as well as Martha and Esther?'

'Not quite,' Elliot said. 'He doesn't appear to have the same knowledge of digitalis, and he doesn't seem to know which potions are which. He swears Esther is Nat's mother, he knew Andrew Trago was his father, and he didn't think it would make much difference to Nat or any of them that Andrew had been told.' He ran a hand through his hair. 'And, somehow, I'm inclined to believe him. But there's no proof, and I've been wrong before.' He smiled thinly at Hugh. 'Occasionally.'

'He presumably does have access to Martha's potions though,' Lucy said quietly.

'Yes,' the inspector agreed. 'But he says they were exclusively part of her enterprise, and he only ever went into the room she used to make them to put up shelves, and that was some time ago. Any fingerprints we have of his in there are certainly old ones.'

'What other prints did you find?' Anna asked suddenly.

'Mainly Martha's,' Elliot said. 'A lot from the girl who helps her, Lissa Trago, and a few of Esther's. Some that are probably from your photographer friend, Hugh, apparently she'd been in there to take pictures.' He shook his head slightly. 'The relationships in this case are so complicated I wonder how they've all managed to live as neighbours for so long.'

'Not that long,' Hugh said. 'The Tragos have only been back for a few years, and it seems that living as neighbours wasn't going that easily.'

Anna said quietly, 'What about Laney? She seems to have been in contact with all the victims, and we don't know very much about her.'

' Not quite true,' Hugh said emphatically, leaning forward. 'I know her.'

'How well?' 'Anna asked and watched his face close up. Rob intervened to say, 'Laney Scholz is having her fingerprints taken right now. She agreed to go into the station.'

Hugh sat back, his hands gripping the arms of his chair.

The inspector nodded. 'And we have no connection between her and the victims. Our main concern now is to determine whether the murders spring from the various relationships. If Martha Zennor or her sister are guilty, it would be for that reason. But if they aren't, I haven't the faintest trace of another motive for anyone.' He ran one hand through his hair. 'At least we can move on one front. Nat had agreed to have a DNA test, so have Esther and Martha, and that will settle the issue of his parentage.'

'What about Tony?' Anna demanded suddenly. 'Does he think Martha's guilty?'

'Very definitely not,' Elliot said. 'Nor Esther. He's talking of bringing in a London lawyer.'

'Oh,' Anna was surprised. 'I heard Shona suggest he get one, but I didn't really think he would.'

'Apparently he's got a cousin at The Inns of Court.' The inspector's mouth set harder. 'More complications. I'd like to get this sewn up before we get bogged down in legalese.' He raised an apologetic hand at Hugh, whose legal background was often overlooked in the success of his publishing venture. 'You know what I mean,' Elliot added. 'If I don't get a confession or put together a cast-iron case, this business will drag on.'

'And there may be another death,' Lucy said quietly. Her words fell into a sudden silence.

It was Mike who broke it. 'Just what I'm worried about,' he said belligerently, glaring at Anna. 'And I'm convinced this is to do with Soldiers' Meadow. Just think,' he spoke louder, to muffle Anna's murmured dissent, 'two out of four of the deaths occurred on or near the meadow. That's suspicious. It links them to the place. But you don't seem to see that,' he glared at the inspector. So,' Mike gestured round the room, 'we need to give you a hand,' he said directly to the inspector.

'That's what I've been afraid of,' the inspector said. 'Just leave it to us, Mike. When the four of you get involved in my business at least one of you gets into danger.'

'One of us may already be,' Hugh pointed out. 'If neither Martha nor Esther is guilty, we've no idea why the victims are being killed.' He looked grimly at Elliot. 'You may in fact have a serial killer on your hands.'

'Bloody hell!' Mike exclaimed. 'That really cheers me up.'

The inspector's face was stern. 'Do you think I haven't thought of that?' His tone was sharp. 'Don't any of you put yourself in their way.'

He pushed his chair back. 'I've really got to get going.' He looked round the room. 'Much as you don't want it to be,' he said quietly to Anna, 'Martha is the most likely candidate.'

He raised a hand in farewell as he opened the door, walking quickly out into the crowded bar, closing the door firmly behind him.

The four people left in the back bar were silent again. Again it was Mike who broke the silence. 'Alright,' he leaned forward, looking at Anna. 'You don't believe Martha did it. Tony seems to be discounted. Who does that leave?' He laughed shortly. 'I could certainly have killed Andrew Trago,' he said. 'The man was a bloody nuisance.'

'He seemed so awful I actually felt quite sorry for Shona yesterday when she came up to the garden,' Anna said. 'Perhaps she killed him because she couldn't stand him any longer.'

'I didn't really know any of them well enough to even guess who's behind the deaths,' Lucy said. She glanced at her husband. 'I guess it's the same for you.'

Hugh nodded. 'Where does that leave us?'

'There's Kerenza,' Anna said slowly. 'She always seems to be in the background, and I've got the impression that she's well aware of all the local undercurrents, all the local scandals. Maybe there's something that affects her that she wants kept secret.'

'Like what?' Mike demanded.

'I don't know,' Anna said impatiently. 'But we could try and find out.'

'That's going to take time,' Hugh pointed out. 'And we've no idea where to start.'

'I'll get chatting to Jed at the bar, he's local, his family go back generations. He'll know something and he likes to talk,' Anna said. 'I'll go out in a minute and get us some more drinks.'

'Just watch what you say,' Mike growled. 'Don't look too interested. You never know who else might be listening to you.'

'What about Fabio?' Lucy asked suddenly. 'We don't know anything about him really. He came here quite unexpectedly, he knows Kerenza and he knew Andrew Trago.'

Anna shook her head. 'I was talking to Will and Niri about him, they've seen quite a lot of him on their visits to Isobel and he's very well known in Italy. So at least he's who he says he is.' She looked at her friend. 'And, Lucy, use your eyes. He's come here with Isobel because he's mad about her.'

'Let's hope mad isn't the right word,' Mike said heavily. He leaned forward to drink his beer. 'There's that woman you brought down, Hugh,' he said abruptly. 'She seems to have got around everywhere, meeting all these people. And many of them are dead now.' He scowled. 'And she knows all of us. We could be next.' His eyes widened. 'I could be next. She wanted photographs of the dig, didn't she? I'll bet she visited all the others just before they died, conveniently poisoning them before she left.'

Anna leaned forward, her eyes intent. 'You don't keep anything up at the meadow that poison could be put into. But she was up on the cliff after Shona left Edward. If she saw him there with the flask, she could have poisoned it.'

'These flights of fancy are all very well,' Hugh said mildly. 'And I'm aware it'll be my fault for bringing her here. But just stop for a minute and think. She's never been here before. She doesn't know any of these people. Why should she start killing them? And why would she be carrying digitalis around with her?'

Anna wrinkled her nose. Mike scowled at Hugh. But Lucy spoke quietly. 'Think what Rob said to Anna. Anna believes what Martha told her, even though she can't know whether it's true. Aren't you doing the same here, believing what Laney tells you? How do you know she hasn't been here before, hasn't met anyone here before?' Lucy answered her last question. 'You don't know that, do you, Hugh?'

SEVEN

Anna was horrified to see the cars and vans parked in the lane outside Carne Farm in the early morning light. They lined both sides, blocking the field gates and the approach to the farm track. 'Keep driving, Mike,' she said. 'It must be the press. I'd no idea they'd be here so early. So many of them too.'

Mike did not need telling, she realised, as he scowled and drove straight at a crowd of reporters who had turned eagerly towards them. They scattered immediately, but she was aware of cameras swinging in their direction as Mike drove on around the corner and out of sight.

She glanced up the farm track as they passed and saw it was just as heavily blocked with cars, and reporters and photographers were pressed against the garden fence. She hoped the geese and the dogs were keeping them out of the yard. 'I wonder if Tony's called the police. He must be under siege in the farmhouse.'

'He can't be,' Mike said. 'He'll have to go out to feed his animals. He keeps cows on some of his cliffside fields. Bloody hell.' Mike's scowl deepened, and his hands clenched on the steering wheel, sending the car jerking across the road.

Anna bit her lip as he righted it. 'What?' she demanded.

'I hope there'll be no bloody reporters at the meadow. That's all I need, heavy great boots trampling the site, as if the police haven't already done enough damage.' He groaned. 'I really can't see that this dig is going to happen. I knew Andrew Trago would do a lot to scupper it, and he seems to have pulled it off. It's just as well Melanie's excavation is going so well.'

Anna forbore saying that Andrew would probably rather have stayed alive. 'Look,' she said instead, 'drop me off on the corner, Mike. I'll pick up the cliff path further down and see if I can get into the farm through the fields. I'd like to make sure Tony is alright.'

'You barely know the man,' Mike said grumpily. 'But I suppose I can't stop you. Just be careful,' he said abruptly as he drew the car to a sudden halt by the finger post. 'If your instincts about Martha are right, and I'm not saying they are, there's a killer still out there.'

Anna got out of the car door and was opening the back door for the collie to jump out when Mike said, 'I'll come up to the meadow as soon as I've got these pottery samples in the post. When you've finished with Tony go up there and wait for me by the rock seat. I suppose the area's free of police now,' he added, frowning, 'so just watch who you let approach you. But,' he said angrily, 'I expect there'll be enough people around to see if you're attacked. Bloody reporters may as well make themselves useful. If they haven't infested the pub, we'll meet the others at Genarren for lunch. We might as well catch up on what's happening and that's as good a place as any to hear about the latest deaths.'

Anna waved as he drove away and then began walking along the path with Ben pottering happily ahead. It was level at first, running between hedgerows that were still bare of leaves. After a while it began to rise steeply as she reached the slope up to the cliff top.

The sun was out, the sky blue and cloudless, and the chilly wind was actually a relief as she walked. A blackbird was churning leaves under one of the hedgerows, searching for insects. He paused to watch them approach out of beady eyes, scurrying into the shelter of the hedgerow as they drew nearer.

She felt her mind clearing a little of the cloud of suspicions and doubts that had been fogging it. There must be an answer to the riddle of what was going on, they just hadn't found the key to it yet. Well, if she didn't think too much about it, maybe the solution would present itself.

Anna smiled suddenly, brushing back her hair as she reached the cliff path. Rob would certainly have something to say about that as a scientific method of deduction. Her amusement faded as she thought of him. She was sure he was not convinced of Martha's guilt. Or Esther's either. How odd that either of the sisters could apparently be the murderer. Was that intentional, Anna wondered suddenly. Had they been set up?

She paused for a few seconds to admire a patch of purple violets and then stood quite still, looking out to sea, watching the gentle roll of the waves as they surged towards the foot of the cliffs. The sound of voices startled her, and she turned to see who was speaking. But the speakers, two women Anna thought, were out of sight beyond the blackthorn hedges that narrowed the path eastward towards the hillfort promontory.

The disturbance reminded Anna that she had better walk on as Ben came back to her side, ears pricked alertly. She glanced down at the farm buildings below, catching sight of Tony's tractor chuntering across the lower field towards Potter's Yard. A few tiny figures seemed to be running after it.

Anna bit her lip as she wondered what to do. There was no point going after Tony, but if she went to the outcrop around the rock seat she might catch sight of him coming back and then she could go down to the farm. But then she didn't know where he was going or how long he'd be away. And she might end up being at the farm when Mike came to meet her. She certainly didn't want Mike coming over to the farm to collect her, bursting through the hordes of waiting reporters and almost certainly giving them a good story to fill their pages.

She set off along the cliff path, with Ben close on her heels. The sun was warm in the shelter of the blackthorn thickets; she was soon within sight of the rock seat and could see the police tape had been removed from the path.

There was a figure moving ahead of her, partly obscured by clumps of gorse and blackthorn, and for a moment Anna wondered if the police had left an officer there. But the figure was on the path, clearly walking northwards around the bay, and Anna remembered the voices she had heard. But there was only one person ahead, disappearing around a rocky corner. Anna had time to see a flash of blonde hair, and was surprised, sure that the blonde head belonged to Shona. Had she been to visit Tony? Surely the woman could hardly feel welcome at the farm, Anna thought.

Her attention was caught by a movement on her right in Soldiers' Meadow. This time the figure moving carefully among the trenches was unmistakable. It was distorted as always by the cameras that Laney Scholz took almost everywhere. What on earth is she doing here, Anna wondered furiously, opening the gate and striding onto the turf.

Laney looked up from the camera she held and grimaced ruefully as she saw Anna. 'Caught in the act,' she said, raising one hand apologetically from the lens she had been adjusting. 'I was getting away from Shona, she stuck to me like glue on the path up. And then the light's so good, I just couldn't resist coming to have a look at the site again. See how dark the trenches look against the grass. Quite ominous really.'

'Does Mike know you're here?' Anna demanded.

Laney shook her head. 'Look, I'm sorry, but I'm not doing any harm. He's a busy man, and he didn't really want to bring me here yesterday. I'm not sure Hugh will persuade him to do it again.'

Hugh, Anna thought impatiently. She seems to have got him wrapped round her little finger.

'I like coming up here,' Laney said, her gaze scanning the cliff top and the sky beyond. 'I know there've been all these deaths, but still it's a special place.' She turned to Anna. 'Look, let's go up to the seat and I'll show you the pictures I've taken, then you'll see there's nothing controversial.'

Mike pulled his Passat to an abrupt halt in Genarren. Hugh, walking purposefully down the street, glanced at it, then stopped as Mike leaned over and spoke through the lowered passenger window. 'Any news?'

Hugh shook his head. 'We haven't heard anything from Elliot,' he said. 'Lucy seems to have a hot line to him, so no news must mean just that, no news.'

'Damn,' Mike muttered. 'I don't like this. Anna is sure to get mixed up in it if Elliot doesn't get a move on.'

'Has she thought of anything else?' Hugh asked.

'No. Nor,' Mike said pointedly, 'have I. You?'

Hugh shook his head again. 'No. But Lucy's very quiet. I wonder if she's got some inkling.'

'She thinks it's that woman you brought down,' Mike said. 'And I wouldn't be surprised.'

'I wish you wouldn't keep referring to her like that,' Hugh said mildly. 'It gives the wrong impression.'

'Does it?' Mike asked bluntly.

'Yes,' Hugh said, 'it does.'

'Better make sure that Lucy realises it,' Mike advised.

Hugh raised an eyebrow in pained surprise.

'The pair of you seem very close,' Mike said. 'You're always getting her what she wants. Like photographing my dig.'

'She's a world-famous photographer,' Hugh said with a touch of impatience. 'Something nobody here seems to recognise. Her photos would bring amazing publicity for the garden, and your work too, for that matter.'

'Then why is she taking pictures all over the place if it's the garden she's really interested in?' Mike demanded.

Hugh frowned slightly. 'It's instinctive, seeing a good opportunity and taking it. I'm just visiting her now,' he said in an effort to change the subject. 'I wondered where she was going today.'

'I'll come with you,' Mike said abruptly. He settled back into the driver's seat and flung the door open. As he got out, he said, 'I want to make sure she's not going up to my dig.'

'Isn't it still a secure area?' Hugh asked, walking on towards Kerenza's cottage.

'No. Elliot had all the tape removed late last night,' Mike said. 'And it didn't affect the dig this time, just the cliff path.'

They stopped at Kerenza's cottage and Hugh raised the knocker, using it to hammer lightly on the front door.

They waited for some time, and Hugh raised the knocker again, releasing it carefully as the door was opened.

Kerenza stood there, surprise on her face as she saw them. 'I've just been trying to ring you, any of you,' she said with relief. 'There's something I think you should know.'

She stepped back to let them enter the hall. 'In here,' she said, leading the way into a small sitting room at the front of the cottage. It was a neat uncluttered room, pale colours making it seem larger, shelves orderly with books and photographs, and a small vase of early daffodils stood in the tiny hearth.

As they sat down in the armchairs, she said, 'I've been worrying about whether to say anything. But now, with Edward dying too, I feel I've got to.' She looked at them enquiringly. 'They're saying in the village that he didn't kill himself, that he was murdered.'

'That seems to be the case. The fourth murder in as many days,' Hugh said. 'If there's anything you know that might be slightly relevant, you must say. Do you want to get Inspector Elliot here?'

'No,' she said quickly. 'I want to tell you first, then you can see what you think.' She sighed, closing her eyes and rubbing them with her hands. 'I'm so afraid it is important, and I could have stopped all this earlier, if only I'd said something sooner.'

'Well, get on with it now,' Mike said impatiently.

Kerenza opened her eyes and considered him. She nodded. 'Yes, it's time. Well,' she marshalled her thoughts, 'you know the village has a strong storytelling tradition.' She glanced at them.

Mike nodded impatiently. Hugh smiled encouragingly, although he had paid little attention to this when Anna had been talking about it.

'The genuine storytellers,' Kerenza went on, 'those who have stories handed down through their families, know many things that aren't included in the public tellings. There are some things I know that I wouldn't pass on. And I'm sure I'm not the only one who knew these things.'

'Who else?' Hugh asked quickly. She had said knew, not know.

Kerenza looked sad. 'Rosa. She always knew things. And probably Edward. He wasn't an official storyteller, not part of our group, although he could have been once. But,' she hesitated and then went on, 'Edward had a malicious streak. He liked to tell stories he shouldn't have when he felt like it.'

'Was Rosa part of the group?' Hugh asked.

'No.' Kerenza was silent for a few seconds. 'She wasn't like Edward, but she liked knowing things about people too much, it wasn't really what we want in the group. Both of them wanted to join us, but we didn't trust either of them to …' she searched for the words, '… to monitor the content of their stories.'

'Censor them,' Mike said bluntly.

'Yes.'

'What weren't they supposed to say?' Mike demanded.

Kerenza took a deep breath. 'Twenty years back there was a group of young people locally. They were all friends, but the friendships were fluid, changing, becoming serious, then fading, although some of them settled down permanently. Others didn't, they got partners elsewhere. Andy Trago was one of those. He met and married a young American who was over here, travelling around. Laurie, beautiful, but fragile.'

She paused, clearly picturing the woman and the times that were past. 'She and Andy had two children and I looked after them both. They were both bright children,' Kerenza's expression softened as she remembered, 'the boy especially. He was always getting up to something if he wasn't occupied. Laurie was glad enough to hand him over to me, even before Lissa was born. Jeremy, he was called, after Andy's grandfather. The next in the Trago dynasty, Andy was fond of saying.'

Mike shifted impatiently, but a quick glance from Hugh kept him quiet.

'Laurie was never quite well after Jeremy was born. She had post-natal depression after the birth of each of her children, although she never saw a doctor about it. She alternated between ignoring the boy or doting on him. He became a difficult child very early on, good at getting his own way. And the other children he played with here were forced to let him get away with a lot when Laurie was around. I did what I could to stop her spoiling him, but he became much more difficult after Lissa was born. Melissa she was christened, but the name was always shortened.'

Kerenza sighed heavily. 'And that was probably what caused the tragedy. He had taken to following Andy around, trying to get his attention. The day he died he went up to the cliff after his father, beginning to run around when Andy saw him. When Andy tried to catch him Jeremy slipped over the cliff. Andy was devastated. And Laurie was destroyed.'

Kerenza's eyes were unfocused, seeing into memories of the past tragedy. 'And then Laurie died, only a couple of months later. She went over the cliffs close to where her boy died. Andy was there too, he was often at the rock seat. He saw Laurie but wasn't close enough to help her. It seemed like history was repeating itself. But he could never be sure if she slipped too and went over accidentally, or if she did it on purpose. Edward was living down here then, and he had just walked up the cliff footpath to Soldiers' Meadow. He saw the whole thing, and always swore it was an accident.'

'It must have been a terrible time,' Hugh said slowly, 'but I don't …'

Mike interrupted him. 'That's all past,' he said roughly. 'What's happening now?'

'That's just it,' Kerenza said. 'I'm afraid what's happening now is because of the past.' She looked at Hugh. 'It's Laney. I thought she was familiar, but it was a while until I realised why. Then I remembered. Laurie had a younger sister that she was devoted to. The pair of them were adopted separately in their early teens when their parents died in a car crash. Perhaps in an odd way that made them closer. Laurie was always down here posting letters and cards to her sister. That's who I think Laney is, Laurie's sister. Laurie had a photograph of the two of them with their birth parents.'

Hugh was frowning. 'That may be so,' he said, holding up a hand to stop Mike breaking in, 'but why does that make her responsible for what's happening now?'

Kerenza studied him for a while. At last she said, 'Locals have always said Laurie's death was an accident, although there was a strong feeling she'd killed herself, perhaps because of the post-natal depression. Certainly, it was thought, because of the death of her son, and maybe too because of Andy's affairs. They'd always gone on, even before the boy died. Most people knew about them, he never bothered hiding them.' Kerenza frowned too, momentarily diverted from her story. 'It was always Lissa I felt sorry for. Andy never bothered about her even when Jeremy was alive. She was down here with me a lot until she was in her teens, then she got interested in Martha's work and got drawn in over there. She's turned out remarkably well with the benign neglect.'

'You think,' Hugh said abruptly, 'that Laney is here to avenge her sister. Andrew, the unfaithful husband, yes, maybe. But what about the others? How do they fit?'

'I think there was probably one of his lovers with Andy at the rock seat. Both when Jeremy died, and when Laurie went up there later on. Whether it made any difference I can't know. But I think Edward knew more about it, and perhaps Rosa guessed. She said something about it just before she died, but Shona came before I could ask her any more. And it wasn't just women with Andy,' Kerenza said. 'He and Edward were close for a time. Martha wasn't one of his women though, it was always Tony for her, but Laurie thought she was. And she knew Esther was. Can you be surprised I wonder now if Laney is behind this? All the people who made her sister miserable, they're dead or suspect.' She sighed again. 'I should have spoken before, but it's just such a habit to keep other people's secrets.'

'Andrew and Edward dead, yes, I see,' Hugh said slowly. 'And Martha and Esther are involved, suspected of the murders. All people who could have contributed to Laurie's death. Yes, it does make a pattern,' he conceded. 'But Rosa? Gareth? How do they fit in?'

'I don't know,' Kerenza admitted. 'But isn't it enough that they might? And why didn't Laney say anything about her sister?'

'I don't like it,' Mike said, getting suddenly to his feet. 'Where is she now?'

'I don't know,' Kerenza replied. 'She went out early, took her cameras and went off.'

'She's gone to the dig,' Mike snarled. 'And Anna's going to be there too.'

He stormed out of the cottage, and Hugh only just caught up with him in time to scramble into the Passat as Mike swung it heavily around in the village street.

'You see,' Laney said, taking her camera back from Anna, 'they're all quite innocuous.'

'They're lovely,' Anna said frankly. 'Really beautiful shots.'

For the first time, she realised why Hugh could be so interested in this woman. He was a fine photographer himself and would certainly appreciate her skill.

Laney seemed to read her mind. 'It's a shame Hugh doesn't do more photography. His work is very special, he's got a good sense of what to take and he often shoots it from an unusual perspective.'

Anna leaned back on the rock seat, the stones of the outcrop behind cold against her back despite her thick coat. 'I wish Hugh would, it might keep him here more,' she said, absently watching Ben exploring scents in the bushes. 'I thought he'd mind you taking photos on what must be his patch, but he doesn't seem to care.'

Laney laughed. 'I'm only skimming the surface. He lives here, he knows the best sites, the secret places, the optimum times for light. He can take shots in all weathers and he'll never get the same picture.' She smiled at Anna. 'My pictures will never make a difference to what he can do. I just can't help myself taking them wherever I am.'

'Why did you come down here?' Anna asked. 'It wasn't just to take photos, was it?'

Laney looked away, out across the sea. 'I wanted to see the place,' she said quietly, so that Anna had to lean forward to hear her. 'I knew somebody who lived here once, she used to send me cards, write me letters telling me all about it. I always wanted to come, I just didn't ever make it before.'

'Is she still here?' Anna asked.

'In spirit,' Laney said soberly. 'She died a long time ago.'

'I'm sorry,' Anna said.

'So am I,' Laney said. 'It was a long time ago, but the past casts long shadows.' She shivered suddenly and looked away from the sea and stared at Anna. 'Go and stand on the edge of the cliff. Look out to sea, let your hair blow out behind you. It'll be a fantastic shot.'

'Isn't it too bright?' Anna asked, getting slowly to her feet.

'I'll adjust for that. It'll be fantastic,' Laney repeated.

Ben raised his head to watch as Anna moved slowly away from the seat, with Laney behind her, already juggling with one of the cameras.

'That's it,' the photographer said. 'Let me just loosen that bit of hair.' She leaned forward, jerking back suddenly at the sound of a voice.

'Hello,' Shona called as she strolled towards them on the cliff path. 'Can I join in too?'

Laney muttered, 'Not if I can help it.' She met Anna's eyes briefly. 'She's still on at me to take pictures of her house, and glamour shots to go in the big British magazines. I think she's got Country Life in her sights. Good luck to her, but it's not my scene.'

Shona had almost reached them, when Laney swung round, fitting the camera back into its case. 'I'm just off,' she announced. 'There are quite a few shots I want to take while the light is so good. I hear there's a storm blowing in.'

She brushed past Shona, striding away up the cliff path towards the hillfort. Anna moved away from the cliff edge, pausing reluctantly by Shona who was staring after the photographer.

'Really,' Shona said angrily, 'that woman's manners. I've been trying to get her to take photos of the house, I'm sure they'll be snapped up by one of the better magazines. You'd think she'd be grateful for the opportunity, nobody else has had this kind of chance, Andy wasn't really keen on the idea. But I actually think this woman's avoiding me, she doesn't want the job.'

Shona shook her head and rummaged in her canvas bag. 'You're the only person to appreciate me,' she said. 'I told you the locals all hate me. But they're only the riffraff. Once I've got proper friends here, the right class, you know, it'll be fine.' She pulled out a flask. 'Want a drink? I could certainly do with it after the time I've had.'

'I had a coffee not long ago, thanks,' Anna said mendaciously, suddenly keen not to drink here where Edward had died. She would like to move on following the collie who had wandered over to Soldiers' Meadow, but Shona was blocking the path.

'It's not coffee,' Shona said, a suddenly sly smile on her mouth as she glanced sideways at Anna. 'Can't stand the stuff. This is something stronger. Vodka. Go on, have a sip, nobody will know.'

Anna shook her head, pinning a smile on her face. 'No, thanks, I've got to work when I get back to the garden, and alcohol always makes me sleepy. I just came up to clear my head and see if I can call in on Tony without getting my picture in all the tabloids.'

'Spot on, you don't want to be bothered with them,' Shona said, pouring a generous amount of vodka into a cup. 'Not the right kind of papers at all. And Tony's not there, no point creeping in the back the way I did. I went to collect the rest of my things, I'd forgotten I'd left them there. Only Lissa's there now, but when is she ever anywhere else. She said he's gone back to the police station to meet the solicitor he's got for Martha and Esther. Gone across the fields in his tractor, can you believe it, to get there without meeting the press. He's leaving his car at Potter's Yard. Of course, there's no one there now to stop him.'

'How is Lissa?' Anna asked, as Shona drained the cup and poured more vodka in. Anna suddenly wondered if Shona had already been drinking, she seemed rather strange this morning. But then, the woman's husband had been murdered on the site just behind them.

Anna frowned. Shona didn't seem at all bothered to be here, it was almost as if she had forgotten about it.

'Lissa,' Shona said suddenly, startling Anna. 'That girl, she always treats me like a leper. And she's forever at Carne Farm, it's like she's always known she's got family there. Just as well really, she needn't bother to come back to the house at all, as far as I'm concerned.' Shona picked up the flask, pouring out more vodka, upending the flask disbelievingly when the flow dried up. 'I'll send her packing once it's legally mine.'

'Why?' Anna asked, a chill creeping over her flesh.

'Well, I don't want her, she can go and live with Martha, who's virtually a mother to her anyway. And she'll have her precious brother to make her feel at home.'

Shona laughed unpleasantly. 'Only she can't, can she? Precious Martha's going to be locked up for a long time. Shame the death penalty isn't still going. I'd like to watch her hang.' She picked up the flask and tried again to get a few more drops out of it. She dropped it and the cup onto the ground. 'Damn. I can't even get a drink when I want it.' She felt in her pocket, pulling out a handkerchief to wipe her mouth. As she stuffed it back her eyes fixed on Anna. 'You know, don't you? I knew you'd work it out, Edward said you would.'

'Did he?' Anna asked as lightly as she could. She was beginning to feel afraid. 'I don't know what there is to work out. I've been so busy with the garden, there just hasn't been time to think of anything else.' She wondered whether try to move around Shona, although the thick masses of gorse would make it difficult. Better not, she thought, remembering how close they were to the edge of the cliff.

She stood still, trying to look relaxed. 'In fact, perhaps we should talk about what you're going to do in the garden.'

Shona's eyes were still fixed on Anna, narrowing with suspicion. 'It's not the garden, no, not the garden. It's those oral histories. You'll find out. You'll know faster than I did.' She laughed harshly. 'Three years I'd been married to him, all that time it took to know he was a murderer. Thank God I wouldn't have children. He wanted them, wanted another son to inherit, but I wasn't going down that road. Spoils the figure, and gives you screaming brats to look after. No thanks.'

Anna was silent, wondering what she could say or do. Her heart was beating so hard she thought Shona would hear it.

Shona had not taken her eyes off Anna. 'He killed her here you know. Laurie, his first wife. Had enough of her, pushed her off the cliff. Andrew *said* it was an accident, but then he would, wouldn't he? He lived with that, kept it quiet all this time, but then he went to pieces when Gareth spoke to him. After your party, that was. Not the proper party, the one you won't be going to now.' Her expression darkened. 'The second-best one we were asked to.'

Anna hesitated, then asked quietly. 'What did Gareth say? He couldn't have known about any of this. He wasn't here then.'

Shona laughed shortly. 'Edward was. Bloody blackmailing Edward. Did you know he had an affair with my husband? Him and Martha, oh, and Esther, just to keep it in the family. God knows how many others there were. It was before my time, of course. I've known about the later ones, and God knows, there've been enough of them.'

She studied Anna carefully. 'You didn't know that, did you? But you'd have found out, Edward was sure of it. Well, you probably haven't discovered that darling Edward had been blackmailing Andrew about the murder for years. Andrew was in such a state when he got home after the party that he told me it all.' She laughed. 'That's why Laurie was so hysterical on the cliffs, she found Andrew and Edward hard at it on the seat. Can you imagine it?' The laugh died abruptly. 'And Edward was there when Andrew pushed her over, apparently trying to control her hysterics. Edward's kept quiet ever since, for a high price, you can bet. But then Edward got carried away, he was so sure he could control Andrew that he told Gareth all about it. Promised that Andrew wouldn't push to buy Soldiers' Meadow and Potter's Field. Andrew didn't want to buy them, you know, but I was going to have them, I wanted them. But Edward was sure his hold on my dear husband was stronger than mine.' Her eyes widened in genuine disbelief. 'And he was so wrong to tell Gareth. I would have known that. Gareth didn't believe in blackmail, it must have been that nonconformist Welsh upbringing of his. Gave him morals.'

'But,' Anna was struggling to make sense of this, 'did Edward tell Gareth about the reason for the blackmail?'

'Oh yes. And Gareth was concerned that Andrew should come clean about what happened to Laurie. As if Andrew would dream of confessing to murder. That's why he attacked Gareth, to stop him telling anyone. Even then, he couldn't do the job properly. But Gareth died anyway, and I didn't have to do anything about it.'

Anna was staring at her, trying not to show how horrified she was.

Shona was too busy reliving it all. 'And Edward, darling Edward, told Gareth about blackmailing Martha too. Nothing much, of course, after all, what had she got that Edward would want? Just the odd little thing here and there to demonstrate his power over her and Esther. But Edward couldn't stop himself from telling Gareth about the "big secret" once he'd started boasting.' She laughed unpleasantly.

'He told Gareth,' Anna said slowly, 'about Nat. That he was Andrew's son.'

'There, I knew you were bright,' Shona said with ghastly admiration. 'Yes, that's it, he thought that was his trump card.' You can just hear him,' she parodied his voice, ' "Ooooh, Andy, didn't you know, you've got a living son. I'll tell you all about him if…" Stupid, stupid man. He should have guessed that Gareth would want Andrew to sort it out quietly. Because Gareth didn't know that Lissa already knew all about it, and he was afraid she was getting romantically involved with her brother.' Shona smiled. 'Gareth misjudged that too. Andrew was euphoric at the thought of a son, he was determined to get him, he didn't care about Lissa and what they might have been up to. He didn't stop to think there were other men who could have been Nat's father either. Oh no. Edward, for one.' Her smile grew. 'Andrew didn't know that, nor did I, until Edward told me later. But Andrew's obsession gave me the opportunity I needed.'

She looked at Anna. 'You really didn't know about this, did you? That's a shame.' She threw back her head and laughed again. 'You can't think I'd let Andrew make any of this public, just when I'm getting a foothold in real society. All this scandal from years back, and probably a murder charge too. It was for the best really, he would never have coped with prison. And he should never have said he didn't need me anymore, now that he had his son.'

She glanced over her shoulder to the meadow. 'It was so easy. It's all been so easy. Edward's inability to keep his mouth shut started all this off. But Rosa had already been hinting, so I guessed a bit of the story, and put paid to her suggestions of little treats. My Gucci scarf, that's what she had her eye on to begin with.' Shona's face darkened with anger at the thought of it. 'It was easy, it was all so easy, first Rosa, then Andrew, so I knew there wouldn't be a problem getting rid of Edward too. There won't be one getting rid of you either. You know now that I'm good at getting rid of people.' She gave a satisfied smile. 'Edward had to go, he had already worked out what I'd done and was trying his hand at more blackmail. Not very bright of him. I was ready when he came up to Carne Farm. And Martha or Esther are the ideal fall guys. I really don't care which of them takes the blame. They're so busy trying to protect each other that I'm enjoying hearing about it.'

Anna did not have time to think about what she was hearing. Shona had put her hand back in her pocket and pulled out a small silver-mounted pistol. It was so small that it fitted into Shona's hand, betrayed only by the round black hole that was pointing at Anna.

EIGHT

'Don't get any closer,' Shona warned. 'I'm a very good shot, you know. That's another thing,' she sounded suddenly aggrieved, 'Andrew wouldn't have a pheasant shoot. I'd have fitted into that, all those local snobs who look down their noses at me, they wouldn't have been able to deny that I'm a good shot, a very good shot.' She smiled as she looked at Anna. 'But of course, I can do that now. Have my pheasant shoot.'

Anna stood quite still, frozen with shock. She struggled to think, and suddenly Mike's voice sounded in her thoughts – *Keep Her Talking*. It was such an unlikely thing for him to say that her mind cleared, grew alert, and she was aware that Shona had been moving slowly round her as she spoke. Anna had automatically been moving away just as carefully and now she was on the edge of the cliff, while Shona and her little pistol were between her and the path.

'It's got a bad reputation, this place,' Shona said conversationally. 'You're going to add to it. You can choose, I'll give you that because you've never sneered at me, although,' her voice hardened a little, 'I thought you were going to at first.'

She waved her free hand at the sea. 'Go over the edge like so many others, or I'll shoot you.' She smiled, never taking her eyes from Anna. 'I'm not coming anywhere near you, I know all about your judo skills. You'll not catch me like that.'

'I'm not going to jump,' Anna said, surprised to find her voice was steady. 'And it'll be hard to explain away a bullet hole in my body.'

'I won't need to,' Shona said gleefully. 'There's always Lissa, you know, I'll find a way of involving her. This was her mother's gun, it's always been kept in the gun room with mine. Stupid little thing,' she glanced at it disparagingly. 'Laurie thought it kept her safe when she was travelling. It didn't do her any good in the end.'

Anna found that her fear was under control now. She thought she was probably going to die, for the first time ever she really thought she was, but she was not going to make it easy for Shona. If, Anna thought suddenly, she could only get close enough she could at least mark Shona, scratch her, hit her, anything to show she'd been in a struggle. And she might be able to deflect the pistol too, maybe getting shot but not killed. Anyway, she thought coldly, she had nothing to lose by trying.

'This will all come out, you know,' Anna said conversationally. 'Nobody will ever want to know you.'

Shona's face tightened, she stepped closer to Anna to glare into her face. 'That's all you know,' she said fiercely, the hand that held the gun dropping slightly.

Anna tensed, ready to move, when a voice drawled behind them, 'This all looks very dramatic. I've got some superb shots. What are you practising for?' Laney stood on the cliff path, a camera held in both hands, as she focused on the women precariously positioned on the slippery grass cliff edge.

Shona was startled and her gaze swung round towards the photographer.

Anna seized her moment and stepped swiftly forward to force the gun out of Shona's hand. It fell to the ground, sliding out of reach on the grass.

But Shona reacted swiftly too, grabbing Anna and pulling her back so that they both teetered dangerously on the very edge of the cliff before recovering a precarious balance. Anna did not dare to struggle again; the slightest movement could send one or both of them hurtling down to the rocks below.

Laney was moving forward purposefully, her camera still held to her face. 'These are going to be superb, Shona,' she said, 'better than the photos you wanted me to take at your house. You'll certainly make a name for yourself once they're published.'

An expression of delight spread over Shona's face, but she did not release her grip of Anna's arm. The delight was wiped out by rippling uncertainty as she watched Laney get nearer.

'Just turn slightly to your right, Shona,' Laney instructed, 'that's your best profile.'

Shona obeyed her for an instant, just as the collie shot round Laney, teeth bared, snarling ferociously, and sprang forward. Anna seized her chance, wrenching herself free and almost falling as she lurched towards Laney.

Laney's camera bounced heavily against her chest as she grabbed Anna, dragging her further towards the rock seat. Their retreat was protected by Ben who leapt between them and Shona, but the photographer's face was a mask of horror as she stared beyond Anna and the dog to the cliff edge.

Shona was tottering there, arms flailing as she tried to regain her balance. Her face was white and terrified as she teetered on the edge of the land, her mouth open in a silent scream.

Anna tried to run forward, but Laney gripped her tightly. 'No,' the photographer said urgently, 'she'll take you over with her.'

Shona lost the battle to regain her balance and seemed to fall in slow motion off the cliff and down towards the turquoise-blue water below. Her scream was audible now, loud and drawn out, fading as she fell, and the sound rang in Anna's ears even after she knew it had stopped.

'Dear God,' Laney said hoarsely. She released Anna and stepped forward carefully to peer over the cliff edge. She looked back over her shoulder and said abruptly, 'She's on the rocks, but she can't possibly have survived the fall. Maybe it's for the best,' she was walking back to Anna as she spoke, almost to herself at the end, 'she had so much to answer for.'

Anna found that she was shaking and picked her way slowly to the rock seat, where she sat down and buried her head in her hands as Ben anxiously pressed up against her, nuzzling his nose under her arm. 'I can't believe it.' Her voice was muffled and she raised her head to speak more clearly, one hand stroking the collie.

Before she could say more the ground under her feet shook under pounding steps, and Mike thundered up, scarlet in the face, perspiration dripping off his chin. He threw himself on Laney, seizing her in a fierce hug that clamped both arms to her side.

'Mike,' Anna sounded both horrified and amused, 'what are you doing?'

'We know all about you,' Mike growled, retaining his hold on Laney. 'It's over now.'

Hugh had brought up the rear with less energy and more composure. 'I think we might have the wrong end of the stick, Mike,' he said mildly. His eyes ran quickly over Anna and moved to Laney, who was standing still in Mike's hold and studying him with amused acceptance.

'Laney just saved my life,' Anna said, the shaking starting again. 'Shona fell over the cliff. She said this was a place of ill-omen.'

Mike's arms fell away from Laney and he turned to stare at Anna. As soon as he saw her white face and her trembling body he was beside her, pulling her into a rough embrace. 'I knew you'd get into trouble,' he muttered into her hair. 'You always do.'

Aaron had retired discreetly to his studio when Rob Elliot arrived at the walled garden in the mid-afternoon. The chairs and benches had been pulled into a small circle, tables scattered among them holding the remains of the lunch Lucy had brought up from the village. Anna sat back on one of the chairs, Ben at her feet, her face turned up to the late sunshine which was warming the enclosed space very nicely. She had not felt like eating at first, but had managed a little of the chicken stew and felt that she had finally stopped shaking inside.

'I was telling Shona the truth at the end,' Laney remarked. 'I've looked at the photos I was taking, and they're outstanding. It's not really my sphere, but any news agency will snap them up and pay well for them.' She looked at Anna. 'It's up to you,' she said. 'You feature in them too. But I'd be happy to donate the fee to the garden fund.'

'I didn't realise you'd actually been taking photos,' Anna exclaimed. 'I don't know, I don't really think I'd want people seeing them. They'll be captioned Murderer and Victim, or something grim like that.'

'But you weren't a victim,' Mike said. He glanced at Hugh enquiringly.

Hugh smiled. 'And yes, Mike, they'd be fantastic publicity for the garden. If Anna can stand being the heroine.'

'Again,' Mike snapped suddenly. He glowered at Anna. 'This can't be good for my nerves.'

She gurgled with laughter. 'What nerves?' she demanded. 'Oh alright,' she flicked a glance between Laney and Hugh, ' "publish and be damned" as a famous soldier once said.'

'Wellington,' Hugh supplied automatically.

'I don't care if it was Napoleon Bonaparte,' Mike growled. 'I just don't want her doing this again.'

'Neither do I,' Rob said as he sat down. 'I always dread the four of you getting together, one or other of you always seems to end up at risk. I don't know whether you are the jinx or whether you are jinxed.'

'Very funny,' Mike growled. 'Never mind the humour, just tell us what it's all been about.'

Rob glanced at Anna. 'You probably know it all, you got most of it from the horse's mouth.' He grimaced. 'Almost appropriate, that, the only creatures Shona ever seems truly concerned about are her horses.'

'I'd rather you told them,' Anna said, bending down to stroke Ben.

'The story started a long time ago,' Rob began. 'When there was a group of rather wild young people here. Andrew, Tony, Edward, Martha, Esther, were among them. Partnerships formed and broke easily among the group, and children were conceived whose parentage was uncertain.'

Rob looked round at his audience. 'You all know that Nat was one of those children. Andrew Trago's son, his only living son. Tony Zennor has certainly always treated the boy as part of his family, and so has Martha, even though Esther is undoubtedly his mother. Those are salient facts.' He glanced at Hugh, fore-stalling a possible query. 'The boy's parentage doesn't matter to any of the family at Carne Farm.'

Rob drummed his fingers together as he thought how to carry on. 'I suppose you all know now that Andrew Trago's first wife was Laurie.' He gestured to the photographer. 'Laney's sister.'

Laney was silent, her attention fully on the inspector, who carried on, 'Laurie had two children with Andrew. Her health was always fragile and worsened after the birth of both her children.'

'It was worsened too,' Laney intervened, 'by Andrew's constant affairs. She wrote me every week, so I always knew about them. He never tried to hide them from her.'

'And then tragedy struck,' Rob continued. 'Their son, Jeremy, fell over the cliff in front of Andrew and Edward and died in a terrible accident.'

Rob's expression was grim. 'Gareth managed to tell us a little before he died. Enough to fill in some of the gaps in the story. When Edward was telling Gareth about his hold over Andrew Trago he explained that they were "in the throes of passion" at the rock seat when the boy came up. Andrew was angry with him and the boy ran off, with his father chasing him. Edward implied, but didn't actually say, that Andrew had caught the boy before he went over the cliff. All this Edward kept to himself, when Andrew told his story of the terrible accident.'

Rob looked round at them all again. 'It seems to have been a similar situation a few weeks later, when Laurie found Andrew and Edward together at the rock seat. Although this time they weren't in a passionate embrace, they were arguing. Edward, I suspect, was already trying his hand at blackmail over the boy, and Andrew wasn't having it, after all Edward was an accessory to what happened. But Laurie heard enough to realise what they were talking about. Whether she had her suspicions, we can't know, nor whether she followed Andrew deliberately. She had apparently taken to long lonely walks on the cliffs after Jeremy's death. But what she heard sent her into wild hysterics, and Andrew tried to restrain her, but then, according to Edward, intentionally pushed her over the cliff too. Right where their son had fallen.'

'It had clearly become a habit for him,' Mike said sourly. 'So easy to push a helpless child and a frail woman over.'

Rob nodded. 'Yes, and it proved to be an expensive habit. Andrew was determined to end the relationship with Edward, and Edward had decided there had to be a fee for all the help he'd given Andrew after the deaths.'

'All the lies,' Lucy said quietly.

'Yes, all the lies,' Rob confirmed. 'We don't know whether Edward had already developed a line in blackmail by then. But he certainly milked Andrew regularly over the years.'

'Is that why Edward moved down here?' Anna asked. 'To be close to the source of his income.'

'We think so,' Rob said. 'They both lived in London before that, and he got here shortly after Andrew and Shona moved into the farm.'

'Andrew must have loved that,' Mike commented. He frowned. 'But where does Soldiers' Meadow come into this?'

Rob smiled, his face lightening. 'It doesn't, Mike. Or only incidentally. It appears Andrew was being harried by Shona, who intended to develop it and Potter's Yard. We've seen the draft plans up at their place. Andrew must have felt he was between a rock and a hard place, with Edward on the one hand and Shona on the other.'

'Somehow,' Anna said, 'I can't feel sorry for him.'

Laney flashed her a sudden grin. 'I know just what you mean.'

'Did Shona know about the blackmail?' Hugh asked.

'Not until recently,' Rob replied. 'And I think she found out because Edward over-estimated his powers of persuasion. We know from Lucy that Gareth had apparently begun to think they should move from their farm, sell it off to Andrew and settle somewhere else. Edward didn't want that, and to convince Gareth he could persuade Andrew to back off he told him some of what had been going on.'

Rob contemplated his hands for a moment. 'We can't be sure how much he told Gareth, all we know is what Gareth managed to tell us and what we can work out from what happened afterwards. But we know that Edward told Gareth about the deaths and that Andrew Trago was Nat's biological father.'

He shook his head disbelievingly. 'I don't know quite why Edward told him so much, but that last fact seems to have been the trigger that exploded the situation into tragedy. Gareth approached Andrew as they were leaving the garden tour. And the deaths started. Andrew asked Gareth to wait until everyone had left then they could discuss what he should do.' Rob shook his head again. 'He'd already decided, of course. As soon as it was quiet, he attacked Gareth viciously, catching him off guard. I've no doubt he'd have killed him, but Hugh's return along the avenue disturbed him.'

'Shona told me that Gareth was worried about the children, Lissa and Nat, who had clearly become close. As far as Gareth knew, they weren't aware they were half-brother and sister,' Anna said. 'Edward, of course, must have known Nat's parentage was common knowledge in the family, but he obviously didn't pass on that piece of information. Maybe he deliberately didn't, he liked to wind Gareth up sometimes, especially about his principles. But Edward can't have realised that Gareth would be driven to action. Edward would have been so focused on how clever he was because he thought he had the means to stop Andrew getting Potter's Yard. It sounds as though Edward probably wasn't able to stop himself from telling Gareth all the secrets he knew once he'd started to talk.'

'How do you know Gareth confronted Andrew about all that Edward told him?' Lucy asked.

Rob smiled slightly at her. 'Shona told Anna. He must have gone home, covered in blood and in a state of shock anyway, and no doubt she saw him. She said in her earlier evidence that she had gone home in the car, and Andrew had walked back along the cliffs. She even saw him set out, and thought he was going to Soldiers' Meadow, but if she was speaking the truth he must have doubled back when she was gone. I think she probably was telling the truth, that she didn't know what he was going to do.'

Rob lifted both hands a little and let them fall again. 'Anyway, it sounds as though he told her everything. She found that far from being overwhelmed by his violence, he was in such a euphoric state about Nat that he couldn't think of anything else. She must have known that he'd try to claim the boy. Perhaps it was that on top of all the other brewing scandal, that made her decide to kill him.'

'So,' said Anna, 'all this was because Andrew wanted a son.' She frowned. 'No, there was the threat to reveal the truth about the earlier deaths too. I wonder if he'd have tried to kill Edward as well.'

'He was used to sorting out issues with violence,' Mike pointed out grimly.

Rob nodded. 'Yes, perhaps that was his default reaction.'

'That has been a confusing case,' Hugh commented. 'Two murderers, each with a different mode of operation. Andrew attacked Gareth, but all the others were Shona's doing.' He glanced quickly at the inspector. 'That is right, isn't it?'

'Yes,' Rob agreed, 'and it didn't make our work easier. The attack on Gareth didn't seem premeditated, although in a way it was. The later deaths were planned, although Andrew's own death was a confusing mixture of both methods. He was dosed with digitalis too, Shona met him at the meadow with her handy little flask, and when the dose began to affect him, she hit him. Again and again, she didn't stop until he was dead.' His mouth tightened. 'We think she had originally intended to make it look like suicide, she had written an email to a friend saying she was worried about him and how he would react if Nat didn't want to know him. She was probably already sure Nat wouldn't be interested. But then something made her change her mind.'

'It was what he said,' Anna murmured. 'He must have said it then.'

'What on earth did he say?' Hugh demanded.

'That now he had a son he didn't need her. If she hadn't already planned to kill him, I've no doubt she'd have done it after that,' Anna said quietly.

'But why did she mind so much about his past?' Lucy demanded. 'She didn't care anything about him, from all I can gather.'

'She wasn't worried that her husband had committed murder, probably more than once,' Rob said. 'She was worried that he would be found out, but more immediately she knew he was going to make a fuss about Nat, which would bring them unwanted publicity. She seems to have been abnormally concerned about her social standing, and was afraid Andrew was going to set back her attempts to progress in what she regards as society.' He looked enquiringly at Anna. 'She seemed to feel you were going to help her with that. I still can't understand why she intended to kill you.'

'Edward told her I'd work out what was going on.'

Mike snorted. Anna ignored him and went on, 'Did she mean to implicate Martha or Esther?'

'Oh yes. One of them might come out with the truth of Nat's parentage, it wasn't something they were bothering to hide. Shona couldn't allow that to happen. So it seems she used a few cough linctus bottles that she found at the farm. Martha realised some were missing, she keeps a very tight accounting system, but apparently Esther is prone to giving things away, and her sister assumed this was why the numbers were down.'

'So naturally they had Martha's fingerprints on them,' Anna said, 'and probably a few of Lissa's. She certainly had plans to get rid of Lissa later on, one way or another.'

'You're right about the fingerprints,' Rob said. 'Shona wore gloves when she drew out most of the linctus with a syringe and topped the bottles up with digitalis. The fingerprints were smudged, that was why we weren't too sure of the case against Martha – it did look as though somebody had handled the bottles after her.'

'Where did she get the digitalis from?' Hugh asked.

'Mike's colleague, Melanie.'

'What!' Mike exclaimed furiously.

Rob turned to him. 'She has a dodgy heart and carries a large supply of digitoxin with her, apparently because she travels in wild places a lot. She hasn't had to use any here, so she hadn't noticed that a few bottles had gone from her store. Shona took them when she insisted on checking over Kerenza's rooms for her employees. Her computer history shows she's been researching poisons. We can't know whether she knew Melanie had the digitoxin or whether she just took her opportunity.'

'Why did she kill Rosa?' Lucy asked. 'She told Anna that Rosa had been hinting about Andrew's past, was that it?'

'Rosa was, like Kerenza, an acute observer, and she had, in addition, access to other people's houses as a cleaner. We've been told she nosed about a bit, almost certainly she overheard things. None of this would have mattered, but she liked to let people know that she knew things about them and expected little gifts to acknowledge her discretion. That was her death sentence when she hinted to Shona about Andrew's chequered past.'

Anna nodded. 'Yes, I've heard Rosa had that habit, but local people didn't really seem concerned about it. They kept her sweet with things they'd probably have given her anyway, and she never spread the stories she knew.'

'Once Gareth had been attacked, Shona probably felt she

couldn't be sure of that,' Hugh said.

'But,' Lucy was frowning, speaking slowly as she thought it out, 'how could Shona get the bottle to Rosa after Andrew attacked Gareth? Rosa died on the night of the attack.'

Rob looked at her with approval. 'It's my belief Shona had already decided to dispose of Rosa before the issue with Gareth arose. She was probably worried that Rosa would get too demanding or let her tongue wag to somebody else. It would have been easy enough to give her the bottle when Rosa went up to work at Trago Place that day. Kerenza said Rosa had a cough and sore throat for a few days, the perfect opportunity for Shona to offer some linctus from her own supply.'

'But what was Rosa so upset about at the garden tour?' Anna asked suddenly.

Rob's lips twisted in a grim smile. 'Nothing directly to do with Andrew's affairs,' he said bleakly. 'Kerenza told us that Edward had told them both he was going to tell Andrew about Nat, and Rosa was concerned about losing her privileges at Carne Farm. That's all it was, Rosa trying to dissuade Edward from talking, trying to get Kerenza to stop him. Kerenza didn't take it seriously, she didn't think Edward would do it, and she knew it wouldn't affect Rosa's treats at the farm if he did. Even after Edward was killed, Kerenza was more concerned about Laney, who seemed to have a better motive.'

'So Shona was prepared to kill, before she even knew for sure what the stories about Andrew were,' Anna said bleakly. 'If she could get rid of Rosa so easily, I suppose it was inevitable she would dispose of Edward once she knew what had happened all those years ago.'

'Oh yes,' Rob said. 'She was sure he would carry on the blackmail too. Probably at a much higher rate as he could have built a pretty case implicating Andrew for Gareth's death.'

'Did he know she'd killed Andrew?' Lucy asked.

'I think he guessed,' Rob replied. 'Who else would have reason to?'

Mike opened his mouth to speak, and Rob nodded to him. 'You had reason, perhaps, Mike, but I'd never suspect you of using poison.'

The archaeologist glared at him. 'Or of hitting him from behind.'

'That too,' Rob agreed.

'Did she deliberately try to incriminate Martha and Esther over Edward's death?' Anna asked.

'Almost certainly. She asked Esther for a flask of coffee, knowing how much Edward liked it. By then Shona seemed always to have had one of her little bottles by her.' He glanced at Anna. 'She had one with her when she tried to kill you, presumably in case she had an opportunity to use it.'

Rob shrugged. 'She'd have had no problem doctoring the coffee. Edward can't have been suspicious, presumably because Esther had made the coffee, so he drank the whole contents of the flask, and was soon feeling too ill to move. That was when Shona left him to die.'

Lucy shuddered. 'He must have known what she'd done before he did die.'

'He was a fool to mess with her,' Mike said harshly. 'He knew, or could guess, that she'd already killed people in her way.'

'Oh yes,' Rob said, 'He seems to have been a very stupid man, as well as a greedy one.'

Mike turned suddenly to Laney, who had been very quiet. 'And where do you come into all this?'

'I came here because Hugh gave me the opportunity to see where my sister lived and died,' Laney said frankly. 'I've always been curious about what happened to her.' Laney was silent for a moment, before adding, 'And I wanted to know where Lissa, my niece, was now, how she was.' Laney smiled broadly. 'Meeting her was a real bonus. She's going to come and visit with me, you know, in Canada. And Nat's coming too.'

'Are Martha and Esther home now?' Anna asked, clearly not much concerned with Laney anymore.

'Yes, there's no case against either of them,' Rob said. 'Thankfully, it would have been a nightmare trying to prove it against one of them, when each was determined to protect the other.'

'So Martha will still be taking a studio,' Anna said with relief. 'With Gareth gone, I was worried about losing another tenant.'

Mike burst into laughter. 'Welcome to the real world, Anna. How to fund your project supersedes everything, even death.'

'You know I didn't mean that,' Anna said crossly. She ran her fingers loosely through her hair. 'What I could really do with is a meal out and a good drink. What about it?' She looked round the walled garden. 'Not here or the pub, I think. How about going home to Roscombe? It would be nice to sit safely near the sea to relax. Somehow, I don't fancy being on a cliff edge for a while.'

'You haven't asked me,' Laney said quietly to Hugh as they walked slowly across Elowen's back lawn, waiting for Lucy to catch them up. She was engrossed in conversation with Anna in the doorway of the walled garden.

'What?' Hugh queried, pausing and turning to look at Laney.

'How much I knew about all this,' she said.

'You've told us,' he parried, walking on.

'You know what I've told the others, especially your so English inspector, and it was true. But I'll tell you the truths I didn't mention if you want me to.'

Hugh hesitated, but his innate curiosity was too much for him. 'Alright.'

'I was coming down anyway,' Laney said, 'but it was true that you gave me the opportunity to do so more easily. I always meant to come here, but I'd forgotten where Laurie lived in the West Country. Neither of us ever bothered to put the address on letters, there just never seemed any point. Then there was an odd twist of fate when I was in London, the day we met, in fact. I was flicking through some old magazines in a hairdresser's, when I came across a photograph of Andrew and Shona at some event down here. Trago is an unusual name, and it rang a bell. So I googled it and got their address.'

Laney sighed. 'I began to remember a lot of things Laurie had written about and I began to wonder about her death. I wanted to speak to Andrew about it, but I wanted to study the lie of the land first.'

'And so you came down, with me as your cover, and you saw how things were here,' Hugh said noncommittally.

'Yes.' She studied him. 'And I used them, perhaps I manipulated them. Just a little, but enough to move things on. I encouraged Shona to think Andrew's scandalous past was a threat to her, that she ought to find out what might come out of the woodwork so she'd be prepared to deal with it. I didn't know it would end in more deaths, but I think that makes me complicit in them.'

'Perhaps,' Hugh conceded. 'But most likely they'd have happened anyway.'

'Do you still want to come to Canada to work on this project we discussed? You hadn't answered before, so perhaps this will make up your mind.'

'I've already decided,' Hugh said slowly. 'I haven't told Lucy yet. But yes, I want to come.'

Rob had joined Lucy as she walked down Elowen's lime avenue to the car park. 'I haven't managed that catch-up with you,' he said wryly. 'I wasn't expecting such a spate of murders.'

'Who could?' Lucy asked.

'I should, I'm always wary when you four are together. It's not a good omen, I've said it before. God,' he said, 'I'm beginning to sound superstitious. No, worse, I'm beginning to feel it.'

'It'll pass,' Lucy said. 'And things change,' she looked towards the gateway, 'we can't always be a foursome.'

'About time,' Mike said grumpily as Anna shut the back door of the car behind the collie and slid into the front seat of the Passat.

'I thought you were settling in here for the night. Sometimes it seems as though you do.'

'I know,' Anna said. 'But now I want a change of scene, and somehow the thought of being home in Roscombe is strangely comforting.'

He glanced over at her. 'You're getting old,' he said, intending to needle her.

'All the time,' she said with complete equanimity. 'It's not so bad. And after all,' she added, 'I've got you to grow old with.'

'God help me,' he said forcefully. 'Many more adventures like this and you may not grow old. And I probably won't either, I'll have had a fatal heart attack.'

'Nonsense, Mike, you couldn't stand a quiet life. But it'll be quiet enough now, and your dig can go ahead. At least,' she added with a gurgle of laughter, 'you know you're likely to find bodies there. No more surprises.'

'With you, I'll never be sure,' he said. 'Maybe that's part of your attraction,' he added gloomily.

MARY TANT'S WEBSITE

Find out more about Mary Tant's world by visiting her website

www.marytant.com

- ❏ Find out more about her plots
- ❏ See which authors' books she has in her library
- ❏ Explore the bookshops she finds
- ❏ Visit the teashops she enjoys
- ❏ Follow her regular nature blog
- ❏ Get the latest news of further Rossington titles.

The twelfth and final novel in the Rossington series will be available in 2026. Watch Mary's website for further details closer to publication: www.marytant.com.